NEW YORK REVIEW BOOKS
CLASSICS

DIVORCING

SUSAN TAUBES (1928–1969), born Judit Zsuzsanna Feldmann in Budapest, was the daughter of a psychoanalyst and the granddaughter of a rabbi. She and her father emigrated to the United States in 1939, settling in Rochester, New York. She attended Bryn Mawr as an undergraduate, and in 1949 married the rabbinically trained scholar Jacob Taubes. Taubes studied philosophy and religion in Jerusalem, at the Sorbonne, and at Radcliffe, where she wrote her dissertation on Simone Weil. She and her husband had a son and a daughter, in 1953 and 1957, and in 1960 she began teaching at Columbia University, where she was curator of the Bush Collection of Religion and Culture. During the 1960s, Taubes was a member of the experimental Open Theater ensemble; edited volumes of Native American and African folktales; published a dozen short stories; and wrote two novels, *Divorcing* and the still-unpublished *Lament for Julia*. Her suicide came shortly after the publication of *Divorcing*, in November 1969. Two collections of Taubes's extensive correspondence with Jacob while they lived apart in the early 1950s were published in Germany in 2014: the letters appear in their original English with German annotation.

DAVID RIEFF is the author of ten books, including *The Exile: Cuba in the Heart of Miami*; *Slaughterhouse: Bosnia and the Failure of the West*; *A Bed for the Night: Humanitarianism in Crisis*; *Swimming in a Sea of Death: A Son's Memoir*; and, most recently, *In Praise of Forgetting: Historical Memory and Its Ironies*.

DIVORCING

SUSAN TAUBES

Introduction by
DAVID RIEFF

NEW YORK REVIEW BOOKS

New York

THIS IS A NEW YORK REVIEW BOOK
PUBLISHED BY THE NEW YORK REVIEW OF BOOKS
435 Hudson Street, New York, NY 10014
www.nyrb.com

ACKNOWLEDGMENTS
I wish to thank the Radcliffe Institute for its generous help and encouragement toward making this book possible; and also the Ingram Merrill Foundation for its very helpful support.

First published as a New York Review Books Classic in 2020.

Library of Congress Cataloging-in-Publication Data
Names: Taubes, Susan, author. | Rieff, David, writer of introduction.
Title: Divorcing / Susan Taubes ; introduction by David Rieff.
Description: New York : New York Review Books, [2020] | Series: New York
   Review Books classics | Originally published in 1969.
Identifiers: LCCN 2020010234 (print) | LCCN 2020010235 (ebook) | ISBN
   9781681374949 (paperback) | ISBN 9781681374956 (ebook)
Classification: LCC PS3570.A88 D58 2020 (print) | LCC PS3570.A88 (ebook)
   | DDC 813/.54—dc23
LC record available at https://lccn.loc.gov/2020010234
LC ebook record available at https://lccn.loc.gov/2020010235

ISBN 978-1-68137-494-9
Available as an electronic book; ISBN 978-1-68137-495-6

Printed in the United States of America on acid-free paper.
10 9 8 7 6 5 4 3 2 1

INTRODUCTION

AS THERE are cult books, so are there cult people. What mysterious alchemy vaults people who were largely ignored, or at least by their own lights insufficiently valued, in their own time to this privileged niche in the imagination of their posterity is never fully explainable and is not to be confused with reputation in the conventional sense. For viewed coldly, the accomplishments of these cult people are almost always slim rather than thick. But this only adds to their fascination and to the aura that surrounds them, as if their lives were meant to illustrate the acuity of Mies van der Rohe's dictum that less is more. These are men and women who attract the interest of posterity through some combination of charisma (always), physical beauty (more often than not), and, at the risk of sounding somewhat heartless, also more often than not death at a comparatively young age. Musing on one of these cult people, their admirers often exclaim, "Think what she would have accomplished had she lived."

Divorcing, quickly forgotten after its publication in 1969, has yet to become a cult book, though it has all the qualities of one, but its author, Susan Taubes, was very much the sort of brilliant, glamorous, doomed person I have been describing. Indeed, the typology of the cult figure fits her so well as to be almost discomfiting—her charisma, her Garbo-esque beauty, but above all, that sense, universally subscribed to by those who were close to her, that she found the burden of being itself too crushing and that her relation to the world always was a radically contingent one. Candor is called for here: I am not speculating about this. In the early 1950s in Cambridge, Massachusetts, Taubes and her then husband, the rabbi and philosopher of ideas

Jacob Taubes, were the closest friends of my parents, Susan Sontag and Philip Rieff. Their children, Ethan and Tania, were my friends and contemporaries. And after both the Taubeses and my parents divorced, and after both had moved to New York, Susan Taubes and my mother remained intimate friends, a friendship that was only ended by Taubes's suicide in November 1969, barely a week after *Divorcing* was published. It was left to my mother to identify her body. Much later, she told me: "I will never forgive her...and never recover from what she did."

A book, the Romanian aphorist E. M. Cioran once wrote, is a suicide postponed. But in the case of *Divorcing*, not postponed by much. A few weeks before her death, Taubes wrote in her journal: "I am sitting in my room. I go out. I come in waiting for time to pass. In about two weeks I will drown myself." My mother, though, always thought that the proximate cause of Taubes's suicide was the bad reviews the novel received, above all a savage and, from the vantage point of today, a startlingly misogynistic notice from the critic Hugh Kenner in *The New York Times*, in an era—how long ago it seems and what a good thing it is that this is no longer reliably the case!—when a thumbs-up or thumbs-down in that paper made all the difference to a book's chances. But whether this was true or not in the most immediate sense, all of Taubes's work and much of her life (or so, again, my mother thought: I am channeling here more than I am opining) were rehearsals for her own death. That was certainly the case with *Divorcing*, a title that Taubes had not chosen but only agreed to when her publishers rejected what had been her working title: *To America and Back in a Coffin*.

Hindsight is not just twenty-twenty, it is usually invidious. And even if it weren't in this case, I want to manumit Taubes from her admirers. She was far more than the doomed artist, or some early recondite precursor of Renata Adler (though in a certain sense she was indeed that as well). Yet it is difficult not to read most if not all of Taubes's work—the only obvious exceptions being *African Myths and Tales* and a book of Native American myths called *The Storytelling Stone*, which she compiled between 1963 and 1965—as episodes in a series of rehearsals in prose of her own death. She had always been fascinated by the memoir from beyond the grave—the title, in fact, of Chateaubriand's masterpiece of that genre—and her work, beginning with her university thesis on Simone Weil, her still-unpublished novella called *A Lament for Julia*, and the handful of stories she produced, has death as its driving force. Even in reviews, the leitmotif of the grave is given pride of place, as when she wrote about Jean Genet's play *The Blacks* and called her review "On Going to One's Own Funeral," though the play is broadly about white racism, and specifically about a murder and a trial, at the conclusion of which there is death but no funeral per se. Later, a revised version of this review would appear in *The Tulane Drama Review* under the more appropriate title "White Masks Fall." The editors' choice in that case was surely correct. But despite what one presumes was the obvious commercial rationale—*Divorcing* may not be the most inviting of titles, but as Taubes's editors surely pointed out to her, *To America and Back in a Coffin* is a profoundly off-putting one—her original title actually does justice to the book she wrote, if not necessarily the book her editors wished she had written.

It is important to be careful. *Divorcing* is not only about the end of a marriage and a woman's struggle to extricate herself from the various holds, psychic, sexual, and otherwise, that her husband continues to try to maintain over her, but neither is it only a novel about death. To the contrary, the book assembles several narratives under one novelistic roof, sometimes masterfully, sometimes unsteadily. In it, the relatively straightforward, almost memoiristic story of the attempt of the narrator, Sophie Blind—Taubes had a weakness for giving her characters somewhat didactic names—to extricate herself from her marriage fades in and out of a modernist conjuring act in which what is dream and what is reality are made deliberately unclear. The book actually begins with a section in which Sophie informs the reader that she is dead and that only thanks to this can she tell the truth. Alive, she insists, she just wanted happiness, adding that all women do (for all its originality and the antinomianism of its narrator, *Divorcing* can be jarringly of its time). But dead she can care about power and about truth. And with that prologue, the novel begins in earnest.

Sophie, of course, is not dead, not in the next part of the book anyway. This first section of the novel is an anatomization of Sophie's marriage to Ezra, and flits from parts of its beginning to parts of its end. For those who remember Jacob Taubes, or have read the many recollections that have been written about him, the portrait of Ezra is an uncannily accurate description of him in all of his charm, intelligence, cruelty, and priapism. The man who would later write boastingly to a friend, "I am impossible," was just that and worse, especially toward women. In the novel, Ezra berates Sophie, then tells her that he loves her for precisely the qualities he is berating her for, then berates her again. Meanwhile Sophie is tallying up the legacies of her marriage all the while imagining her own death, at one point fantasizing that she has died and that Ezra and her lover Nicholas have come to identify her body and as they wait exchange erudite views about Judaism, Heidelberg University, and a painting in Chartres Cathedral. Such exchanges are everywhere in *Divorcing*. It is in many ways a novel about erudite people written for erudite people, to the point that Sophie notes that when she spanks her son Joshua in front of Nicholas, the way that her lover formulates his distress over her having done so is with a reference to Franz Kafka.

It should be too much, above all for a reader in the 2020s when the large consensus among even non-woke academic intellectuals is that these forms of erudition and this inventory of references mask all sorts of oppressive structures, and badly need, as the jargon of the day has it, to be interrogated. And even for the reader who is indifferent or hostile to such contemporary proscriptions, and I'd wager that there are many more of these than are willing to show their heads above the ideological parapet at this particular moment, the range and sheer quantity of intellectual and philosophical references are likely to be overwhelming. This should not be confused with pretentiousness. *Divorcing* is a novel overflowing with arcana, but its portrait of psychological pain is so searing, so universally recognizable, and Sophie's efforts not to succumb to it so convincing, that the cultural references are more like background music than barricades, background music to a funeral that is also a movable feast. Contemplating not just her former husband and her former lover but her own family from beyond the grave, Sophie is sardonic. "I am dead," she comments. "They can all relax and celebrate."

To the psychic brutalities of Sophie's conjugal life, add the deforming legacy of family. It already seeps into the early part of the book, including in the burial scene in which, at the graveside, Ezra says to Sophie's father, "At her funeral at least she is decent," and her father does not demur. But about a third of the way into *Divorcing*, Sophie the unreliable narrator of the breakup of her marriage gives way to Sophie the entirely trustworthy narrator of her childhood as part of the extended high-bourgeois Jewish Landsmann family (another telling name) in pre–World War II Budapest and later Vienna. Taubes is deftly savage in her portrait of both her overbearing psychoanalyst father (modeled, as Ezra was on Jacob Taubes, on her own father, a distinguished psychiatrist of the period in Europe and later in the United States) and her mother who is sedulously and unapologetically unfaithful to him, and eventually divorces him and marries a much younger man. All of this takes place just before the union of Nazi Germany and Austria in 1938. It is followed by an equally straightforward section that takes up the story of Sophie and her father after they have emigrated to America. After that, though, the realistic narrative once more gives way to a phantasmagoric one.

As in the early parts of *Divorcing*, Sophie is dead; at least presumed to be: intentionally, it is not entirely made clear. Ezra, Sophie's father and mother, and eventually Sophie herself speaking from her coffin appear before a Hungarian rabbinic court. Sophie's entire life, from early childhood to wretched marriage, is debated in increasingly hysterical terms. In the end, the court grants Sophie her divorce, after which Taubes wrenches her narrative back toward realism of structure and tone, though not of chronology. Sophie is with Ezra during their marriage, she is in America in the years after she and her father emigrated, she is back in Budapest, then in America once again. Toward the end of this section, Sophie has a kind of reckoning with her mother, but it is without reconciliation or even understanding. After that, the book tails off: Sophie with her children, Sophie writing her novel in New York, Sophie headed back to Europe again. This is unquestionably the weakest section of *Divorcing*. To me, it reads as if Taubes had not quite known how to gather all those interiorities and externalities, and lay them out once more with the same force and inventiveness that she musters again and again in the novel. Or perhaps she was bowing to an editorial desideratum for an ending that at least left open the possibility of redemption. Both explanations are the purest of speculation on my part. It may simply be instead that because *Divorcing* is neither fully a realistic novel nor exactly an experimental one, no ending would have been entirely satisfactory. Instead, the reader is left with what Taubes in the penultimate sentence of the novel calls "the anguish of abandoned dream places."

It is tempting to take refuge in the observation that had she lived Taubes would of course have gone on to write better books. But then about what writer can that *not* be said? I do like to think that she would have found a way to harness the ecstatic qualities of her writing which are so striking in her truly remarkable letters to Jacob during 1951 and 1952, when she was largely in Europe and he was studying in Jerusalem with the great scholar of Kabbalistic Judaism Gershom Scholem, and of which there are a few intimations in her university thesis on Weil (the letters were published in Germany in 2014). But despite its limitations, Taubes's novel has stood the test of time. There were many interesting experimental novels written during the same period in which she was composing *Divorcing*. It hardly seems controversial to say that today very few are worth reading. *Divorcing* is one of these rare exceptions.

David Hume is supposed to have said of Rousseau that he was like a man walking around without his skin on. The same, I think, can be said of Susan Taubes, which is what caused her such terrible suffering in life and which also makes *Divorcing*, whose deepest subject is anguish, at once so relentless and so remarkable. This is a novel that bleeds.

—DAVID RIEFF

DIVORCING

to
ELSA FIRST,
who knew this book before it was a book

ONE

SHE OPENS her eyes with enormous effort but it's in another room; then she is hurrying down a busy street past fine shops, the window displays on Place Vendôme attract her, watches flat as coins; but she knows this is wrong, she knows she must open her eyes as she lies in bed in a room. Repeatedly she closes and opens her eyes, now she is in bed; she recognizes the room; the light on a high floor by the Hudson River. But she can't keep her eyes open long enough; each time she blinks the room changes, the window is on a different side, or a dark mass blocks the view. Now she discerns a man's shape, she recalls the pain that rent her, for which her body was not prepared—is it her lover?—he stands in his coat beside her bed, she wonders if she screamed like a savage, if he heard her wild ravings and blasphemies burst on vaulting blood. If he has heard he pretends he hasn't, from kindness or indifference, because he prefers not to believe what he has heard or seen. Beautiful and dignified he wants to remember her.

She begins to speak, she is far away now, her own voice remote, surprisingly rapid and fluent. She is laughing. She has never laughed like this before. The man's shape has blurred, a dark inert mass, it swings slightly, now she sees the white of his bare soles—he's hanged himself!

Sophie Blind doesn't believe this, of course, she knows just because something gives you a fright you don't have to believe it; she has studied philosophy, epistemology, published papers on the problem of verification. Besides, now she doesn't see a thing. Perhaps it was just a coat on a hanger swaying as the plane lurched. Or stroboscopic vision.

The pain has lifted, literally rising. First she did not see. What was that white caress? God was painting the world on her retina with the softest brush; stars, snow falling, blossoms, rows of wild chestnut trees in bloom, each leaf a green tickle. She had never laughed like this before. This was not to be believed either. Just because something puts you in a rapture it is not necessarily to be believed.

She is in a room in bed; to this familiar notion Sophie Blind held on while she was having the wildest dream.

But is she dreaming?

She is in a room writing. The only trouble is that all the pages of the small pad are already covered with words in some foreign language. She sits up in bed. The room is unfamiliar, high-ceilinged—a marble washstand with a pitcher, the armoire, provincial French—a room in an old-fashioned first-class hotel in a seaside resort in Normandy. Clearly a dream because now she remembers the industrialist from Milan, they were streaking along the Amalfi coast in his Alfa Romeo—that dates and places it; but what has become of him? She must make a note of all this—quick, before he comes—on the lace paper mat on the breakfast tray. The room has changed again but she is used to this. Sophie Blind is used to unfamiliar rooms. She has been traveling all her life.

This room with printed muslin curtains tacked on the window frame, the drapes an obscure color, bedding piled high, could be in her grandmother's apartment in Budapest. Pictures of bearded men in silver frames cover the wall. There is the bustle of backroom deliveries; rugs clapped over the sill, brushes scrubbing stone; guests are ushered in and shown out; the door of the buffet creaks each time another wine glass must be fetched.

She is looking at a page of Dore's illustrated Bible, a picture showing the deluge, whirling throngs of nude bodies at the bottom, the dead draped voluptuously over rocks, the great white Ark approaching from above; in another second someone turns the page to a pastoral scene. The shadowy figure poking around the room, pulling things from chests, could be a cousin or uncle. Odd, the gaudy paraphernalia—boots, petticoats, hats and fans from the nineties and the twenties. The quick, sure grace with which he handles things and moves suggests her lover, her lover teasing her, putting on her great grandfather's fur kaftan, next her aunt's stole of silver foxes; his impersonations go too far. Stop, she pleads, but he is already pulling her mother's sequined dress over his head: a woman's painted face appears, a perfect likeness, the blond curls, the black beauty patch just below the left corner of the mouth; she is sitting, in tight, low-cut dress, legs crossed like Marlene Dietrich—Someone shakes the room like a kaleidoscope; chandeliers blossom and drop in mirror-lined ballrooms, there is too much glare and reflection. Now Sophie Blind isn't sure whether she is dreaming. There is another question on her mind. When you are under their devilish drug, can you remember taking it, even supposing they didn't slip it in your tea, the dirty bastards, supposing no foul deal, you volunteered like a fool, can you remember when you're actually under the drug? Sophie Blind doesn't remember.

She is looking up at her lover, astonished by the phrase, "... that happiness, so improbable, we call it love ..." He sits on the edge of her bed, smoking gravely. She wonders why he looks into the distance, his head thrown back; she wants to see his eyes. "... because you're dead Sophie," she hears, like a voice out of a letter she is reading, "Dead."

"We've been through this before—" she wants to say. Instead her eyes leap for a last glimpse of his dear face. It's gone. Where? Disappeared. Into the wallhanging? A medieval hunting scene, the background faded greenery; a castle floats sketched faintly in the upper left; in the foreground spotted Dalmatian hounds on their hind legs, painted full-face, are jumping outward—such virtuosity of foreshortening in the Middle Ages; it's astounding! Modernity, Reformation, Renaissance are classroom jokes after all, as she always suspected—the world ended when it was supposed to in the year 1274, if only they had believed it. "... Why there had to be a twentieth century—?" She hears a familiar voice repeat a student's question in a heavy German accent. That was in another dream. She can't see anything now. Actually she sees too much and too fast. It's the same whether she keeps her eyes open or shut. Her lover is in the room and he wants her to be calm. Who's having a hunting party in her head? Birds shot in flight are plummeting darkly from all directions and new ones are thrown in as fast, their cries piercing shrill.

She knows it's over. She can't stop now. She must get used to her new voice.

Yes, I'm dead. I knew I was dead when I came but I didn't want to be the first to say it. Not just as I arrived. I wasn't really sure, you see. Everything looked so new, the water tanks on the roofs, the wide avenues, and heavy glass doors; boys playing touch football on the sidewalk. As if I were in New York for the first time. My sense of things is sometimes distorted. But I never felt so intensely alive as now. That's what's confusing me. And your presence. Listening. Or just watching my face in sleep, always calm, you said. When I know you're far away... Perhaps you are speaking to me the words to make everything clear. No need for words perhaps. Women want essentially only happiness, you said, happiness more than power or truth. But I care for truth. Now I am dead I care only for truth.

I died on a Tuesday afternoon, struck by a car as I was crossing Avenue George V. It was raining heavily. I had just come out from the hairdresser. The time, judging from the traffic, increasingly violent but not yet congested, was shortly before six. I sighted a free cab, waved to it. I stepped off the curb watching for a chance to cross. Just then I saw the doorman of the hotel on the opposite side head toward the taxi with an oversize umbrella, blowing his whistle shrilly. I made a dash for it. I was flung into the center of the road by a car and struck at once. The rest is blurred. Because of the rain only a handful of bystanders gathered. The police and an ambulance arrived within a few minutes. And in less than half an hour normal traffic was resumed.

It happened so suddenly, and besides my mind was on something else at the time. But it's quite certain I am dead. It's in the newspaper. The doctor's statement lies on the desk of the police even though an official death certificate can't be made out till tomorrow morning; *"Femme décapitée en 18° arrondissement,"* it said in *France Soir,* and the sensation of my head severed from my back is still vivid. My body growing enormous, its thousands of trillions of cells suddenly set free, spread, speeded, pressed jubilant, rushing to the seven gates of Paris, out Porte de Clichy, Porte de la Chapelle, Porte d'Orléans, Porte de Versailles; the fingers of my outstretched arms plunged into the woods of Boulogne and Vincennes.

Dearest,

I'm coming. Don't be misled by the Crillon stationery. I'm on my way, flying out of Paris tonight. Five days in Amsterdam (I wrote you about the conference); perhaps I can cut it down to three and be in New York by Sunday morning the eleventh by Icelandic. Will cable when I know exactly. Leave a key under the loose tile just in case. I hope this reaches you in time. It was impossible to write the last weeks. Work deadlines, settling the children with my sister-in-law for the summer, and then the final clearing out—a depressing amount of stuff. But now it's done. I am free at last, the keys turned over to the new tenants, my one suitcase checked at the *aérogare*. I walked all day, wonderfully light with only my papers and your picture in my pocket.

Wandered through different markets staring at the same varieties of cheeses and beautifully displayed fruit, even the green string beans arranged in perfect rows; got lost in the flower market. Sat in the lobby of the Crillon for almost an hour trying to write to you. Then strolled around Place Vendôme looking at window displays. Not till all the stores closed for noon did I begin to think perhaps I should have a plan for the afternoon—shop, visit the Musée Grévin, see the new exhibit of ancient Chinese calligraphy or take a last look at the Cycladic heads in the Louvre. But continued in a daze past Châtelet looking into every junk shop along the *quai*, blocks of sporting goods, fancy tropical birds and fish for sale and back on the other side of the river felt suddenly how senseless all this delight, the fine blue sky, a sudden impatience and anger as I saw women starting homeward with small children from the playgrounds and crowding before butcher shops and bakeries. Braced myself for the standard tourist sunset boatride along the Seine, the ferry packed with a crowd of boys from some German youth organization, the "Wundervogel." And now it's time.

Forgive this late and hurried note; I hoped to get it off earlier this day; now I might as well mail it at the airport. Haven't even begun to think about paper I have to give on Spinoza. Count on spirit of place. It will be my first visit to Amsterdam.

Love, SOPHIE

WHILE traveling, Sophie Blind carried her accumulation of some thirty-five years in boxes, suitcases, trunks, barrels, crates and the like. Not on her person, or necessarily accompanying her person. On her person she carried only what was necessary depending on the nature of the journey—whether by boat, plane, train, bus or foot—its length and destination and, finally, the number of persons traveling.

This seemed the obvious way to deal with things: pack and unpack and pack again if you were traveling, and Sophie had been traveling all her life. When she married she continued traveling with her husband. Ezra Blind was working on a book that might take all his life to complete, or at least the next twenty years; his work required going to libraries and meeting scholars of different countries. Fortunately Ezra managed to get invited as a visiting lecturer to good universities on both sides of the Atlantic as far as Jerusalem. So they lived in many different cities, sometimes for only a few months, sometimes for as long as two years, and traveled to other places in between. Sophie liked traveling. She also liked to have some things she cherished, a few familiar objects around her, wherever she was, beyond the more or less same sky with its same sun and moon and more or less same walls. Some things she found, some she stole, some she bought. Sophie liked traveling. For a wedding present from her father-in-law Sophie asked for an extension of their honeymoon trip instead of a fur coat. Not want a fur coat? Their daughter-in-law must have a fur coat. When at the birth of a son a fur coat was bought, it was for their respective family pictures. She wore the coat for them. She was their daughter-in-law. But did she have to take it along with her everywhere while traveling with her husband? Yes, because Ezra paid part. His father had said, "I want to buy Sophie a five-hundred-dollar fur coat." Ezra said, "Buy her one for seven hundred dollars. I know a man through whom we can get a nine-hundred-dollar coat for seven hundred dollars. I pay the two hundred and we save four hundred and she will have the best coat." With Ezra Sophie wore the fur coat and jewelry he bought for her. Whenever Ezra felt desperate about their future, he bought Sophie a piece of heavy silver jewelry.

He liked her to dress in black. Black was what she was wearing when he proposed to her and it suited her best and went best with the jewelry he bought her. He was always ready to buy Sophie another good black dress. A good black dress was for a lifetime. What Sophie always dreamed of having was a white nightgown, long and soft of the finest cotton or flannel. But Ezra couldn't understand why she wanted it. She looked better naked. Sometimes he asked her to come to bed in the fur coat. A nightgown? That was a luxury.

Not everything Sophie kept accumulating followed her in boxes and by freight in crates and trunks; that was difficult and expensive and complicated. Besides, if they were going south, they wouldn't need all their coats and woolens, although they might need them the year after or at some future time, for they never knew where they would proceed to next. Similarly she would store outgrown children's clothes which could be useful for the next child. Of course most of the things she collected from different places on the way she could not take with her but stored, depending on where they happened to be, with friends and relatives who were settled. Everything had to be kept for the time when she would be settled and have a great big house with many wings and floors, a cellar for storage, an attic to keep all the pets she had promised the children. In her mind it was all together, she was always in an imagined house, leaving for a trip and choosing one or two things to take with her. But perhaps all she really wanted was that imaginary house and she would always go on traveling and collecting things and living everywhere. In the meantime she managed quite well storing a box here and a suitcase there, with friends or relatives who were settled. Then, if she stayed in the same place for more than a year, even though nothing was ever definite, she could ask for certain things she wanted to be sent. She always wished she could have known and packed in view of future circumstances.

It was a weakness, she knew, to accumulate and to keep and to remember where she had left things. Things got lost, but that was part of traveling. Not only individual objects, but packages, a whole suitcase, mysteriously lost. She did her best to take care of things, and if they got lost despite her efforts she was cheerfully resigned to it, unlike Ezra who recalled the lost object over and over again. Whether it was something precious to him or simply something he needed that moment, each time a new loss was discovered, he would mournfully enumerate every single item that had gone astray since the day they embarked together. This Sophie did not do. Or she kept it to herself. There was the moment the loss was discovered, the anguish felt. Once is enough was Sophie's stand. Lost objects wanted to be mourned. Ah yes, you could never grieve enough for those earrings bought in some back street of Genoa. But it was against Sophie's principles to suffer the loss of anything more than once. How could Ezra take the side of *things*? Not that Sophie was absolutely sure. In fact she was haunted by those lost things in spite of her principles and it didn't help to say: Good riddance, I wouldn't be seen dead in those earrings today! They sent their ghostly eidolon: on the dresser of some hotel room. It was in the nature of things to do this, Sophie concluded, and in her nature as a woman of principles to resist. If that thing still haunts me, Sophie considered, it must be because I did not suffer its loss as truly, profoundly, as I should. But in that case there is nothing to be done. I have missed my moment; or the thing has missed its moment; that is why it keeps coming back. As for the loss of anything that caused her true anguish, that loss she carried in her very marrow, compacted with it. If at any time she had wanted to know the total of what had been lost, all she needed to do was state the last thing lost and Ezra would begin reckoning, today this, yesterday that, all the way back. But Sophie wasn't interested. Keeping count was men's business. That's what her father did and both her grandfathers.

Yes she loved traveling. It's the only way to live, Sophie always said, the only way to live in time: fly right with it. Sophie got nervous when they settled too long in one place.

Sophie made every effort to avoid arguments, but it didn't always work because Ezra was not content with simply worrying and complaining: he wanted an argument. Furthermore, Sophie had some grievances of her own which she could not always contain in silence. So they quarreled.

Ezra always won. Whatever the issue and regardless who started it, Ezra always managed to make her come out in the wrong. Sophie didn't understand how he did it. It must have been his special talent. And in the end he always said she was the most wonderful woman in the world.

Ezra began with a very small point. So small that Sophie didn't realize at all that he was starting a quarrel. A little thing that can be settled in a minute, she thought; or a little thing there's nothing to be done about that can be dismissed in a minute. Then as Ezra went on developing his point for an immoderately long time, it dawned on Sophie that the issue wasn't simply a particular tie he couldn't locate and blamed her for failing to pack, or her having failed to pack other items on other occasions, or her disregard for his appearance, or for her own appearance—her disregard for appearances in general. The issue was really all the consequences this had on their lives and would continue to accumulate. The issue was enormous.

Ezra pursued his point with mounting pathos; now pacing heavily, now standing still so as not to distract from a rhetorical flight, or to anchor a dramatic pause. Sophie watched his index finger: it was tracing circles or stirring some mysterious brew. It launched on a vertical course to the sublime. Loopdiving into the horizontal it stood pointed at her. The index finger started wagging at her increasingly menacingly as if it didn't know what to do with itself. At this point she took a deep breath, either to come back at him or storm out of the room.

Sophie hated arguments. Mostly she kept her grievances to herself. Or it burst out of her suddenly. She would be undecided whether to bring up the matter, or the best way to go about it, and while she was still debating with herself, how and whether at all, it burst out of her, surprising both of them—probably surprising Sophie more than Ezra, who was used to being screamed at by his family, while Sophie was not used to hearing herself scream.

Ezra listened attentively in a reclining position, very calm. Did he take advantage of a moment when Sophie was too caught in her passion to notice, to sink down on the sofa or slide into bed—or is that how their quarrel started? With Ezra lying in bed when Sophie was up and about and things wanting to be done, more than she alone could cope with, and Sophie's instant realization that her life reduced to the hopelessness of ever getting anything done. The vision of Ezra reclining, sprawling, yawning—this may have been the true beginning of her rage.

Sophie Blind didn't believe the devastating words that erupted from her mouth, or that she was saying them. Besides, Ezra did not register dismay, disbelief, or shock. She saw a pleased expression: sitting upright now, looking at her wide-eyed, he nodded, approving woman raging as woman should, suppressing a smile not too successfully, his face definitely softening, assuming a mask of sternness or simply fright, then vanishing under the blanket when her lunging arms, hands clawing, threatened to bear out the intent of her words on his tender skin, and hiding, he waited for the storm to spend itself. He had little to fear under cover, this was only a woman, throwing her weight on him, fists pounding mostly wall, air, mattress; at worst a jab in the ribs, her fist passing through the barricade of arms and knees. Just a woman, and now increasingly molten, pliable, fluid with rage; his own beloved wife, he knew what to do with her, and in nine months there was a baby.

Or if she did not leap on him, he would wait till the storm exhausted itself, as it was bound to eventually. Wait till the furious lashing rain thinned into a mere dribble, to take upon himself the last soft droplet of Sophie Blind weakly repeating, "... always have to do everything myself..." Then Ezra, wounded to the soul by the mere implication of a reproach, would begin to recount, remind her of the instances where he had helped her, done things for her, lifted burdens from her shoulders, bought her gifts; one after another all his good deeds toward her in general, only a few of the inexhaustible store, as long as she could hold her head up, till she was quite overwhelmed by all his good deeds so lengthily and feelingfully listed. The weight of so much consideration, devotion, service of so many years made Sophie quite faint and numb. She wasn't sure whether she was standing, sitting, or lying. She was asphyxiating. When she finally felt his body surround her and felt crushed under his weight, it was a relief. And in nine months there was a baby.

When Sophie was growing a baby she was happy; nothing bothered her then. She slept and walked and ate when she pleased. When Ezra asked her to do something, she mostly didn't hear. She was pregnant. My wife is pregnant, Ezra said significantly, when people noted her absence or commented on her absent air at parties. Sophie couldn't be bothered with social twaddle when she was growing a baby, and even less so when she was nursing and raising. She couldn't be bothered with shoes that pinched or arguments for or against. She stayed home and oiled her belly or her baby, or both.

Ezra saw how happy Sophie was when she was pregnant and gave her another baby. She soaked in the bathtub. When there was a baby she took it in the tub with her as many as there were and they played with all the faucets and the shower, or just splashed water at each other. When they were older, she gave them paint and clay and beads and old clothes to play with and make things.

Ezra complained; Ezra was appalled by beads and clay and stuff and rags and paint, especially by children painting on the wall. It washes off, his wife assured him, and proved it with a sponge. But Ezra was appalled by the idea of children painting on the wall. It was the end. It was sinful. Ezra proclaimed he wanted order in the house. Sophie watched his index finger wag menacingly and his mouth tighten into a thin line. For a long time she refused to believe in Ezra's transformation. Was this Ezra talking through his nose like his father? He grew a belly, developed strange ailments, he screamed at the sight of a crack in the wall, anything spilling, a missing button; it had to be repaired immediately.

Ezra ordered her to have the floors waxed. The children will slip, she protested. They should stay quietly in their rooms and walk carefully on waxed floors, Ezra bellowed. But it was pointless when they were moving in a few months, and besides, it was expensive, she tried to reason with him. We can't afford it, she pleaded, citing unpaid grocery and doctors' bills. So the children will have fewer toys, said Ezra, stomping into the bathroom with a stack of foreign journals.

Sophie was happy with the children; they went on making things even if it messed up the house. Ezra was mostly away and when he came, always unexpectedly, there would be a row, and that was part of family life. Only somehow, as the years passed and the children grew, the fighting became worse and Sophie saw herself losing and him winning in a way she could no longer accept because now he was keeping count of all of them, her and the children, keeping score of what each lost and did wrong and, having persistently failed and done badly, would continue doing. He was not only recalling past wrongs, but prophesying all the wrongs they would commit. By the time they became men and women he had them on gallows and in the gutter. Sophie Blind, who had never come around to defend herself, now had to begin to defend two and three and more against words and sometimes blows, the words especially, because they were more lasting. Also, now with more children Ezra had a longer inventory of his own favors and kindnesses and exertions in their behalf from the day they were born, which he recited at unrelenting length, till some turned faint and others screamed and stamped and Sophie didn't know at all what she was doing, let alone what she should be doing, except that obviously this could not be resolved or survived in the way it had been, and that however great and pressing her inclination, she must neither scream nor faint, but do everything else. So many things had to be done: to shield or argue or sometimes just stand stock still like a statue, or get them out of the room and tell them to do as their father said, or try to get him out and try afterward to comfort and cheer. Years afterward when she tried to remember what she actually had done, or what she could or should have done, it was as muddled as then. She didn't know what she was or should be doing and yet she went on from day to day. And from one country to another, packing and unpacking and traveling more on her own, till she was tired of living in remote, backward places, islands to which the ferry went once a week, mountains without roads, accessible only by foot or mule. She was tired of traveling or just tired and wanted a bit of city life. Both she and the children began to miss and want their things—books, toys, clothes, all the nice things they had bought and used in different places, and left in boxes and suitcases, stored here and there, lost perhaps (the suitcase sent to Ezra's sister which had all her notes from Italy, and the fine glasses from Venice). She was tired of being shabby and of other people's bad taste and wanted a place where she could have all their things together once and for all, and not have to move and pack and worry, but be settled in her own home to raise her children, and have peace and quiet to write one of the books she had always thought of writing someday.

All she really needed was money and a happy love affair, Sophie was told by a retired Englishman in Ibiza.

Sophie remembered she still had the money her father put in the bank when she got married, "in case—" She never let him finish his sentence; it was the day before her wedding and Sophie was afraid her father would say something that would spoil everything, so she refused to listen. In her life there was not going to be any "in case"; everything was going to be right, and none of his cynicism and doubt the day before her wedding.

Sophie made plans to settle in Paris. Ezra protested, then approved. Ezra's delight in her choice of Paris and his ironic comments were to be expected. To their friends, Ezra boasted he was granting his wife what every woman dreamed: to live in Paris. To his father-in-law, he wrote reproaching him bitterly for aiding his daughter to run away from her husband with the children. Ezra mocked Sophie, but he was pleased at the prospect of visiting her in Paris and spending some weeks or months of every year in his favorite city. At last she had come to a sensible decision.

Ezra urged that the children stay with his sister Renata in Bern so that Sophie might arrange things in peace.

"But I'm leaving you, Ezra," Sophie said.

"I only want to make it easier for you," Ezra protested. "You are still the woman I married and the mother of my children," he added with emotion. "Facts cannot be changed. The children will have the best care in Bern and your hands will be free. Renata will keep them for as long as you need to get organized."

In the spring of that year Sophie went to New York to pack and ship things she had left there and to straighten out her finances. Was this the right time to have a happy love affair?

It was done.

Sophie returned to Europe to spend some weeks by the seashore with the children till their apartment in Paris was ready. On the plane flying from New York to join her children, her thoughts circled in sweet confusion. She would have many more happy love affairs. Or maybe just one more for the rest of her life. But perhaps just one was allotted in a lifetime, and that she had had. It didn't matter if she hadn't quite finished packing.

THEY ARRIVE at Orly airport in the usual gray drizzle. Sophie Blind in her traveling cape, a child dancing at each side, the oldest forging ahead with one of the huge straw baskets in which they put the heavy things—knives, shells, camping equipment, the typewriter, the iron wrapped in still-damp beach towels. What plane are we going on next? the children ask. Swissair? Pan Am? Air France? Lufthansa? Why don't we ever go Air India? We're not taking any more planes. This is where we're staying. Settling for good. The mother's tired and distant voice continues in the taxi racing along the quay, while Paris monuments sprout up around them.

They stand before a building under construction. The last floor, where the windows have been put in, she points. A five-floor walkup. I knew it. I just knew it! Joshua comments, hoisting the straw basket. It's good for your heart, Toby says. Why do they start at the top? Jonathan asks.

The place is not quite ready; the workers are just putting in the moquette. No, they can't go in till they're finished in the evening, but a lot of things have arrived—boxes and suitcases stacked against the wall beside the door, and some letters on top of the trunk. Did Daddy write? Why doesn't she open it? Not on the stairway.

They walk out on the boulevard: TABAC, BOULANGERIE, kiosks pasted with last month's concert announcements, the Credit Lyonnais, the urinals; and single file through narrow side streets: DÉFENSE D'AFFICHER on pocked walls; yes it's all there, rivulets streaming along the gutter and the little man in the blue *tablier* guiding the garbage toward the sewer hole with his whisk broom; at the next turn

Notre Dame appears. So what are we going to do? At least it stopped raining. Go to a movie?

She writes to her lover while they sit in a corner café waiting for the workers to finish. Rereads his note, tears up her own. Arrived this morning in the usual gray drizzle and found your note...she starts a new sheet. Isn't it time to go, Mum?...Paris is not the same. She crosses out the line and crumples the page.

Yes, there is a carpet under the brown wrapping paper. What fun for the children to rip it off and roll. Gold, if Jonathan insists. Shade called *moutarde*, when she chose it last year. No furniture? Who needs furniture. On a gold rug they eat, play and sleep. Good thing they brought their butane gas camping equipment till they finish putting in the pipes and the *inspecteur du gaz* comes around to...

The children are curious. Who sent her that fat letter from New York she is reading while the spaghetti boils? Who is Ivan? they ask. Is he rich? Is he good-looking? Will you marry him? I want to marry a rich man, Toby says. You're rich aren't you? Jonathan says. Joshua is never going to marry. Eating on the floor Japanese-style, who are they, these little people? We'll need some furniture, Toby insists. For guests. What do you think? We're going to have parties here. It's true you can't invite people properly till you at least have some chairs.

But people come anyway. X who heard she was no longer living with Ezra. Y who heard from Ezra that she is living in Paris now. Z who heard from X. They've been waiting all these years. Pointless to apologize, *Je ne me suis pas encore installée*. The carpet is perfectly suitable. It's out of the question. She can't, the children might awake. She can't, she's exhausted. She can't, she must unpack. She can't, she has fifty letters to write. No, she can't, she must work on her book; she can't tell them what it's about. She must sleep. She must really write those letters. To Ezra. Can't. Business letters. Can't. To her lover in New York. Can't. Finish unpacking. Can't. Can't sleep. Can't work. —What is the proper way to dispose of a wedding gown one can't give to one's daughter or daughter-in-law? No proper way.

The plaster still hasn't dried. Can't dry in this damp..."Quartier pittoresque et malsain," as the *Guide Bleu* said. Long after midnight she paces in her fur coat.

Where are you going, Mum? Joshua stands blinking in the hall on his way from the toilet. To a ball in her nightgown, where else? She waits till he has scurried under the sheet in the next room before she puts out all the lights.

The room is crowded with people in party dress. They pass in and out. Some are out drinking on the terrace. The doors have been thrown open and the sun pours in.

Wake up, it's Wedding Sunday! shrieks a flushed blond woman. Her nude, prominently veined arm upraised waving a chiffon scarf like a general rallying an army, she sweeps across the room, a maenad, leading a group of seedy European intellectuals in her train. They cast furtive glances at the silver trays of garnished hams being carried out on the terrace while noting the disorder in the room: the unmade bed, old magazines, castoff garments, dirty cups and full ashtrays on the floor and the furniture. It's an artist's room, someone explains. Little girls stand around the desk rummaging through the stacks of papers and notebooks. Their cheeks are rouged and their eyes lined with blue eyeshadow. Such little girls wearing makeup! one of the guests laughs disapprovingly. They begin to throw the papers around while from the terrace the opening bars of a piano piece come through faintly.

Just then the Bridegroom enters in black, followed by his clan, a noisy procession of bearded men to the seventh generation. They swagger and lurch about, dragging their boots, flushed and perspiring under their kaftans, they press into the room. The air has become asphyxiating, but the women keep bringing in more crystal vases with huge, waxy, odorous flowers.

The Bride is led in, heavily veiled. Jangling silver bracelets weight down her wrists and arms. She enters barefoot like a slave, reeking of ether. The Bridegroom's clan has formed a group, the youngest squatting in the first row, the little patriarchs in the back standing on stools, they pose for a classroom picture. The Bride kneels down, her hands crossed behind her back, waiting to be beheaded while the Groom chants in a high falsetto: "You are my pride and glory! Without you I'm a beggar..." The kinsmen file past, grunting approval. Each places an iron collar around her neck till her head buckles. The Bridegroom joins kinsmen as they chant.

The Bride is placed in a coffin lined with pink satin. The Groom invites the menfolk to enjoy her in turn. All the children press around the coffin to watch. The men clamber in with their boots, the patriarch first, down to the youngest nephew, a boy with a girl's face and the smile of a gentle clown, while the Bridegroom blows smoke rings up to the ceiling. Soft as silk, the little nephew says, and they have to drag him away. Indignant women replace the coffin lid. The wedding has been consummated. The guests adjourn to the terrace where there is a reception for a famous actress.

The children have propped up the lid of the coffin with the handle of a rake. Now the little girls climb in and out. A head suddenly emerges from the coffin to deliver a speech: "Woman is part less than human, part more than human and part human."

The Bride and the Groom are playing "It" in the garden. She staggers around uncertainly, blindfolded, her arms stretched before her, and embraces a tree trunk passionately.

In a wall panel quite high and to the left practically behind her, a scribe or an angel is writing; perhaps a reproduction from a book, her eye caught only the gesture of the moving hand overlarge, violent... one of the Evangelists? An angel with a message for her, she persists in believing, because of his troubling presence, not bookish at all, grimacing and gesticulating to catch her attention. It's a bearded angel with a comic Jew-face, bible in hand, that changes into a cherub on a Renaissance fountain, then a faun...

How did Ezra get in?

How did Ezra do it? She wonders dimly, as she walks toward the kitchen still half asleep. It's past four. She will have a cup of tea.

How did Ezra get in, by what fraud, cunning or magic, when her door was locked? She always said no; to all men; to Ezra. Her look, her walk, the way she dressed, spoke, or kept silence, stated it clearly. She was waiting for someone else. Or perhaps for no man. She meant it when she told Ezra that she could not marry him because she was about to resolve something; she was not yet resolved. Ezra understood; it was his right to try to persuade her otherwise, to dissuade her from walking this path alone, wherever it led—she said she did not know in her confessed state of ignorance where her paths would lead. But Ezra was sure. She remembers only that he kept translating both her words and silences into another language, dazzling, polyglot; the foreign phrases from Greek, German, Latin, Hebrew, French; verses from the Old Testament. She was trying to make out his features in the dark: the face changing like reflections in water; the hands now in her hair, now fingers groping between blouse and skirt, skirt and slip, then lightly up her thigh; the voice, breath weaving, brushing over cheek, ears, throat; the fingers, cat-like, padding through her bush and before she knew it her palm came down over his hand and she had said, I want the real thing.

And lay smiling, pleased as if it had been done already while he asked anxiously, Are you sure you really want to, and What if I give you a baby, It hurts the first time; already driving in, having propped her up, mounted, and whispering in her ear while she clutched his head. It is not easy work deflowering a woman, he said. Then she let go, her hands falling away, her head rolling to the side, eyes open, saw the room in the sweep of a full circle: his shoe with his wallet in it on the floor to the left where her head was turned; the patch of dawning light in the window to the furthest right, and in the center Ezra straddled upright his knees hugging her ribs, tall and erect, looking out, out far, riding over miles of steppes, and still driving, she thought he would break straight through her skull, then breathing once more, breathing comfortably now, full of pleasure, the warm liquid trickling down her thigh his member slipping out, resting on her thigh, after rider and mount tumbled and fell together, and they both went to sleep.

It was something else she wanted. They both struggled against their own dreams and inclinations. Ezra wanted to be different, she, perhaps, wanted simply to stop dreaming, waiting, virginal; he lying that he wanted her, still wanting what he could not wean himself from; wanting to believe himself, her to believe him: that he wanted her; lying himself into believing. She, silent, still holding truth dearest like a last coin in her palm—perhaps a worthless coin—in the twinkling of an eye she flung it away, leaving her so empty-handed that Ezra could.

Scenes from another life played over, of no value now, she thinks while sipping her tea. She lies in bed, quietly watching the window. In two hours the alarm clock will ring.

The deception is endless. To laugh. To cry. To curse. To breathe is actually most that she can manage. The night is paling. Soon it will be dawn. Day will be starting. The light dim, thick at first, clears till it is entirely weightless; there is only the pure surface of day, the city of streets and buildings, the walls inside and outside, all will be surface only, on which other surfaces cast precise shadows.

Things couldn't be so monstrous, or frivolous or senseless as they appear to Sophie in Paris. Nothing she does is serious. Even though she has finally unpacked and even fixed up one room with curtains for her daughter, bought an expensive sofa, not serious. Not her relationship with any of the men she is seeing. It's simply in the nature of things; being the one-day-a-week mistress of a married man cannot be serious. As Roland keeps saying, if she were in love with him it would be catastrophic. He brings her bird-of-paradise flowers, limited-edition art books (he holds top position at a publishing house and can give her introductions); afterward they always have a feast of oysters with choice white wine, and he is a big man, and his expression when he speaks of his little boy, she likes that, but what is she supposed to do with it all between Tuesday and Tuesday? Better not be serious. Wasn't it a mistake to take her marriage seriously? But it's clear she was not cut out to be *la petite maîtresse*. No better at being the "other woman" as the "one woman," just the other side of the same bad coin. Most men want deception. But an outright bastard and pervert like Gaston is positively refreshing. He wants a woman to be a whore, he pulls the paraphernalia out of his drawer, he is going to humiliate you, nobody talks of love or pleasing one another, there is a tussle, and curiously, contrariness results in pleasure. Perverse? Just coping with Gaston is an achievement, but certainly not serious. As for Alain, he is a bore, but she needs him for circulating. Then there is, among former admirers, Nicholas, now settling in Rome with his pregnant wife and twins, who fancies he's still in love with her. He wants her for his Paris mistress and Sophie thinks it's a revolting idea, but there are the old ties. And actually if she were going to settle in Paris for life, being his Paris mistress in the long run might be a nice steady sort of thing, like the annual Budapest quartet or the Russian ballet...To fill in her life. A revolting idea. As for that young man in New York, it's not at all clear why she keeps up this strange correspondence, unless she is really in the grips of fate or the wildest folly. Absurd and maddening that his image continues to haunt her when she should be settling into her new life in Paris. It's simply to survive, she keeps telling herself; to regain something of herself in the form of a letter. Because nothing can come of it. He is simply too young and crazy. She has to think about her children. It was ridiculous for them to talk about the future. They parted with that understanding.

But now these letters stating his and her sorrow or resignation, the very fact that these letters are being written... It's really demonic, because whenever she believes it's over, that she will never hear from him again, invariably the first day she feels free of his phantom, a letter from Ivan arrives. She replies to it, of course. It's a week's job to put him together again from all the pieces, collating what he writes with previous letters and memories till she can send him on his way, in the sealed, stamped envelope in slot of the CTP box. Then the period of anguish, hopelessness, recovery. Till his next letter, the mere handwriting on the envelope sends the Chinese puzzle man flying, and once more she is in tears of bliss and misery and cursing him as she sits down to construct the ceremonial object making it seem like a letter.

And yet the letters to Ivan also are unserious. Each plotted elliptically between two impossible extremes of rushing to him and forgetting.

She must be practical, sensible. A woman needs money and a man. She needs a man to get started earning money. A man to manage her money. She has to know how to manage men.

She is really doing quite well. It's only her third month in Paris.

She is really quite mad.

Is she serious about her book at least?

It is not true, as their father claims, that Joshua is a mindless brute, or that her daughter is a cold fish or as Joshua describes his sister, a natural genius for making herself useless, why is there so little love in the family?

Jonathan is not stupid as his brother claims and screams at him or late in the evening alone with his mother, intimates with a tone of sadness and intimacy reminiscent of his father: I hate to say it, but

I think YoYo is just dumb. He is not to call him YoYo; he is taking his time, that's all, doing all right in school... Better than you did, if you must know. Well, he shrugs superciliously—his father's professional gesture—he started at a progressive school, I had to go—if you hadn't sent me to that—Enough is enough, now they're all going to same school and it's time to take his bath. Maybe by midnight, he says, testing the water heater, assuming the gas pressure stays constant. True, there are two inches of hot water, the rest of the water tank is ice cold. She continues ironing. He persists about his brother (not about his sister now—that's an evening for itself): Confidentially (having suggested his meaning by mimicry), you know what I mean— He's plump, she suggests. That's part of it, the whole thing, his sloppiness, the way he smiles, lets people push him around. I really think he's stupid. Sophie knows Jonathan is not stupid, or a ninny. Just quietly making up his mind, or trying to. And will he be able to with this older brother who is a combination bomb and Iago? Why do you look so mad at me? Joshua asks innocently. If you would worry half as much about yourself as about other people... And now go to bed, she cuts his next sentence. You can take a shower in morning. Hot shower before going out? Swedes do it all the time. So now we're Swedes. And he displays his filthy feet creeping under sheets. He's about to show the rash on his buttocks, but she prevents this with firm hug and goodnight kiss. Sleep well, darling. G'night, Mom, as she draws away, one eye opening slyly, I can tell when you're angry.

Back in kitchen, Sophie paces muttering to herself before she resumes her tasks. A curse. A punishment. Upon her has fallen the ungrateful task to which Ezra Blind's mother was not equal. Out of her womb another Ezra. But when she is done cursing and praying to God to prevent her wrath from falling on this innocent child— rather let another Ezra Blind come to her bed that she might strangle him if it must be—when she is done cursing and praying, she knows Joshua is not an evil reincarnation of his father. Knows, even if Jonathan does look a bit like Uncle Joske who became a bum... As for Toby, she knows she has spoiled and indulged her daughter. She is terrified she'll end up being raped while riding on a white horse dressed in her Sunday best, like in that awful Swedish movie. But she knows all this is nonsense. She knows Toby is all right, knows—

The notebook lies open on its first blank page—blank but for the speck of a mosquito-like insect, late survivor into autumn, that had dropped onto the sheet and stands trembling on its bent legs, near transparent, paler than its shadow. Obviously you can't write with an insect on the page. Try blowing it off, shake the notebook, try with a deft flick of the finger—the moribund little ogre won't be brushed off, it clings on, rooted fast, tiny claws invisible to the naked eye, gripping the porous pulp of the paper. There is only one solution, slide a hand under the hard cover, raise it and slam down firmly. Hold it pressed down tight. Another ten counts. It happened so fast it didn't feel a thing and you know it. As soon as it's dry and set into the paper properly you can start writing. Well done. The blow has fixed the insect in a very graceful figure, legs hanging as in flight, one stretched out, slightly longer than the other, wings folded angel-wise. A nice golden brownish color like old prints.

. . . coming into consciousness, a lifelong struggle. For countless departures, few arrivals—mostly false. The beginning can be dated from the momentous, if unrecorded, event when for the first time a child's hand wrote Sophia Alexandra Landsmann (actually, Landsmann Sophia Alexandra, as is customary for Hungarians) on the cover of her class notebook; or one of the first times the child's hand wrote the name for without time there cannot be memory. A child writing its name on a class copybook marks the beginning of a struggle, not of coming into consciousness. The coming and going, not marked. No first time, no difference between coming and going. No count:

drops from a faucet leaking in a deserted house. The struggle is in time and against time, that much is certain. The object is not so clear. To set up the start and finish lines. Chart a course. To salvage from the morass of memory and the diffusion of the present—what?

She remembers her happy love affair in New York.

His raining tongue laps under her eyelids herds of woolly mammoth, bison, leaping reindeer, a tusked wild boar. Her head fills till it's so heavy it rolls away by itself.

How would you define our relation? he asks. Technically we are lovers, she says after a while.

And nontechnically? (She cannot think of the term that would cover everything.)

She has gotten quite used to the way he leaps about and walks on top of the furniture. I don't ordinarily behave like this, he says, tossing up the blankets in the air with his feet. Don't, she says in her sleep, you're letting out all the water. And in protest has curled into a ball. Don't you have any more covers? He has heaped on her everything in the closet. He teases her with a hairbrush. But she knows it's not him, grabs his wrist and pulls him in. They realize all this is very silly. They will get up and read the newspaper.

The day hangs suspended—a dull golden weave on which an impressionist master's brush has sketched, placed at random, the familiar furnishings of a New York City apartment: the whiskey bottle, jar of instant coffee, cans of soup and spices on the shelf, a torn bag of sugar, ashtrays, magazines and a bowl of fruit on the floor. A tropical garden painted on the air. At this moment the mind, which has sunk deep into the trunk, a migrating organ, passing through the clapping

valves of the heart and the belly toward the bowels; the mind, especially lucid, observes with surprised amusement an old riddle unfold-
ing into a simple demonstration. Irrespective of will or will-lessness,
the arm plunges into space, the hand reaches out to seize a pear and
as gratuitously arrested, lies still on the fruit. Movement and rest,
irrespective of will or will-lessness. The mind, sunk comfortably in
the liver, finds a wonderful significance in this. It would like to make
a note of it; but does not, in fact, any more than a fat man submerged
in a hot bath will make a note of his revelation. He cannot. The paper
would get wet. Besides, to lift his arm out of the water is inconceiv-
able: it would damage his insight.

What are you thinking, he asks; you are so silent. She smiles. All
thoughts have been driven out of her head. Her face is only flesh.
Outside her now, a little harpy perched on the bookstand or hanging
from the ceiling, Worry wrings its hands.

She is laughing. Over her lover's sunken shoulder she sees in a brief
phosphorescent shimmer the smiling ornate head of the goddess
whose whim has undone her, and laughs back. These visions are only
to distract.

He promised to help her tie up the boxes today. Predictably, after a
shower, they make love instead. She must finish packing. It's terrible
to be in love. He's up again, taking another shower. Are you crying?
he asks. He has just finished shaving, lies down beside her. Aren't you
getting dressed? he asks. And they lie gazing at each other in a silence
that does not lengthen or gain weight. He composes her face of half-
moons.

He doesn't care. It's obvious. All the chairs are broken. There is no place
to put the clean dishes and laundry. She will put up shelves on her
own ... So that, at least—, she doesn't finish the sentence. Everything
depends on it, but she cannot explain. He is playing with a silver measuring tape; he pulls out the steel band. It springs back by itself, recoil-

ing in its tiny metal case when he lets go. He stretches the steel ribbon across her shoulders: eighteen inches. She wants it now to measure his spine; then he winds it around their waists, then their necks. Giving the figures so fast it is impossible to record them. Why must it be like this?

He is measuring spaces, distances. Between his right elbow and her nose. Her belly button and his left pelvic bone, her right nipple and his left eye. The rest is conjecture, he says. Three, two, one. Zero. Minus four, minus six, minus ten:

I don't care, she says. I don't care either.

Almost time to fetch the children and she hasn't even made the beds. Can't face thinking about what to serve for dinner. The effort of putting on her shoes is too much. She remembers how different it used to be—up at sunrise, on her bicycle, with baby in front, balancing laundry and groceries on each handlebar, another child strapped to the back. She remembers the young wife, stoical and innocent. It was beautiful to be always busy, harried; being used up, this was what life was all about, she was becoming almost transparent. But now she is stuck with herself, a grubby phantom that fattens on her days.

It's like the unmarried girl, her hair all snarls, big as a house—the old shapeless woe, panting for a man to find some use for her. Rubbish. She was the best student in ... She played Salome in ... And if not for Ezra, she'd be ... Rubbish.

"So what are we having for dinner?" Standing in line at the meat market on Place Maubert; trays heaped with glossy glands, hearts, brains and livers. The plucked chickens lined in rows all in the same coy posture: rumps pointing up, necks twisted and tucked under their breasts with the head peeping from under one wing. And rows of skinned rabbits laid out on their backs in furry boots, their forepaws tied over their heads, their flanks spread apart—"Well, Mum, what are you going to buy?" This is the way the world ends.

"Let Toby decide today...We'll take turns deciding—" she manages to say, but the children won't play this game.

"No, you have to decide, Mummy; we want you to decide."

Can't give them spaghetti again..."How about *le Self-Service?*"

"Oh, yes! There's a slot machine there."

"Then we can have spaghetti!"

"Yes! I want to play the slot machine."

"No," she announces. "I'm going to make a roast." But they're pulling her out of line, then dancing ahead, all excitement, and Joshua taking her arm, festive, kindly and superior, "Cheer up, Mum," he says, "I know you think the slot machine is bad for my character. But you don't realize it takes a certain skill...So, it's really educational," he concludes and adds, "C'mon Mum, don't look like that. You should have more fun in life..."

"But why?" Ezra gasps.

He stands stunned in the hallway, still in his galoshes, coat half unbuttoned, a night's train journey written on his face.

"I don't want to be married to you," she repeats.

"But why, Sophie?"

His look of utter bewilderment belies the least suspicion of a rift between them. Hardening his face, biting on his pipe, he struggles to maintain calm. A shattered man, he has not lost all pride. It is difficult not to be moved. Ezra has his moments of beauty: just now, staring expressionless, an animal dazed by a sudden blow, he seems so solitary and forlorn—a stranger, as if he were already deserted, the person she cast out into the street, cut out of her life. If he were to walk out now without a word, she could not bear it.

"So," he says, and takes another deep breath. "So this is what I must hear when I come to see you. A twelve-hour trip." He puts a small oblong jewelry box on the table. "A present. Please take it and don't thank me. *Na ja*. I am a fool," he says dryly, gnawing on a pipe stem.

"We have discussed this matter before," she says, "and I have written you..."

"I thought the matter was settled, I thought—What has possessed you?" He speaks brokenly, tearfully, but with utmost composure, of how they had discussed and settled matters during the three days he visited her in Paris last spring—they had resolved matters, discussed their difficulties: Paris was the solution.

"I think I have been more than generous. How many husbands do you think permit their wives to live in Paris?" As for breaking the marriage, he did not take that seriously, of course, he never took that seriously, he says sternly, and with bitterness and superiority now; takes off his coat, his galoshes, and continues. A responsible man, under great strain, a reasonable man, a patient man, speaking to a woman undeserving of his patience, an irresponsible, childish woman, seething with spite and vindictiveness, driven by impossible dreams, lacking all sense of reality; a woman he once loved, against whose folly he must now protect the home, the family. A man cursed to perform this grim duty. "It's bitter," he says. She says nothing. One is never prepared for the queer, horrible way these things really happen. It's unbearable.

"Could we have some tea?" he asks. She is in the kitchen. She really likes to make tea for him. It's a comfort. It's crazy, but it's a fact. Such small comforts make life bearable. Perhaps Ezra is right and she is mad. Perhaps Ezra is wrong and she is still mad. Drop the whole thing. A lot of crazy talk. Receive him with a hot bath, breakfast, clean sheets; because she wants it, even if he doesn't want it and has to reproach and quarrel, even if she has contempt for him; do it simply because she needs it for her sanity. He comes into the kitchen.

"Have you something to eat?" he asks, opening the icebox. "As usual, only food for the children." It was always so. Her asceticism. She is so tired of the old complaints she is ready to cook a goose with dumplings. But it's just too late. She wants him out. She really wants him out. He weeps into the teacup. "We will not survive this. I know I will not survive it." So perhaps he has accepted. Weary and dumbfounded, she waits for him to finish weeping. In an hour the children will be home from school. She must get the papers for him to sign, however pointless everything seems at this moment. Yes, it's too late for everything; too late to end the marriage. Still, it must be done.

"So," he says, and takes her hand. "It is settled. Please may I hold your hand? You've taken off the ring, I see; but we are still married. We must both try. But Sophie! But why, Sophie!"

"Why?" She is up, clutching the back of the chair. "I told you in New York and in Ibiza, I told you in Genoa and in Paris, last year and again this summer; I've told you and told you and told you and I'm telling you for the last time: The marriage is over. It's over. The marriage is over." She screams.

"Please," he protests, clutching his ears.

"I'm screaming so you'll hear me, yes I'm screaming: The marriage is over."

He rushes to the door muttering to himself; she follows him. "You're not going to slither out."

"I'm not. I just wanted to make sure the children..."

"The children are in school and I don't care if the whole house hears me screaming. THE MARRIAGE IS OVER."

"Please control yourself and let's sit down and discuss this quietly in a civilized manner." The reasonable man to his crazy wife. "It's a life decision involving the lives of three children!"

"We have discussed this matter, Ezra, for seven years. We have discussed it and discussed it and discussed it. I have nothing more to say."

"I am sorry," he says with a perplexed air, "you must forgive me. I have a different sense of the situation. I remember we had such a nice dinner at the Coupole the last time with the old crowd." Speech fails. "Perhaps I really don't understand. Forgive me, but I must have a drink. This is really too much." He sips the Scotch she has served him. "I want only to understand. I won't stand in your way, hold you against your will—what would I have from that?" It's the voice of the lover and friend. "You are a just and noble person. The woman I married. I know I have failed you—please allow me to speak—I am not asking you to forgive me. I am resigned. You will have your freedom, I promise I will not stand in your way, but I must understand why. Why *now* after all these years?"

"It's seven years Ezra," she says, staring out the window. "Seven years that I've been telling you."

"Was it really so terrible with me?" he asks, smiling at her and pouring himself another drink. "Tell me, Sophie, I want to understand the woman I married—the woman I divorce. You can talk to me. We are friends."

"No," she says coldly.

"But why, Sophie?" He is offended. "If there is another man... Look, I don't care who you screw around with, the marriage is sacred. We promised each other. It's Nicholas, I know. But that's neither here nor there. Maybe you suddenly don't like my nose. You're capable of any frivolity. No, I can't give you a divorce unless you have someone else to marry you. I am responsible for you. You have no reason to want a divorce. You just want to break the marriage. Why? Are you evil? Are you bent on my destruction?"

"I don't want to be married to you."

"But you don't see me. We live in different cities. I give you complete freedom. I visit every so often, we spend a few weeks of the year together for the sake of the children—Look, Sophie, it's not easy for me with you, but a marriage is a marriage. You can live as you please and with whom you please. What more can you want? What do you gain from a divorce?"

"The thought of being married to you drives me insane."

"Then see an analyst. I have no more time to waste on these discussions. We have more important things to talk about. When do the children come home?" He looks at his watch. He wants to spend the afternoon with the children. All this has exhausted him; he really needs a nap but he must meet someone at the Deux Magots. He will be back in time to take the children for dinner. They have important matters to discuss...

Soon it will be Christmas. Sophie is still trying to come to terms with the future. With the fact or the idea? She doesn't know what the future is. A pseudo-problem, she resolves, strolling through the courts of the Louvre, and not to be taken seriously. Anyway, time passes of itself, it runs without gasoline, it can't stop.

As she walks along the sandy paths of the Tuileries, the possible relation between the force of gravity and the temporal flow whereby all this mass and spectacle, the Louvre included, was hurtling into the next instant is tantalizing her mind, when she notes that a man whom she had seen standing before a white Alfa Romeo at the Carrousel entrance of the garden when she entered is now standing at the rue de Rivoli gate, looking at her, on her way out. It is the same man in the same expensive cashmere camel's-hair coat, tartan scarf, beret, pigskin leather gloves, the white Alfa Romeo parked visibly near the gate. He watches her approach: a civilized man's predatory look. In a situation like this (not yet actually accosted but simply alerted to the strong probability), a woman disposes of a series of mysterious adjustments whereby she can, while maintaining her nonchalant pace, and without altering the diffuseness of her gaze or appearing to scrutinize...

...pleased to attract the attention of an obviously wealthy and well-built man still in his prime, and perhaps behind the clothes-horse—she suspects he has facials, and why not?—there is a soul. (More likely a drunk, looking for a woman with a soul.) Of course, once more she has been recognized by a dim-sighted worldling.

Where would she like to go? Urban setting is always a problem in these preliminaries, unless the man himself is the lure, but there is a place in the Bois de Boulogne she has eyed dreamily on Sundays with the children. Her capacity for self-deception goes only so far; it's clear as she leans back on the leather cushion that she wouldn't be interested to be with this man except as a partner in a pleasant journey; a walk along the beach might be just as nice—in the city it needs a fat wallet. He is delighted to be conducted to such a pleasant place; she looks out over the white tablecloth, and silver bowl of bouillon, at the bare branches. From the fine lines of branches threading into mist she draws her smile, which elicits some remark about her being un-*parisienne*, Nordic, her mystery— Fortunately the language barrier —her limited, his incomprehensible French—puts some restriction on inane conversation. Having begun as usual with jokes (Are you a model? Did you rent the car and outfit?) it's a variant of the old story. Lives near Milan; owns some factories. Wife and children. Nice family; he just isn't a family man. Doesn't know what he is. Once interested in mountain climbing and Indian philosophy.

. . . go somewhere else for coffee and dessert? No, she will finish the wine, it's marvelous. She must remember the name—no, it's better not. It's quite wonderful not to be Sophie Blind just now. It's wonderful enough to be this someone else in the car. He asks why she is smiling. She answers with a new smile which turns into a kiss. She is thinking of what her aunt told her when she was twelve: Always be sure your underwear is clean even if you're only going across the street; you never know when a car might hit you and people will see your underwear. While they wait at an intersection she hears him tell her about the garage; it's three blocks from the hotel, does she mind walking? He could ask the doorman, but he doesn't want *n'importe qui* to drive his car. She doesn't mind walking; it's right, his tenderness for his car, it's such a delicate, sensitive, powerful beast—she's in love with it herself. They talk about cars. He finds it unusual, her enthusiasm for machines, women don't usually—she hasn't had the opportunity of course. She chatters foolishly about typewriters, phonographs, a motor scooter she owned once. She wonders how long this euphoria will last. Whether it will last her through. In the elevator (perhaps just the stupid situation: sealed in this ascending coffin with him, a separate individual who doesn't mean anything to her) the reflection that she is a bitch taints her euphoria; doesn't interrupt her ease, only changes its color, which may be for the best. Undeluded, she walks with the same ease, it doesn't spoil her pleasure. There is no regret when she awakes to herself, all the wine drained off in the act of pleasure, leaving her utterly lucid, alone, curiously purged; after a while, just empty and becoming restless. She recalls other rooms in other places...the men...It's really quite nice, this elegant suite at the George V. Faïence knobs high in the wall so you don't have to bend when you take a shower. Nice, the thin white blankets—Does she really have to go in half an hour? They could have an early supper served in the room. He is explaining about his trip to London: He would invite her to come along except that his brother-in-law will be waiting for him at the airport. But she could join him in a day or two, and they could drive through Scotland or fly off to—

She is dressed. He wants to know how he will find her. She smiles, her hand on the curved brass handle: Perhaps they'll meet again some afternoon in the Tuileries...

Strolling out the carpeted lobby (a fleeting glance at the newspaper headlines reassures nothing has changed for better or worse), she is feeling rather good, the hot bath in particular, till at the entrance of the métro she discovers she has lost her gloves in his car or the hotel. (Perhaps in view of such an eventuality, or for unrelated motives, Sophie had stuffed her bag full of hotel stationery and soap, a faïence knob from the bidet—nothing from the Milanese gentleman, in whose reality she did not entirely believe.)

Nice for an afternoon—but too strenuous a business to incarnate some guiding star or even an exotic fish for a floundering millionaire.

Has she missed her calling? She recalls backing out of a very attractive offer two years ago: a yacht, villa in Nice, apartment in Paris. Wanted her to fly to San Francisco with him. Took her three days to realize the futility of it. Sorry now? But then other things wouldn't have happened. As for the tyrannical rich man who was usually on the other side of fifty, that too was impossible in the long run—and anything over a day ran into a long run or just a waste. No, it was just too much trouble to comply with an assured, vain man's whims, or revolt, or get around him—that was the kind of patience Sophie knew she didn't have. It naturally occurred to her that she might use a floundering rich man for her ends, indeed this was mostly on her mind. It wasn't so much a question of the means; it wasn't at all a moral problem, but simply that if you've set your heart on going to Rome, the Shanghai Express won't get you there. You're better off walking. The Shanghai Express might be great fun, you might fall in love with a station master, it could make you forget about ever wanting to go to Rome, revolutionize your life or be just an adventure. All this was possible but it wouldn't get her to Rome.

In her coat pocket is the letter to New York she wrote last night, which she decides not to mail.

Ezra lies on her bed when she comes home late at night.

"Don't look so shocked," he laughs. "I'm still your husband."

"Where is the baby-sitter?" she asks.

"I paid the baby-sitter and sent her home. I am glad to see my wife goes out. But you don't seem very pleased to see me. Please try to make a friendlier face," he says rising, his smile affectionately indulgent. "Should I have stayed outside till you returned? I wanted to see the children."

"You could have let me know that you were coming."

"Sophie, I have taken this time out from my lecture schedule just so I could see you. I must be back in London by tomorrow noon and fly to New York the next day. It wasn't easy to arrange and you are not very friendly."

"All right," she says, "then let's settle things. I wrote you a month ago."

"Yes, I received your letter." He rises with a gesture of grief. "I didn't know what to write. Sophie, I would not hold you against your will. But a divorce! Sophie, are you aware of all the difficulties, professional, medical; the real problems we must face together? How do you imagine a divorce—it's economically unfeasible, I can't afford it. Divorce is a luxury of the rich. Poor people have to stick it out together. I have been lenient, generous, I have yielded on many issues, too many, but I have let you go too far. It's obvious you are bent on the destruction of the marriage, a compulsion clear from the beginning. No, I will not permit it, someone has to be responsible."

"Ezra, you promised."

"Sign? Out of the question. What kind of papers? You went to a lawyer? I can't believe it. My own wife to whom I entrusted myself and our children? You went to a lawyer. My own wife has turned into my enemy." He weeps, but in the next instant collects himself. "It's unworthy of you," he says with disgust.

"If you don't sign the agreement, I'll take you to court."

"So that's what you are. A bitch. *Na ja*. I am not the first man to . . ." he mutters to himself, pacing angrily. He wants to see the papers. "Please," he demands, it is unworthy of her to entertain the thought that he might tear up the papers. He is offended, disgusted. She has no sense of him, sees him as a common brute, uncivilized— only proves how far out of touch with reality—he demands to see the papers, must he scream? Holding the sheets, he stares at the first page. "Legal gibberish, what kind of language is this? A piece of paper. *Zum arschwischen*."

"Sometimes one's life depends on a piece of paper."

He cannot look at it now. It makes no sense. If she has problems she should see a psychiatrist, not lawyers. It's a psychiatrist she needs. Or a lover, or a beating. Beat her blue. "I'm not going to beat you. Oh no." He kicks off his shoes, throws off his jacket, pants, pulls back the bedspread and gets into bed, muttering to himself in German and Hebrew.

She stands glaring, speechless.

"You don't like me in my drawers? I know I'm ridiculous. You have made me ridiculous." He lies on his back, smiling, his eyes veiled. "I know you think I'm undignified, a boor," he mimics the disgust her expressionless mask of dignity conceals. "I know. I know. I know everything you feel and think. Sophie, you are a child. A pure and noble child; I understand you," asking her to come to bed, his out-stretched arm invites her, his smile is seraphic. "Sit down, I am leaving tomorrow. It may be our last chance to..."

She wants to be out of this room. Her coat lies on the back of the chair; she wants to walk out, simply to move and breathe. But she can't simply walk out because of the children, because she must get him to sign the papers. "Consider it as a business proposition," he pursues with gentle irony. "I am not pleading with you; I will not use force. We are in the twentieth century; you are a free woman and I want you to make a rational choice. I hope one day you will feel some affection for me. I have a right to hope, after all, but I accept your present feelings of hostility. I want you to look at this as an offer in terms of your interests, professional ambitions, your taste. I know how important it is for you to live in the right setting. We have struggled through such difficult years; now for the first time I can offer you what you always wanted." A city of culture, he pursues, and reminds her that she always wanted to live in Europe; and she could go to Greece every summer. As for her Paris apartment, he can think of any number of solutions. "Isn't it reasonable?" he asks. "Be reason-able," he says.

She can't be reasonable even if his proposition appears reason-able—reasonable and attractive for someone else. She cannot be that person. Even if her own position is groundless, the fact is she has no position, she has no plans, she is nowhere. She has only her feelings to rely on. And she must say no. Perhaps she is really in another room, a young woman listening to Ezra Blind's marriage proposal fifteen years ago. Must this time say no.

"We have made mistakes," he is saying. "But we are not children any more. I have changed, Sophie. I promise you."

Even if he means it, she can't forgive herself for making the mistake the first time, or risk making this mistake again. Even if it's not reasonable. Sometimes it is imperative to be unreasonable.

"I am not pressing you, you don't have to give your decision now. But think about it. I will be in Paris again in two weeks. Think about it, Sophie," he concludes. "And now, after we have spoken as friends..." He is asking her to come to bed. It's three A.M., he points out, it's only proper after all. "But Sophie, why not?" he laughs. "Come, I'll woo you. Sophie, you know even if I fool around with other women, you're the only woman I ever loved. You're the only woman who arouses me." He will prove it to her right now. She won't lie down. She demands he get out of her bed. He rises laughing, puts his arm around her, pulls her toward the bed.

"No, Ezra. Please. The children will wake up."

"But why? How odd. You're really strange." He smiles at her, baffled. Not sleep with her own husband when she sleeps with other men? He knows all about it—her affair with Roland and some rich young art collector she got to know through his girlfriend. He knows everything and it's all right if she's enjoying herself. No one can say he isn't the most generous husband. "Come, be nice... Don't be afraid to put your head on my arm," he laughs. "All right, put it on the pillow."

"I can't," she whispers.

His hand moving to caress her breasts, still laughing, "But Sophie. Baby. Are you crying? I know how you feel. It can't be so bad. Pretend I'm a stranger. Don't cry, please don't cry..."

She gets out of bed. "What's the matter? Come back, Sophie."

"I can't," she says, putting on her coat.

"What can't you?"

"I can't forget that I loved you once."

"Where are you going?"

She needs to take a walk, she tells him quietly. No, alone. She needs to be alone. It's all right, she tries to soothe him. She'll be back at seven in time for the children.

"Go back to bed. I'll go. Take off your coat."

She won't take off her coat till he's out. She wants to see him go. "Now. Right away."

"I may put on my clothes. You really want me to go?" Maddening to watch—he can't tuck in his shirt properly. He boohoos shamelessly like a child, the tears drop on his shoe. Wouldn't it have been better to go to bed with him—for the hell of it, do anything, pull each other's ears . . . "I'm going, I'm going," he sobs while she is trembling with rage. But he does it very slowly. He is out. She latches the door. But he hasn't really left. She can hear him crying on the next landing. "The only woman who really loved me . . . I know . . . I know . . . no woman will ever . . ." she hears Ezra howling up the stairwell. It's how Ezra wants it. Ezra always wins. He leaves after a while. Of course. He is mad only so far. And he'll be back in two weeks once again to die the old comic death.

It has narrowed down to a lack of choice. Rereading the long letter from New York—not a love letter, she decides—and yet it's clear he is as powerless as she to break off their relation. He does not accept her silence as a way of ending. A right ending is impossible under the circumstances, but no ending is intolerable. It's maddening like an unfinished book, you know the missing last pages exist in someone else's hands; at the address on the envelope before her—or, if in the hands of fate, all the more reason for her to take this trip. A folly . . . A necessity . . . She must make a trip if only to destroy the mythic personages that feed on human time, growing larger with each letter, created by a barrier of water, mere miles, that convert into flight hours, that convert into French francs . . .

Perhaps he simply wants to continue writing to her; wants her to continue writing to him . . .

What exactly was contained in the letter Sophie finally stamped and dropped in the slot of the blue CTP box is out of grasp. When Ivan's reply came a week later she was climbing the dingy stairway with bottles of *limonade*, Vichy, *vin ordinaire, baguettes*, the envelope on top of the bulging bag of groceries steadied by her chin; resisting the temptation to lay down her load and read it, till on the fourth landing she yielded. Another letter from him in the next mail—with ". . . disregard the first, written in a fit of madness," but saying essentially the same—she tore open on her way out and read striding down the boulevard. The first letter made her cry. The second made her laugh.

WHAT SENSE did Sophie make of her life on the plane bound for New York when she was heading there to arrange her affairs so that she might settle properly in Paris? None.

What sense did Sophie make of her life on the plane leaving New York after having had a happy love affair? None.

What sense did Sophie make of her life as she boarded the plane at Orly, going to see her lover again? What sense would she make of her life after she arrived, a week, a year, ten years after—?

Thinking about the sense of one's life, trying to make sense of it, was an idle and useless preoccupation, Sophie had always believed. Worse than useless, it was positively unhealthy. In short, a bad habit. And like most bad habits, this one was foisted on you and fostered by other people, their judgments whether in asking or stating. Confronted with the senselessness of other people's judgments, Sophie naturally preferred her own brand of senselessness. In time she learned that if she was to avoid arguments she must be more agreeable. There was no appeasement through keeping one's peace, even nodding and smiling was not enough.

People wanted a statement. Mostly Ezra spoke for her. When he expressed her view in company, she thought it was just as well he did. She would never express herself in such a way, certainly not as artfully or persuasively as Ezra; she couldn't have—she could never make a statement of this sort at all. When Ezra made statements for her or about her, he put them together from their conversations, her remarks on the books he had her read. The statement that came out of this would be neither true nor false; it was simply Ezra's creation for a

49

roomful of people who might otherwise have been offended by his wife's silence.

It was strange, slightly embarrassing, to have Ezra speak for her and about her in her presence as if she were in a trance or absent. It is true she would not be listening—not even aware of not listening. She did not forget, however, that she was Ezra's wife sitting in company; that it was under this cover that she could be anywhere or nowhere, anyone or no one. Perhaps she enjoyed it too much, as Ezra reproached her in private. He complained how she made him do all the talking, she who regarded talk so much shit, made him, poor fool—! Wasn't it easy for her, wasn't she fortunate to have a faithful servant and interpreter. What would the Delphic oracle be without an interpreter? *Ein stinkendes Loch.* While Ezra was parodying himself and her in these roles, Sophie may have wondered where she really stood.

Even when Sophie couldn't bear Ezra, she loved the marriage. It was a many-layered shroud whose weight she relished. To carry it eased, simplified entering a room full of people, it justified her presence in the room. There it was, a costume ready-made for public occasions. Ezra's wife; this was the answer to anyone who wanted to know her. She was the woman Ezra Blind married. It had weight and power: like an impermeable cloak it warded off the inevitable swarm of prying, talky, argumentative, interrogating people. The shroud served to receive the obligatory marks and tags, it absorbed unavoidable stains, its fabric wrinkled and stretched obligingly. It saved her skin. How not cherish a garment so serviceable?

As for Ezra, he may have joked and complained about his wife but he knew he had a treasure. She was not like any other woman. He told her about other women while they lay in bed, women he knew before her, or was just coming from—because he had lied, he hadn't been in the library or taking a walk with Rabbi X; he could tell her the truth now in bed together because she was the only woman whom he loved. "I don't know why," he said, and gave a stream of reasons why he knew he ought to love her and yet it was unnatural for him to do so. "I really don't know why I love you," he said, because she was not like other women he had known or desired. She was difficult and impossible, yet not in the way other women were, with their nagging and clinging and demanding—except when she was in despair, then at least he knew what to do with her: mock her, beat her, screw her, flatter, abuse, comfort; then she was just like other women. But not enough, Ezra complained. He told her what other women did in desperation, depths to which they sank, obscenities, perversion; how they were ready to mortify, demean themselves, begging to be trampled on. She was not masochistic essentially, he sighed. The beatings were functional, not an erotic experience like with another woman who crawled around on all fours begging to be whipped, wanting to eat his shit; yes, she implored him. Sophie wasn't impressed. She couldn't even be properly jealous or offended. Her father had explained to her when she was a girl why men needed obscenity to get pleasure, why it couldn't be simple. So now here it was. And if she still wanted it simple, it was, Ezra pointed out, because she was a child and hopelessly romantic. If Ezra's practices did not appeal to her that was a matter of personal taste; to judge him by society's rules, as a principle she refused. She hadn't asked for a bourgeois marriage; and if ever the depressing thought took hold of her that she was trapped in a bourgeois marriage, Ezra's behavior assured her that she was not. What kind of marriage did Sophie want? She didn't want to get married in the first place. Ezra wanted to get married. Ezra had been profoundly shocked when she had answered his first proposal with the suggestion that they live together in free love; and she had been surprised, amused and finally touched by his reaction, for he had presented himself as a cosmopolite, a free spirit, and they were in fact in bed together at the time; Ezra, still wounded by her frivolity, claimed he had deflowered her in the certain hope that they would marry. His insistence on this point, which he could not explain, intrigued her. Ezra did not believe in bourgeois marriage either, or in orthodox Jewish marriage. Was it the Jew in him? The man in him? Something she as a woman could not grasp? While she was trying to make up her mind about whether she liked or disliked Ezra, his solemn insistence on the marriage still preoccupied her most, and when she assented, it was to the marriage, before having quite made up her mind about Ezra. Once she was married she was thankful that it had happened so; who knows if she would ever have made up her mind whether she liked Ezra? And how unimportant that was! She didn't fully realize till after they were married that it was the only respectable and natural way to be. Two people, a man and woman, living together was intrinsically right; and to have established this as a settled matter once and for all so you didn't waste your time looking around or endlessly analyzing your feelings—this was the virtue of marriage. Thus Sophie found herself, while still frowning on marriage in principle, enjoying it in practice, enjoying the sheer twoness that endured independent of moods, likes and dislikes, that did not need reasons and that wouldn't be destroyed by reasons; and was more baffled than hurt by Ezra's running around, his need for distraction, which she knew did not arise from her insufficiency, just as her fidelity did not spring from any feeling for Ezra; they had different ways of being.

Her innocence was maddening, Ezra raved. He put her in obscene postures, but whatever she did she was hopelessly chaste. "A *kouros*—a chaste boy," Ezra called her. It was maddening, maddening, and yet he adored it. "Nero would have been wild about you," Ezra said. A dubious compliment, Sophie understood; and to perform the duties of wife to husband under these peculiar circumstances seemed most paradoxical.

"Why don't you find yourself men—?" She asked him finally. "Buggering is between men, after all."

"I thought of it," Ezra admitted.

"Then why?"

"I am afraid I'd be the she," Ezra confessed.

Didn't want to be the she. The Jew in him.

"Why do I love you?" Ezra raved in the night. "Why do I always come back to you?"

And in his way of asking he gave the answer that he preferred to intone with a question mark rather than a period.

It was strange with Ezra. Ezra was always on stage: at one moment

Sophie was up there with him speaking the lines, and at another she was like a street urchin peeping through the boards to watch the great comedian perform; so it went back and forth like a badly edited reel, and all the time there was a woman waiting, a woman already in bed, perhaps with the light turned off; a woman waiting for him to come to her wordlessly in the dark; a woman wanting something from this man, that he alone and no other man could give her and that he could give only to her. A woman waited for her husband. As for the comedy, she enjoyed that too, especially since Ezra was enjoying it enormously; ·perhaps she began to believe in the parts he assigned to them, perhaps she was living it and enjoying it, as Ezra reproached her.

Another woman waited and wanted reality. Sophie understood more clearly and hopelessly with time that all this clowning was the awful reality between her and Ezra, that it could never be otherwise, and perhaps she knew this all the years she was married to Ezra, knew it could never be otherwise with Ezra, and all the time she was another woman waiting for another man, however she denied it to herself because she wanted her life to be proper and decent. Ezra saw it, Ezra understood from the beginning that a man like himself couldn't make Sophie happy and he was always teasing her about it. "I know the kind of man who would make you happy," Ezra said, describing now mockingly, now solemnly, the kind of man his wife would like, some improvisations, others real men he invited to their house; and Sophie never showed the least interest because she wanted her life to be decent and proper, that's all she wanted, and wanted all the more fiercely since Ezra laughed at decency and propriety.

She had accepted as part of marriage two people walking together in solitude and opposition. But that her faith and will and pride should be used up, this Sophie could not accept. And when it was used up she could not forgive Ezra or herself. However much she blamed Ezra for his foolishness, it was herself she blamed more strongly and endlessly for being defeated by Ezra's foolishness. She tried to believe that she was leaving Ezra not because she was defeated, but refusing both her own and Ezra's defeat in this marriage, even if there was nothing else left of her than the power of this refusal. But this didn't really make sense; and finally she couldn't explain to herself why she was leaving Ezra, why just now, not three years ago or next year. Now she had to explain to other people—Ezra, her lawyer, family, the children, friends in Paris and in New York. To herself she had nothing to say.

She did not wish to discuss her marriage with Ivan, whom she had just met. "A misadventure," she summed up the matter, annoyed by the way he forced these statements from her, not so much by questioning as by cutting under her evasions and drawing his own conclusions, which she had to protest before he went too far. In the beginning it was simply annoying to have to fend against his oblique probing when they met to talk about his underground movie or her book, but as the discussion progressed from week to week and she realized that Ivan was better at this game—both in inventing evasions and building theories—she began to wonder why Ivan was so interested in understanding her relationship to Ezra. Was it to understand her? But it wasn't her any more, not what she wanted him to know about her. Was it to understand why marriages broke down, what in particular a woman would not forgive a man; was it because of the future ahead of him, or for a movie he might make? And that she couldn't answer either.

Whatever clarification for himself Ivan may have been seeking, he was really trying to make her see her own life differently, Sophie sensed from the beginning, touched by Ivan's tone of jealous concern and his irreverent joking about Ezra. Her situation roused his anger. To see men like Ezra win, Ivan pursued (and he feared that she might in the end return to Ezra, sensing behind her evasiveness irresolution), this was what he could not bear to see happen. But why should it torment him?

And why did she continue to want to see Ivan? Even when these conversations unsettled her, and his company, so often gloomy, sullen, silent or speaking as if he occupied some space outside this world, made her uncomfortable. Only after they embraced did she know that this was what she had wanted to happen for the past weeks.

Now she would have liked to speak truthfully to Ivan and she didn't know how; suddenly she had to question whether she had loved Ezra at all because of the way she loved now. Behind her will to love Ezra part of her was hiding and not caring. There was something that didn't change in her by marrying Ezra and she had thought it a good thing at the time; only now that loving someone had changed her did everything have to be revised.

Realizing that she had merely loaned herself to Ezra for a life-term lease, but withholding part of herself—as to her unpremeditated, unthinking surrender to Ivan with whom she was prepared at most to enjoy a happy love affair of three weeks—she didn't know what sense to make of it. Perhaps it was in the nature of the situation: marriage required a loan; the true and complete giving occurred only where there was no thought of continuation. But she couldn't honestly believe this; even now her quiet happiness with Ivan was mixed with some falseness—accepted and sensed as wrong by both. What was simple had to be veiled; wanting to be more than her lover, he played being her lover with a touch of tender theatricality. The tenderness was true and she had to protect herself against it, escape in a false selfishness, making believe for both of them that she had left the real person behind even before she took the plane to Paris. And all the time their eyes continued to say: we are only pretending that we are pretending. True mixed with false, it couldn't be otherwise they both knew without knowing where they stood; even if Ivan still tried to define their situation, he knew it was hopeless and that all statements between them were to protect the silences they had come to enjoy.

"What will you do in Paris? Why Paris?" Ivan asked. "And what are you doing here with me?"

... AT ORLY you're equally remote from Paris and New York. Chimes follow you up the escalator, through glassed halls with shops and perfume counters, everywhere the two chimes prelude the same drowsy voice announcing *passagers de destination* —— *passagers arrivant de* ——. *Peau Douce* is playing at the Cinéma Orly. I shouldn't be writing to you now. Terrified when I think of us in our different times. In your room the light is just changing. Here numbers roll through the slots on time indicators, a picture marking each minute, faster than on a clock ... Must stop writing. They've announced the gate.

... and now it's over. We've boarded at last. Left my remaining eighty centimes on the plate in the ladies' lavatory. FASTEN SEAT BELTS and NO SMOKING signs are on. The plane crawls along turning paths sentried by blowtorches; and waits, engines roaring, for its turn on the takeoff. I have made none of the usual preparations for this trip: the dress, thoughts, reading, proper for a sky journey. Packed away linen dress purchased two weeks ago specially to arrive in. Left behind volume of Heraclitus. Better so. Up alone without talisman. Good so. Tired of being on ceremony with God. Left everything behind. Even my memories are outside me, stored in boxes, burning in the incinerators of Paris. We've taken off. As we turn over the city, the captain's voice points out Paris monuments. The plane climbs steeply and noses into a cloud bank. They're announcing altitude and winds, flight time to —— didn't catch the name of the city. Surprised the plane is so empty. A small party of businessmen, Bulgarians or Turks, have struck up a card game in front. Family across the aisle, young couple with three children; trying to quiet children. Americans.

Keep dozing off. Oppressive dreams of other crossings. Pink lakes in the sky, flying over new volcano near Reykjavik. Wake up in a stupor. All the engines are on. Still trying to rise over cloud banks. Water streaks black panes, roar of motors drowns out speaker announcing altitude, speed, winds in four languages.

Windows dark. No point looking out. Will sleep. Motors deafening. Men in front still playing cards; crew has joined them. Plane lurching. All the signs are on. Family vomiting. Card players have ordered more drinks; screaming their bids. Windows dark. Can't sleep. Motors seem to have stopped. Silence. Something wrong with my ear... Crew still drinking. We're not moving. The motors have stopped. Such stillness...

On the street before his apartment house a lobster-faced doorman shovels the flying snow. It is he who slips the letters under his door. He who smiled as she entered when it was spring, the same old man who shall greet her when it shall be spring again. With a smile of greeting and thankfulness, swiftly she steals past him in a white flurry, her lids glued down with snow. In the elevator a slender Puerto Rican dozes on the stool. To the roof. Could you please take me to the roof. Yawning, he turns the lever a full half circle.

"Just a quick kiss..." But he clasps her face. "It's so nice to have you here."

"Don't stop working," she says. "I am happy just being quiet together."

But he isn't working. He lifts her up, leads her leaping around the room—where? On the roof. On top of the desk, in the tub, on the rug, into bed. A naked man crouches over her, his knees hold her clinched by the waist while he bends over for matches on the floor.

He lights two cigarets, puts one in her mouth, bites her chin. He won't let her go. But maybe she's had enough?

"Oh no..." She wonders how long they can keep this up. Of course she loves it when he locks his arms around her like a cage. She is just worried about his work.

"Work is a dirty word," he says. "Don't you know nothing I do is work?"

"Still, shouldn't we..." She doesn't know any more what.

"Stop?"

"No. Please."

How can she worry about resuming normalcy at such a moment. "But will we ever?" Not that she wants to.

"Wait. You've just arrived. It will be over all too soon. Didn't you know I was like this? Lazy. Sensual. Foolish," he tells her softly, then laughs. "You look so surprised."

"Everything is still so new."

"Are you sorry you came? Your voice sounds so sad."

"I'm sleepy," she murmurs, "in Paris it's five hours later."

He puts out the light. But she can't sleep.

"What is it?" he asks.

"To think that I almost didn't come because I wasn't sure how you felt. I had no idea it would be like this."

"Did you doubt that I love you? How could you doubt—?"

"Then why didn't you come to Paris?"

"I went to Paris three years ago to see a girl I loved. I couldn't do it again. Don't you see? I thought I told you. It's a crazy story."

She listens to him tell how a young man arrived in Paris three winters ago...

The air is mild as they sit on the roof. It must be almost spring. He has brought out some blankets and a bottle of Scotch.

"Everything is so right," she says.

"I was just thinking that," he says. "Everything except me. I don't see how I can be right for you. Aren't you worried?"

She smiles, deaf. A woman in Paris worries. Their tongues, changed back into loving seals, frolic and laze. Her head is solid marble.

"The fact is that you shall leave me," he pursues. "Who cares as to the reasons. There are always reasons."

"They're your reasons."

"Laws," he says. He speaks of facts, fate and laws. But she is not listening. Such a sense of vastness love gives; the night running up the Hudson River, what bays and inland lakes lie in this embrace—Alaska is her palm.

"Can you see me in ten years?" he asks.

Even with her eyes shut she can't see further than his face. The space behind his back is a night dotted with foreign places and dates, equally past and future.

"I am asleep," she mumbles.

"No you're not. Why won't you let me see your eyes? I know you're wide awake. Open your eyes. I want to see your crazy eyes."

Weeks before the day when Sophie Blind walked up the ramp into the upholstered belly of a jet prop, weeks before she made her flight reservation, before she wrote her lover what she wanted, back in January when Paris was leafless, a bleak wet wash, and New York as bleakly wind-swept; in January at the unrecorded hour of its birth, her naked desire had started walking toward him.

She stands on the terrace outside his window. It has stopped snowing. She sees him at his desk in the brightly lit room. It cannot be, she has realized. She will leave without knocking, as perfect love commands. But she can't move from the window. The white of his shirt holds her enthralled, the cloth right next to his skin and the clean edge of the collar; she yearns for its delicate taste of heart of lettuce. She will leave. One glimpse of the wild green of his iris and she will leave.

He looks up suddenly, his eyes on the pane. Has he glimpsed the blurred face with its pupils pierced back into the outer darkness and the space between the parted lips running into the endless night? No matter, she is inside now. A figure detaching itself from the frost-grizzled pane, she glides boldly into the room.

"I shouldn't have come," she says, filling the room; her hair bristles in all directions, a shimmery halo of snow, very bridal. But it's all melting very fast. She embraces him hurriedly, looking for something to cover herself with.

"You look great," he says. "Of course it's respectable. The gods always go nude." She has come all this way to tell him something and now she can't remember what it was she came to tell. There is no need now that they are together. He apologizes for the cold turkey; he wasn't expecting her. She eats ravenously.

"It tastes like rabbit," she says, sucking on the bone. She insists it has a gamey taste.

"You're out of your mind to come like this," he says suddenly. "It's the kind of recklessness..." Taking little sips of wine, she listens to him rage. "You wouldn't have liked me when you were twenty," he pursues, "at twenty a woman like you wants a man like Ezra Blind. They all do." He spits out the last words and draws her into his arms with sudden fury. Such a violent kiss. It's bestial. They are staggering backwards, as in a love scene from an old silent movie.

"What do you expect?" he says smiling, and they both realize that they are dreaming. She doesn't care; it's her only chance. They are flying high over the city.

It's day, the smell of snow in the air, a winter sky of long ago. Children are skating on the frozen river. She can see the pure bright colors of their mufflers and knitted caps. They soar upward, high up into the blue cloudless sky. He is going to fly straight into the sun. Blinded, she searches for his mouth—just once more. But she too has realized that everything has become pointless.

"... just want to tell you quick before the dream ends, I'm on my way. Coming. With Lufthansa, Air France, Icelandic..."

*

She arrived at Idlewild airport early in the morning. The plane was on time. With only one suitcase she passed quickly through customs. Still half asleep—it was best so. Heading toward the exit she thought she caught a glimpse of him standing right by the door in white pants, the familiar striped polo shirt over wide shoulders, caught brief glances of the long torso, the sullen mouth, the heavy jaw. Keeping a serene face against the strain of a suitcase and six bottles of duty-free whiskey pulling at each hand, and her own growing excitement, she advanced still looking straight ahead. Turning her head slowly toward him only after she passed through the door. It was not Ivan. A gross imitation, she noted uneasily; only the crudest resemblance. She looked around but did not see him in the lobby. She watched the crowd thin; the last passengers met. He was not coming: the numbing thought dawned on her with each passing second; she wouldn't go out through the glass doors and on to Manhattan. She hadn't arrived. Another woman stood in the lobby, still clutching passport and customs papers—or was it possible that they hadn't recognized each other? She looked around again. The young man in the polo shirt still stood by the door, leaning against the wall. It wasn't Ivan. Her memory couldn't be totally false. Besides, neither his posture nor his expression showed expectancy. There he stood, wide-shouldered and expressionless, staring into space; she was just about to take a step toward him when she was embraced from behind. Ivan spoke her name. She turned in his arms and looked into his face.

"You're here. You really came," he said, hugging her. "How do you feel?"

"Not quite down here," she laughed weakly and looked at him, amazed. "It's really you," she kept repeating dumbly.

"I saw your plane fly in," he told her. "I've been here since three in the morning up at the observation tower—I couldn't sleep. It was beautiful to watch the first jets streaking out. I expected you on an earlier plane—I don't know why. I was so impatient. I didn't believe you'd really come."

It was so strange sitting beside him in the big black car on winding thruways, past supermarkets and brick towers. It was the first time she had seen him in a dark suit. He told her how he had borrowed the car from his grandmother and driven it down from Providence. Every so often they looked at each other and smiled. His look softened and the corners of his mouth turned infinitesimally up. Her face felt like a fragile papier-mâché mask behind which her eyes slid furtively from the skyline to his hand on the steering wheel. It was all so strange. It would have been easier if she could have been delivered in a crate. Of course she didn't believe it. There was something she had to tell him. But she couldn't in the car, not just after he had said, "I'm kidnapping you." She could not tell him when they got out, standing briefly on the Manhattan pavement with a side glimpse of the fogged Jersey shore. In the elevator, held in his arms, she could not speak at all.

In his room the sight of all the familiar objects filled her with such gladness, suddenly she felt completely at home, alive, completely awake. Even if she was here by mistake, she thought. Especially if she was here by mistake—

She looked at him coming toward her naked.

"I tried to write you."

"I know," he said, opening her blouse, "I know."

They smiled at each other curiously as they lay down.

"You have invented me," she joked in the middle of the night.

"No, you have invented me," he replied, a trace of sadness in his voice that made her silent.

"Arrivals are always unreal," he comforted her and put on the light. "*Angst*," he said after studying her face. The German sounded funny from his mouth. "You can tell me. It wouldn't be natural if we were always happy. Are you sad because you came? Because of Ezra?"

She shook her head, trying to smile. "Tell me all the German words you know."

"*Geist. Blitzkrieg. Heldentenor. Liebestod. Lebensraum. Sauerkraut. Blut und Boden. Ewig Weibliches. Weltschmerz. Kaputt. Angst.* We'll make coffee and read. You can't tell me?"

"It will pass," she said, getting up. "I'll take a shower."

"Here," he said, and winding her in a big white towel, held her. "I don't know if I can let you. Promise you won't disappear."

Crying under the shower, she has never been naked like this. Had she really intended to tell him at the airport? Tell him what? That she is not the woman who wrote from Paris? Dead? Mad? It's just that she would have liked to arrive in better shape. But actually, as she reviews her past selves, what she was before Ezra, with Ezra, even her most recent self in Paris, it horrifies her how false and insubstantial she was, a lot of poor contrivances; the fact is that she has never been as simply herself as now, wrapped in Ivan's towel. But it's terrifying to be this naked, to have given up all personhood, the old wraps and cloaks, some never worn, all burnt up. This nakedness, she knows, can never again be clothed.

"I dreamed that you deflowered me," she said, smiling in her sleep.

"And what will you do now?" he asked. "Have you thought about what you're going to do about Ezra and the children? I suppose I'm not the person with whom you want to discuss this..." His voice pursued in the dark.

Outside it's snowing and night; naked under the blanket, January of another year...

Lying motionless, she reflected how strange it was to have beheld him in fact outside her, moving about the room, her lover and yet a stranger who had been her own dream; odd, delightful, ridiculous, lovely and illicit, to awake in the morning of a particular day to the hum of street noises, to look out on the water tanks and soot on the window sill, with his head on the pillow beside her.

But their last hours are not to be described—the sensation of his weight descending, the impropriety of the mattress tilting when he sat beside her the last time. The freshness of winter in the sleeve of his coat, snow and just-peeled oranges, perhaps her last sensation. Fragrance of spices from another world in his sleeve, his cool hand on her throat.

He shrugs, rises smoking.

"Was," he says, standing before the dark window. "Was what was."

"What was?" she wants to ask, but she can barely whisper.

He sits smoking on the window sill, watching for daybreak.

"Go on," he says, his face dark in the blinding light, "you were telling me your dream."

"I told you. I was sitting strapped in my seat in the plane. I wondered if the engines went dead. Then I felt a sudden drop; it was endless like a movie still, the sensation you get after taking sleeping pills—everything stops, it really stops and the lights have been left on."

"That's a good one. Death is just..." his voice trails off.

"What? Death is just a bad high? Is that what you said? The last part of the dream is really funny. The scene changed, everything was clear. It was in a square in Prague: women beating rugs over the railings; the Emperor had sent a man to give the Jews a name; everybody was singing like in a comic opera—I realized it was really on a stage. The dust from the carpets filled the square but the women continued singing in passionate sopranos. I heard the messenger call out the name Staubman and I was sure it was me."

"Are you asleep?" he asks.

She is not sure whether she is making any sound. He is sitting on the edge of the bed. He has just come in, his cool hand on her bare shoulder, the freshness of winter in his sleeve.

"Why is everything so strange?" she asks. "Why?"

"Because you're dead," he says simply, his voice quiet and comforting. "Dead, dearest." And rising with sudden energy he strides to his desk. "Sleep, Sophie," he says, his voice far away, and writes: Day is breaking.

THIS PLACE must be the morgue. Yes, that's why Ezra is sitting with police blankets over his winter coat. It is Ezra, the crying face, I know by the way he sniffles and blows his nose. Muttering to himself, *Na ja. So ist es*. It's cold like the night he sat up with me in the hospital after the miscarriage when they couldn't turn the air conditioner off. In the most expensive private room in the hospital, just after we were married, the only room available that night. He blows his nose in a handkerchief the size of a towel, one of the old batch from his father, and he's got the battered old briefcase on the ground beside him. Some things never get lost. —*Na ja*, he repeats. Then with finality: *Ecce homo*.

—Mulier, I want to correct him. But he means himself.

—*Na ja*, he starts again, his nose very full. Now she is *jenseits*. She got there before either of us.

There are two huddled under the blankets. Master and disciple. Naturally he had to bring someone along. There must always be at least three people for Ezra. Terrible to be alone with me, alive or dead. Nicholas is with him; he's grown a beard. A ghoulish, goat-faced Jesus-after-the-deposition lights up in the flare of a match. He chuckles and coughs. Ezra is showing him the present he bought for our fifteenth wedding anniversary. Eternal watch. Self-winding. Has day of month. —Paid five hundred marks, he says. Won't need it. *Jenseits*.

His crammed briefcase bulges open. I see the titles of the old periodicals: *Acephalos, Empedocles, Chimera, Exodus, Second Coming*. He has brought with him material he needs for a paper on the woman messiah in Auguste Comte. Due the day after tomorrow at the conference in Amsterdam. He will write it tonight. But it's dark. They light matches. —I understand why it's cold, but why does it have to be dark? Ezra complains. They give up lighting matches.

Nicholas begins to recite in ancient Greek. You recall? he asks wistfully. He wonders if it was my hour to die. He continues to quote lines from Hippolytus' speech in Euripides' *Phaedra*. For my benefit? He knows Ezra doesn't understand. They are the passages he read to me the first time we were alone together. —Missed her true moment. Her *kairos*. He concludes solemnly.

Ezra puffs rhythmically on his pipe, thinking aloud to himself. —Wouldn't stand in my way if I really wanted to sunder what ... If I could conceive of ...

He was supposed to come to Paris in a week to sign the divorce papers. How convenient for him.

—An act of God, Ezra says. In the eyes of God, eternally married. Could be no other woman for me.

—She loved you, Nicholas muses.

—She loved you, Ezra echoes significantly.

Five years ago, the winter I was in New York and he wrote to me from Palermo, I thought I was in love with him.

—She is dead, Ezra says with gusto, now we can talk truth. You knew her, Nicholas. I want to know what you think—your image of the woman I married. You knew her, biblically I mean. I know all about it.

—She told you?

—Her postcard from Delphi. "Spent Sunday with Nicholas at Delphi. The gods descended." I know what that means when my wife says, "The gods descended."

Meant the gods. Incorrigibly carnal Israelites. Will never understand.

—And what did you do? Nicholas asks sternly, his lips compressed. What did you do?

Afraid Ezra beat me? Was terribly upset when I spanked Joshua. Little boys so delicate. Remember poor Kafka, he said.

—Sent her the postcard from the Cathedral of Chartres of "The Woman Taken in Adultery."

Sent it from Heidelberg. Bought a supply of that picture when we passed through on our honeymoon trip.

—I forgive you, he says magnanimously to Nicholas.

Nicholas frowns, stamps out his cigaret with suppressed fury.

Should have beat me but didn't. Him he loves. Was only go-between in romance between master and disciple. Exalted for their purpose. A beautiful feeling to be their symbolic object. The bastards. Would like these mortal remains to decay all over them. Smother them in my carcass.

—How do you find life in Heidelberg? Nicholas asks. They've just created a new department for comparative mysticism in Lima. Old Beelzebub has gone to Tokyo, has he heard? Tokyo may be the place. Only for two years. Returning to Jerusalem. They talk through the night. Heard all this before. X's review of Y's critique of Z's book on the ——. It's turning into an endless Passover service.

A dog's life alone, Ezra complains. There is Irmele in Heidelberg and Bettina in Paris, an extraordinary woman but getting old, has asthma too. Then Frau X in Frankfurt takes care of his laundry, excellent woman, Ph.D. in Roman history. A delightful girl in London, only eighteen, a Renoir, speaks Latin fluently. But in the end one is alone.

He dozes off on Nicholas' shoulder. He is awakened by an attack of diarrhea. Nicholas holds the pot. She is dead, he howls. Who will take care of me?

—Did you observe, Nicholas asks, the number of corpses that have been brought in between midnight and dawn?

Another batch is being brought in. Nicholas wants to know if this is usual. —*Ah oui, Monsieur*, the night watchman whispers excitedly, flushed with pride. *C'est la fête.*

It's almost noon when the inspector arrives. Ezra is frantic. Burial arrangements must be made at the latest by Thursday, according to Jewish Law. Even with extenuating circumstances. There are complications. City regulations require burial in the eighth arrondissement;

he shows cemetery on the map. Or Ezra can file an application for a permit to release the body at the *Préfecture*, open between eight and six o'clock. It will take another day to get customs clearance. Transport by plane expensive. He tries to persuade secretary to postdate death certificate. Rages against French bureaucracy, medieval laws. Required to bury his wife within forty-eight hours according to Jewish Law. Why this comedy? Wants body—body of his wife, mother of his children; recites my genealogy to the seventh generation, raves about resurrection and Judgment.

Wonder myself why the comedy. Always this embarrassing business of the body. Should be possible to disappear clean and simple. Whisk one's self out of the world whole—dress, shoes, gloves, purse and all. So heavy-handed, the way God—

Nicholas has returned from coffin maker. Delivery promised by six. Fear journey ahead. French Railways on slowdown strike. Nicholas suggests cremation. Tries to persuade Ezra that fire is my element. —All signs indicate, he pursues with smile and clownish shrug, that the gods are opposed to her being committed to dust. Earth is not her element. It will cost two thousand francs to ship the coffin by air freight. Old or new francs? Ezra is considering. A friend of Nicholas' is driving to Naples tomorrow. Could share expenses... Easy to smuggle coffin across Italian border. Scatter her ashes over Aegean Sea. Ezra rushes out to make long-distance calls before the post office closes. Nicholas is studying timetables of ships going out of Naples. The *Grimani*, with stops at Palermo, Piraeus, Cyprus—departure Saturday, too late. Ferry boats out of Naples three times a week to Capri, to Stromboli Thursday morning.

Always wanted to see the volcano.

THE RABBI has agreed. It seems I shall have a Jewish funeral after all. Ezra's family is holding a reception at his sister's house in Vienna.

All the silver—trays, bowls, goblets, platters, candlesticks—shines festively like at Passover in Renata's apartment; only now the big table is pushed up against the wall to make room for the coffin, the chairs have been taken out and the mirrors are covered. There is a happy bustle near the hall leading to the nursery—the little round woman with the long red hair surrounded by children. I'm sure it's Ezra's mother giving chocolates to the children—but I thought the poor soul died; remember going to the unveiling of the stone on our way to Paris; on a beautiful summer day in the cemetery: didn't believe it. Her smug, slit-eyed cat face beams, of course it's she, chocolates in her palm; clucking as if she were feeding chicks. Dear old Sosie—one hand passing sweets, the other fumbling in the back, resticking the pins in her hair that won't stay up, or groping for a buttonhole, grabbing the arm of someone who's trying to pass to convey a compliment. Ezra's father, with dandy rabbi beard and proudly displaying his belly, is trying discreetly to brush white specks from her Sabbath dress—flour or powder, lint, bed feathers. She forgot the zipper in the back as usual, but the best story is the time she got dressed for Passover in such a rush (late as always, the guests already beginning to arrive) and appeared festive in diamond earrings and a red dress, only she forgot to take off her nightgown. I am glad for her it happened this way. Couldn't really leave Ezra. Had to stay with him for the sake of his mother. Entrusted her son to me. Remember in the delivery room when the doctor said, Bear up, Sophie and you'll have a fine boy—it will take a while, he's coming buttocks first, it may last another three hours—but we know it's a boy. When I finally heard—I was screaming so loud, he kept repeating, *boy*—when I heard *boy*, I thought it would make Ezra's mother so happy; if it was true, because I couldn't believe it. Then when I came to, Ezra told me, ceremonious, impressed, surprised, struggling with himself, awe finally triumphing over cynicism; and I knew it was true . . . My first thought was, Won't Ezra's mother be happy. Ezra, myself, unimportant; my father with his "a boy is a big problem"—one all-knowing Freudian eyebrow drooping, the other raised, smiling ambiguously. Not important, Ezra, Father, me, nurse showing Eskimo-faced newborn. Heard him scream, as they tried to pull legs straight to measure length for hospital records. Thinking only of Sosie's happiness when she got the telegram. Perhaps my one moment of real unselfishness. Will I go to heaven? Never understood that scheme of heaven-hell—except to enrich the language. Sosie's bringing in huge steaming platter—can't be jellied fish. Wonder if she knows I'm dead. Doesn't take cognizance of coffin, perhaps she misheard, as Ezra told me before we got engaged: A truly good soul, hears only the good, tell her the women at the party thought her dress a disgrace, and she'll smile and say, I'm glad they liked my hat; let her husband complain the meat's like leather, and she'll say, I knew you'd love my spinach . . .

She is blessing the pictures. Photographs of me that Ezra sent when we got engaged, mounted in silver frames. The wedding is in New York, she explains to everyone, just about now, because of the time difference. Mad little Polish woman. Whatever is good in Ezra came from her. Boasts like peasant, showing pictures around: her daughter-in-law, pretty like a movie star, the father a professor—a psychoanalyst, she adds impressively after a glance at her husband who looks away, pained, his mouth puckered, afraid she's spilled the beans; poor Sosie never got further than that: embarrassing Herr Rabbiner with the wrong word, lint on her dress, serving meat carelessly in a *milchig* dish. Bride's father is son of lamented chief rabbi of . . . Her husband elaborates pompously while she polishes glass on picture with her sleeve.

Nicholas has just come in, his chest in a cast, apologizes for being late; broke a rib skiing in St. Moritz.

"*Goyim naches*," he laughs.

Getting more Jewish every day. Fooled even Ezra as a freshman in his Hegel seminar. Had a wedding cooked up with a girl from a wealthy Sephardic family. Surprised to discover his star pupil was a pure Polish Catholic (son of a small-town New England pharmacist—corrupted by Marxist piano teacher, Nicholas explained with cynical Semitic shrug). Ezra decided his mistake was not a mistake. Claimed he could smell a Jew, developed trans-racial theory. Nevertheless, the wedding didn't materialize.

"At last!" Ezra embraces him. "I was waiting for you."

"Were you worried about the papers?"

"It's all settled," Ezra assures him. "Yes, you may smoke."

Nicholas leans over the coffin, he stares like a man looking down a well for something lost. What is it? Afraid his eyes will fall out. His mouth moving without a sound. Kiss me? Well do it. Kiss me on the forehead like the years you slept on the living-room couch, calling me sister. Remember you in long shirttails falling over hairy thighs. A brother to count among my blessings. The third time you came to visit at night, Ezra was out. "Have you come to see the master or the master's wife?" I asked and caught your hands as you came toward me. It was in New Haven in 1954 but it could have happened in a Polish ghetto in the seventeenth century—the strange slow-motion dance, only our fingers clasping—it happened in a book: you were holding my hands up high like in a minuet; you kissed me on the forehead and smiled. "Good night, sister," you said and let go. I went to my room.

You were kind. Read to me aloud from Hölderlin and the Greeks. When you kissed me in the grass years later it was another book: My eyes were closed. Your hand slid under my coat, up my bare side, you took my breast; you said "*Wurm.*" Why? It was startling. Woman's flesh brought to mind the wages of sin? Or did you mean something good? Because we were lying on the damp, loose ground in April, the earth wet and cold, the last year's dead grass and new grass just beginning. I remember coals strewn gray and black on the path lead-ing to the bank of the river, and our slow-motion descent to the ground. You stared at me (like you do now) as I lay there; my face felt painted on, the damp coming from the earth up my back. The sky baby-blue with white clouds over the campus, looking up through the willows—the whole thing fell straight out of Wedekind's *Früh-lings Erwachen*. "*Wurm*," you said. "Why?" I asked but you only re-peated "*Wurm*." Didn't know whether to be flattered or offended. Did you mean death? Is that why you are staring? I wish you'd say something. My name. Anything. A quote. Once when we sat on another patch of grass and I asked you what you were thinking you said, "I'm thinking that I am unnecessarily fortunate to have two worlds when I am perfectly content with one." Perhaps you haven't another good line like that.

"The folly of it," he exclaims angrily, turning away from the coffin.

The guests file by the wall, circling slowly toward the coffin. They pause to admire expensively framed wedding pictures on display. The gifts have been put on the table again: sets of silver salt pits, sugar bowls and ashtrays. Pairs of candlesticks in assorted sizes. Crystal vases and dessert plates. A pile of tablecloths, satin and damask, still as good as new. Boxes still in their wrapping and ribbons are stacked under the table.

Jonathan stands in the doorway. The children were told to stay in the nursery but he sees Toby and Joshua playing hide-and-seek between the forest of legs. He wanders into the room asking, "Have they opened the coffin?" Grandmother catches his arm and holds him pressed against her jutting belly.

One by one people move up to the coffin. "...done by big-name experts. Latest American techniques," Renata boasts as the guests murmur admiringly, "The sunglasses are *haute mode*."

Grandmother, her palm clamped on the child's forehead, makes a little push forward. He takes a step, but she pulls him back. "It's not her," he says, "that's not her face."

The child is hushed. They had the best mortician in town restore my face. Sixty fingers working all morning produced half a dozen different faces—impossible to please every member of the family. It was Ezra's choice in the end. She looks exactly like in the wedding pictures, the guests remark.

The bereaved husband receives condolences with a festive air; positively aglow, he waltzes through the crowd on waves of sympathy. He holds a large handkerchief over his mouth to cover a leer. From every part of the room he casts triumphant and amorous glances into the coffin, and blows his nose vigorously. Such a loss and a cold on top of it! A thick layer of talcum white to cover up the mourner's stubble makes his lips appear unusually thick and pink. He loves public occasions—a wedding, a funeral, circumcision, inaugural address or political rally—who cares, as long as it is an occasion. There never were enough occasions for poor Ezra. As he confessed to me sadly, but for the fact that he was born a Jew he would have become Pope. He is relieved that fate spared him the dubious status of the divorce. It feels great to be a widower. He has forgiven me, forgiven himself. God has forgiven us all. Once more I am the woman of his dreams, the bride of his youth.

"She was a great woman," he says solemnly.

I am dead. They can all relax and celebrate.

Renata, too, is relieved. It was hard to love me. The strain of having to love me gave the poor soul migraine. She envied me the children. Now she has them.

More guests keep arriving. There is excitement at the door. A raspy voice rising above the general hubbub sounds like my father, speaking louder and with a heavier Hungarian accent than normally. He keeps asking how much all this cost—the shipping, the rabbi, the mortician, the total sum; he will write a check—so loudly it's embarrassing. While Ezra placates him, he mutters on about religious atavism, back to the primal horde. There is Uncle Joske, the soccer player from Budapest. Have they all come? The aunts and cousins from Australia, Canada and Paraguay? I see my mother enter, wrapped in a crystal cocoon. No, it was only a reflection. A little draft lifted the edge of the drape over the mirror. Renata has fixed it already.

"I looked," the child says. "Will I die?"

He didn't see anything, his grandmother tells him.

It is raining. The guests are becoming increasingly restless. What are we waiting for? someone asks.

I hear my father groan in Hebrew.

Ezra, trying to cheer him up, makes a joke.

"At her funeral at least she is decent. *Bekovet.*" They have stepped away from the coffin. Ezra, his arm around my father's shoulder, continues talking heatedly through the noise and confusion. Death the final test "... In the end gathered unto her fathers. The great granddaughter of Reb Smuel Nyitra, after all ... Shame how you lived. The parents, she. Freud. Homer. Joyce. *Kultur.* Cyclon B. Auschwitz. Holy Land." His hand rises, a finger wags menacingly. "God will judge us!" The finger grows gigantic. The whole room turns a gangrenous black.

Judgment? Not yet.

No, it was only a warning. A window was thrown open. Everything is all right. Ezra emphatically denies rumors that I was to be tried as a witch by a council of orthodox rabbis. Grandmother screamed but Renata is quieting her. The sudden gust raised the drape from the mirror and she saw her daughter and granddaughters thrown into the flames, she wails. Always these little excitements. Renata fastens the windows. Only a vase turned over. The coffin bearers have arrived. Renata tries to pick up the broken pieces. Can't under the herd of shuffling feet as the guests are leaving. The children are told to wait in the next room.

A man whose face is very familiar leans down over the coffin. One of the coffin bearers? His final look as he lifts his head is blank. They are putting on the lid.

The child, his face pressed against the streaming window pane, straining to see the coffin bearers as they come out on the street, is disappointed that there is no funeral hearse with plumed horses. They watch the men maneuver the crated corpse into the big black limousine. The car slides out of view.

At last we're outside. Small group stands under umbrellas listening to the rabbi's voice drone on while the rain whips the earth around fresh-dug grave into a yellow froth.

At some moment, just before lowering the coffin, the rabbi will have to turn around and, facing the congregation, ask if anyone present wishes to object.

The coffin hangs suspended.

THE SKY is an intense blemishless blue. Cables stretched taut on derrick booms zone the sky; distant vessels present odd foreshortened silhouettes. Napoleon's tricorne. A cow hangs in the sky. It was on our honeymoon trip, waiting to board the Greek ship. I watched them load all afternoon while Ezra was writing postcards. They were hoisting cattle onto the freighter. I saw a cow strapped in a halter, its feet rising from the ground. The crane swung out over the water and the cow remained there, suspended midair, motionless and inert as if the soul had simply deserted.

Dearest, I hang in the sky. The world has come to an endless stop. My head miles from my crotch—this can't be Amsterdam. How will I ever find you? The conference isn't at all what I expected—"Conference on Drugs and Extrasensory Perception" it says on the runner. An ad?

The hall, oppressively monumental. Imitation of what? Somebody said, imitation. Egypt. Rome, itself an imitation. Train station: Death. When you are not going anywhere. Not leaving or arriving. Turmoil. Are those ticket counters? I hear Spinoza speaking. In Latin, of course, translated into American for my benefit. Incredible the service you get in this century. Simultaneous translation into five hundred and seventy-nine languages. It simply awes me.

There's a crowd like at the *Préfecture de police*. So many heads—is one of them mine? If this is really the Last Judgment—not just the latest Franco-Italian production—the real thing, unrehearsed, as it comes, bound to be bedlam. Refuse to be taken in in spite of preponderance of bearded men and Egyptian décor. Even if it should prove—no, refuse to believe it. If God appears I'll pretend it's an actor. More people keep coming in. We must wait. For more people? Not crowded enough?

We have arrived. People spreading the word. Some monks in white praying silently. I didn't hear the announcement. This the place. America. The next world. Can't believe we really arrived. Don't see Statue of Liberty. Empire State Building. Is this America? Must be the waiting room.

Gypsies sitting on the ground, playing cards. People are grouped by nationalities, not alphabetically. I see they've dressed me as a child in high laced shoes and Tyrolean cape. Everybody filling out forms. I don't remember anything. Mother's maiden name. Date and place of father's birth. Former residence. Name of vessel. Good thing I brought along some books to read. Immigration officer still studying my papers.

"...why weren't you in Auschwitz?" he repeats, hard to understand: rats have eaten away half of his face, part of the vocal cords; touchy about it, naturally. Now I see yellow star badge around his arm. A delicate situation. Certainly don't want him to inspect books I brought. People in group I'm with whisper in my ear different answers, trying to help me. Woman's voice urging, "Kiss his foot." I see customs officer delicately extending foot in curved pasha slippers. Afraid slipper will fall off. Kiss his foot, woman hisses in my ear, It's only a dream. I'm careful not to breathe through my nose. Prepared for everything. Worms.

Matzah being served, I'm told, and jellied fish. Where? Still preparing. Lot of talk about Messianic Banquet. Roast Leviathan. Always lot of talk. Aren't they ashamed? There are some Dominicans nearby and a group of Irish immigrants. Now I see the little old man—like the ones in Jerusalem selling kerosene on a donkey—he is offering tidbits on a paper plate. Where is his donkey? Looks like leftovers. Or hors d'oeuvre? Offering it so ceremoniously, I can't refuse. Tastes like—

A drug, I knew it. Hate this kind of high. Trying to hear Spinoza on a crazy roller coaster. It's a guided tour. Guides ranting in different languages, "... and now we come to the furthermost reach ... a place referred to by many authors ... the fall into the past ..." Missed the classical reference. And frankly, the sensation—like when I was little, sitting on the round hole of the outdoor privy—the moment I felt I was falling with it ...

Counting on miracles of technology somehow this will reach you ... A trap, as I suspected. My head on the table (they've strapped my legs in some gynecological rig-up). I'm to be subjected to trial—not serious, just disgusted by silliness of it all, more delay and afraid of not holding up, losing my temper (must keep my head)—wish you were here to advise me—confusion and intrigue as usual. The charges, I forget how many, filed by different individuals. Particularly worried about what defense has cooked up (Ezra's doing, can't decide if he is mad, stupid or a devil) in way of an insanity plea. Been explained it's standard form in my situation and have nothing to worry about—said something about extraterritorial rights. Don't understand. And O.K. if I deny it, more vehemently I deny it, more convincing—not legally responsible, that's the point, lost my head, head on the table to prove it. Pointless to try to convince them my head even if miles away still connected to my crotch ... question on my mind is whether my acquittal depends on confessing the truth or making up a story. Difficult either way. Awful feeling everything I say will be turned against me, including my silence, everything, and that when I try to speak, the words carefully formulated (whole paragraphs like in Spinoza—proposition and axioms), it comes out in grunts and screeches. Ultimate fear that I'm being manipulated, psychedelic drugs, nothing more insidious (have resisted ether, hypnosis, etc.), or just surgeon poking with rubber gloves and instruments up my cunt and ass hole, would explain screaming, blood, grunts but mind lucid as you see writing to you. Must resist fear of being manipulated must absolutely disbelieve, only chance, only hope, legitimate like Pascal's wager you understand—don't know how much time I have to prepare, they're still at preliminaries: screening witnesses, interviewing jurors—you would enjoy some of the characters, old Eastern European types. The whole thing very informal, my father's been called in to serve as judge. Flew in few hours ago; first thing, before even taking off his hat made his ritual speech, wants everyone in court to hear in presence of his daughter oath of impartiality then some anecdote about how Solomon managed to avoid personal discussion, then his "I knew this would happen" look and talking about his accommodations, food at the hotel, some questioning about what I did with trunk, fur coat, where I was staying, if there was telephone, TV in my room; bluffed my way through that somehow but really terrified. I think he really wants me put away in the "fun house," as they say in New York, because he kept telling me about this wonderful new loony bin they're building, with private bathroom, wall-to-wall carpeting (some suites for families, an adjunct experimental school), even concert hall that converts into skating rink (Budapest String Quartet, rock groups booked), whole big center dedicated to him—why is he telling me all this?—really believes in cause, that's what's so confusing; they're all mad and believe they're doing right. Ezra claims they got hold of my notebooks, diary, letters, may be ruse; sometimes suspect whole trial is his invention to keep me under his thumb; even got my father to cooperate. My one hope is that prosecuting attorney will be sane.

Wish all this would be over and I could come to you. Miss your letters. Wish I could at least send you an address. (Try Morgue on rue Bobillot or Amsterdam *poste restante;* maybe Bern would forward—no.) Forgive my frenzy. Not really important. You must have enough to cope with in New York. I shouldn't be writing you all this. Won't mail this letter. I'll manage. Just make your film. Feel much better. Quite calm. Bells calling.

They want me to testify. Everything so efficiently organized here. My head far away on the president's table. Reading paper. Mistake to think God old-fashioned. No difference between inside and outside.

Distinction even in the mind based on matter. It's simple what my world is now, as simple as—

My name? Don't confuse me.

Miles of ticker tape curling from my mouth. Floor littered. A news office? Oh, they've plugged my nerve ends in an intercontinental— can't read label but it's . . . it's lovely, lovely. Messages from all over and under the world—larvae at sea bottom, maggots deep in the earth, a flying seed. God.

It's unimportant; still, you could have the courtesy to translate me . . .

Coherent discourse? How do you expect me—? Begin to explain now in my present state of decomposition? . . . Having begun at different points accounts . . . No, nothing accounts. Totally unjustified. Incomprehensible. Absurd. You can't imagine how horrible— No, not the pain, not the— Ice water? No thank you. I wasn't like this before. I won't say I was perfect, maybe not all of a piece, still, however elliptical, at least I was neat—I managed somehow, as you can see . . . plurality of parallel existences . . . not my words . . . thought I put it in different books—not the case . . . What do you expect on this planet mud? . . . all human bumbling programmed billion light years ago in pseudo-substance as predicted in the Pistis Sophia . . . not my opinion. I have no opinion. Personal what? What personal? Don't understand the question unless you mean the legal person, but you have all my papers, passport, *carte de séjour*, insurance policy, my naturalization papers, birth certificate, my grades and medical reports through grammar school, chest X-ray, you have my body—you can assess its condition better than I—almost forgot my publications, of course; college papers, dissertation, etc., on file; have your secretary look up suitcase full of notes left with . . . Can't expect me to remember everything. Must repeat have nothing personal to declare, everything about myself is public, you have it. I'm telling you you have all the baggage. What comes to me through this apparatus—whatever you call it, self, ego, brain, don't know the latest jargon—this is not the moment to split hairs; I can only name you the pieces, already in your possession . . . for all I know they lie on the dissecting table in their proper place, or side by side like automobile parts: the four limbs together, the skin carefully folded, the glands in a separate bowl—not conversation for the table? Sorry. Didn't see them bring in the trays . . . as for the actual memories asked for, the original imprint can't be removed. Everything I'm telling you, the words, gentlemen, language is your gift, I thank you for it, indebted, your humble daughter, etc. The matter, what my sponges have sucked up? My membranes? The matter . . . Where my voice comes from? Of body awareness only my cunt curiously, a hole, a nothing, a *negativum*—it was you who just remarked, waste to give vision drug to women, all they feel is their cunt . . . I'm only repeating. But who am I talking to? Earphones. The conference, of course. You know what I mean—in any museum with a good Greek section you can see it painted on vases, something in the shape of a winged little man, or bird, or insect, shown flying from the mouth or ear of the deceased—psyche. Perhaps I was never much more ever—

Gentlemen, why are you so old and ugly? Good grief, if I should need further proof that this whole thing is a fraud, it's your presence. You who said we'd meet in the next world. Afterlife, soul, Judgment, God, One People, One Law: never believed a word of it. So now. Greatly regret, infinitely sorry, unspeakably ashamed of stupidities I got enmeshed in by some particle of belief in your lies. Enough . . . The fact that you invade my privacy, sprout in my dreams, however unpleasant, debilitating, more proof that this is not the true death here with you. When I'm truly dead, my friends, I won't see you standing around me. I will find a way out, I'll get back my arms and limbs, my head, even my heart, I'll find it whatever you've done with it.

"I UNDERSTAND it must be very difficult for you," the man with the drooping walrus moustache murmurs sympathetically.

"How do you mean?" she asks mistrustfully. The moustache gives him a pleasant bearish aspect and the smell of his cracked leather jacket is positively reassuring. But dare any man presume to fathom just how difficult her life is; can a man know? Does she want him to know?

"A woman with your potentialities," he proclaims wide-eyed, his arms outthrown to illustrate her far-flung positions. "You are not one but many women. You've got a fantastic problem between Spinoza and being a playgirl in Acapulco," he exclaims. "How will you resolve this?"

She senses her peril. In a minute he will make the initial move to resolve this conflict for her which she cannot, which no woman alone can resolve for herself.

"It's no problem. I told you I am writing a novel. The truth of the matter is that I've never read Spinoza."

"Baby, I saw your publications on display in the lobby, but it's understandable that you should want to deny it; the conflict between your intellectual passion and your femininity, just as I was telling you. It's obvious you're worried I'm less attracted to you because you read Spinoza."

"I swear to God I've never read Spinoza. As for my degrees and publications—ancient history. If you must know, my husband made me do it."

"How?"

"I was in a state of physical bondage."

"He screwed you so silly you wrote a dissertation?"

"That's right; I didn't care. I wanted to live in a kibbutz and pick oranges. So he made me read Marx. I didn't agree with Marx so he made me read Kierkegaard and all the German romantics and mystics—that's how I got involved in philosophy. I know I was a fool; I should have said Eckhart fits me to a 'T' and I would have had my peace. Look, I'll admit Kant turned my head as a freshman in college, but already in my junior year—"

"Darling, stop trying so hard. You realize all this talk is very sexy."

"The point is I find a woman who can take philosophy seriously after twenty-five pathetic."

"Then you're saying that women are intrinsically superior to men."

"Not at all. Men are superior to women in practically any field you can name—philosophy, military science, music. But every sensible woman knows *au fond* that the things men do are stupid; she can't take them seriously; part of men's charm is that they pursue these things seriously, so we encourage them, then men call us a civilizing influence."

"Baby, culture stinks. Let's screw."

"No, you're too cynical."

"I hope you know you're crazy, darling," he remarks kindly. "I've been listening to you for ten hours and it's obvious from every word you say. Don't look so unhappy—it's not your fault," he continues pleasantly, rolling a cigaret. "My wife is crazy, did I tell you that?"

"You talk exactly like my father and my husband. It's the one thing I can't stand."

"Of course, you told me you had a Freudian papa—forgive me darling—that must really be hard. You realize you've really had it, baby?"

"All joking aside, I want to know where I am."

"Darling, you're in a state. You haven't been screwed in the last ten hours; you're in a state, that's all. My dear, it must be this hashish. Suddenly I can't think of your name. Don't tell me. I know it. It will come back in a minute. Sarah!"

"That's interesting, a few days before I died someone said that ought to be my name."

"I told you this hash is fantastic. Let me guess again. Ridiculous. Your husband's name is Blind—and you're going to keep it?"

"A souvenir," she shrugs, smiling. "Like from the war. Call it a misadventure. Still a ten-year stretch of my life."

"Blind. Blind. Miriam. I got it! That's it, isn't it Miriam."

"No, the name of the heroine of my first novel."

"I have one more guess. Of course: Sophie. Sophie Blind."

"That's really strange."

"True?"

"No, but it's just the right name for the character I want to write about in my new novel."

"Listen there is nothing like this hash—I told you. Darling, take me to your room and I'll screw you."

"I can't. I'm not in love with you. But I'm sure there are a lot of pretty girls who want to be screwed. Why don't you try the ballroom?"

"Darling, I'm too tired for that. I can't be bothered with girls—it's a whole operation; they want to dance, they want a Big Thing—please stop giving me the old nonsense. I just want to screw you and go to sleep. Look, we got to get out of here, the chars are coming."

"I can't imagine making love the way things are."

"I know you're in a mess. We're all in a mess," he sighs, his arm around her shoulder, leaning on her unsteadily as they walk down the thickly carpeted corridor. She stops to look at a bulletin board announcing the events of the week.

"You're worried about missing something important?" he asks, drawing her away. "I'm telling you everybody important will be at the party. We have time to screw—one hour exactly. I need three hours sleep, five hours to wake up, I can prepare my speech on the way. I've got to speak to an audience of five thousand; televised, of course. Haven't even begun to think about it. Stop worrying and take my advice. We go to bed and to the party, O.K.? And don't tell me you're tired. I haven't slept for three nights."

"I'm involved in litigations; I have to face a jury," she protests.

"You'll tell me all about it in bed."

"How do I know you're not one of the jury or a witness for the prosecution?"

"All the more reason you should take me to your room. You realize you're being very selfish. It doesn't occur to you to think of the risks I'm running. Don't you know everything is forgiven a woman?"

"It's this room," she says turning on the light.

"You don't mind if I lean my head on you. I must sleep a little."

"Johann, listen."

"Baby, I've been listening eleven hours now."

"I don't care what you think, I want to know what's going to happen."

"If we don't go to bed, nothing will happen. Darling, you think I'm joking but it's a very serious matter," he says flopping on her bed. "You know the story of the Viennese opera singer who couldn't make the high C unless she was screwed five minutes before. They always had at least three studs prepared for her in the wings. It was public knowledge. Darling, I only want to help you."

"Seriously," she asks, "what's wrong with me?"

"Just one thing," he gurgles under his Nietzsche moustache, pulling her down on the bed, "the simple fact that you were not born in 1890."

"What else?"

"Darling, you will need a lot of money to get out of this mess. Write a book that gets you a fifty-thousand-dollar advance and it's simple. You're as free as a bird. Tokyo, Lima, Istanbul, anywhere. Spend your life on an airplane or cruising. It's obvious you have to travel."

"You really think so? O.K. I'll try."

He's shaking his head. "You don't believe it. If you could, really believe that, my dear. Can you think fifty thousand dollars?"

Each time she tries to think fifty thousand dollars, her lover's image lights up. "No, I really can't. There are things I should attend to. Besides, I should be somewhere else."

"Darling, you are somewhere else."

"It's impossible."

"Baby, I'm already in you."

"It's not right."

"You prefer another position?"

"What about your lovely wife and children?"

"They're three thousand miles away," he yawns, "and you're right here. Don't tell me you don't like it. You can laugh. It doesn't bother me. Go on, laugh like a witch. It arouses me. Can you tell me now you don't like how I screw around in you?"

"That's O.K. But why do you have to have such a pot belly? What do you have in there—quintuplets?"

"I'll tell you why. When God made me a genius he said, 'Johann Tobler, I have made you a genius and I am giving you a big pot belly so you shouldn't be vain.' There you have the answer."

"How sweet. Is that what you tell every woman?"

"What do you think? You would like me to invent something special for you?"

"Leaving me, darling?"

"I have to make a phone call."

"You forgive me if I don't get up . . . so tired. You know how to get to the party?"

HELP BUILD PARADISE, she reads on the poster on the bathroom door.

"Oh, that's a project we tried some years ago," Kate Dallas shouts from the shower. "Environment chambers; everybody create his own. We got fantastic donations and bought five hundred acres of land in Colorado. The idea was happy pleasure. None of the old puritan masochistic stuff. But as a concession to human weakness we had what we called an Id-Lib chamber with whips and boots and girlies, the old sick bit. And you know, they spent all their time there, so we closed up the place. Just in time, too. So now we're working to change people." She emerges smiling and monumental in a long Greek robe Sophie remembers from the days they played together in *The Trojan Women*.

"I hear you've been doing LSD research—"

"That's right. Do you want to go on a trip?"

"Christ no. I want to get off."

Kate is combing her long hair before the mirror.

"I could have been another Garbo," she sighs, "if only I weren't six feet one."

"Couldn't you still?"

"As a matter of fact, I had a call just this morning... But no, I'm involved in this new project which will revolutionize consciousness. What a pity you missed my lecture! Do you realize all of psychiatry will be over in another decade? Freudian psychoanalysis will be looked on as the strangest witchcraft. It will have about as much relevance as Babylonian astrology. But tell me, what's this about your being on a trip?"

"Well, I was on my way out of this world. An accident. It felt so fantastic I was sure this was it. But instead everything turned funny. Here I am on another trip, back on the old merry-go-round with Ezra. I have to appear at a trial tomorrow—my dead grandmother will be there and Reb Smuel of Nyitra, my cousins who died at Auschwitz."

"The place will be crawling with ectoplasmic Jews! So what else is new?"

"Kate, I can't stand it. I'm afraid I won't hold out. If God appears, I'll scream at Him."

"He won't."

"How do you know?"

"I know God can't appear. He is still becoming. I happen to be, well, personally involved in His becoming . . . but that's another story. How much time have we got?"

"I don't know. I should be back there already."

"Why didn't you call me earlier?"

"I was in a coffin."

"Baloney! I went to your wake ten years ago and the next morning we had blueberry pancakes. Every time you get a little bit up-tight, you pull the Osiris bit. Atavism, sheer atavism. The eternal return. What a lot of crap. Entelechy, my dear . . . That's the ticket. The purposive universe. The burgeoning processive, dynamic continuum. Alfred North Whitehead. The Teilhardian vision . . ."

"Ezra."

"Ezra is a bad thought in the divine mind."

"But why do I still have him on my back?"

"I threw him off mine. Oh, yes. Once he tried to make a pass at me. I picked him up, put him in an airplane spin and threw him across the room. He lifted his head from the floor and said, 'The only thing for you darling is a very cerebral orang-utan.'"

"With me he was not so funny."

"Listen, O Shulamite with your teeth chattering 'like a flock of shorn sheep,' Ezra is finished . . . The Jews are finished. Out of the past with you, down with the wailing wall. Yes, that's it. We will demolish it brick by brick. Hot dog! You mustn't tell anyone, but we've just started working with an extraordinary new substance. Actually, it's a virus—attacks the duodenum of the Arkansas wood louse. But on humans—marvelous—it's a forgetting drug. Memory, we discover, is stored in a glutenous protein substance—mucopolysaccharides— a cell glue. Fuzz collects around the neurons. Now, in studying brain waves it turns out that there is a best fit pattern in which a wave closely resembles the one where the original information is stored. The waves are whispering together."

"So that's what it is. The chorus of murmuring! Old Israelites in my cells."

"Correct, and it's time they shut up. We're going to dissolve that old glue. One whiff and you've got a clean slate."

"And there goes that beautiful moment ten years ago, and the taste of the kiss that killed. Tell me, does it blot out everything?"

"That's the whole point, you'd start from the beginning. Don't be afraid, we'll take care of you. We've got marvelous laboratory facilities, trained staff. In six weeks, you'll be fit to walk out on the street."

"What about sex?"

"Under our program, the sexual drive in the pathological forms in which we have known it will disappear. There will be love and physical enjoyment, but no fixation—a sane and happy world. It horrifies you?"

"The vision is not exactly original."

"Of course not. It's as old as sin. We have finally found the way. But you have to be spiritually ready. We are taking only convinced members. Did I tell you we are founding a new Church? Only way you get anything done in this country . . ."

"God help us."

"Admit it, you can't live without those murmuring Israelites. 'May my tongue cleave to the roof of my mouth if I forget thee, Oh Jerusalem!'"

"But of course, to part is painful, to part with an old rag, even a tumor. It's part of human nature to love one's tumor. But seriously, Kate, I'm not hanging on to the old psychology, ego hang-up, continuity bit, the whole business of being a person, it's absurd. Of course I believe in science. Glue around the neurons. Sure. But a chemical solution is simply not interesting. It's not respectable. Or am I hopelessly sentimental?"

"Sophie, you're a nut. You better go to your trial. And remember if you need anything, we've got it."

Two-fifteen. Due for routine psychiatric examination. All these stupid formalities. Nicer office than her father's. Abstract paintings, wall-to-wall carpeting and Scandinavian glass—must produce different free associations. She lies down on the couch. Just to show him she can do it. Not inhibited.

"What do you want me to talk about—Sex? Father? Mother? Bedwetting? Electra Complex? Penis Envy? Anything you want me to—just let's get it over with quick because I've got a ticket."

"Sophie love, dear child, my darling, sweetheart, sweetheart, sweetheart—!"

It's her father's Hungarian colleague ——. His wife died recently. Suicide most probably. Father said should consider his marriage proposal: fine man, has humor, father's best friend, loved her since she was born, flourishing practice, first-rate mind, little paranoia belongs to it. Something to consider. Age difference often a positive factor. Marriage great temptation at sixteen. Couldn't at sixteen; dreaming of a dark man.

He stands in the middle of the room, his plump hands clasped; drops his head dolefully like a priest while he repeats: "Before you do anything you need at least seven years of analysis. Minimum five; absolute minimum." His head tips to the other side, he waits. He pulls his chair closer. So different from her father. Bright blue, popping, bloodshot eyes; delicate, moist, pink skin; speaks excitedly. Hoarse whisper with an undertone of choked laughter, choked terror, implores her to reconsider before she makes a life decision.

Fatman: not the heavy, trapped kind, entombed in a motionless stupor or twisting uncomfortable in his fat. No, the opposite; bubbling, volatile, excitement puffs out his face, swells flesh on his fingers. Bursting out of the skin. Pink from continual state of explosion.

He speaks to her in Hungarian, she answers in English. His use of diminutives, the first-person possessive suffix, it works on her—my dear, my little Sophie, she hears the nouns wrapped up in the "my" ending.

Can I love this man? He is imploring her with all his chins not to throw her life away. She dare not make any decision before she's had seven years of therapy. She paces impatiently. Nothing can sway her from her purpose. He must understand. She must settle things. Divorce. Find school for the children. Check shipment from Paris. Five articles due. Contract for her new book.

"But what about your life? Your life!" he sings. She has made her decision. It's clear she could love him. Sees some part of her lover in him.

"I must repeat my mother's life," she tells him firmly.

"You can do anything you want after your analysis, sweetheart," he pursues, "go on the stage, study metaphysics; you can have all the affairs you want with cavalry officers, Olympic skiers, artists; you can be an aviator, a *femme fatale*, or marry and have ten children; anything, dearest, that makes you happy, but not before—" He is beseeching, hands clasped on his knees, embracing her in a cascade of possessive endings: not to make any final decisions, to wait—not to rush headlong—

"I must. I must."

"What, my sweet, tell me what you must. I want only your happiness."

"I must cross the Atlantic on the first plane. Visit the volcano. Must take the ferry boat down the Danube from Belgrade to Silistra and up the Volga from Astrakhan to Knibyshev. Explore the Galapagos Islands, the Amazon. By helicopter. I must travel all over the world. I can't begin to tell you about all the journeys ahead of me. To Rome, Athens, Jerusalem, Prague, Lima, Tokyo, Moscow. Someone I love is waiting for me in every city and places not marked on the map. Along the Trans-Siberian Railway. The road to Delphi to consult the oracle. Down to Piraeus from the Agora. Must make a long sea voyage to Knossos; track down the minotaur in the labyrinth."

He listens wide-eyed, with a stricken look, mouth hanging open, beautifully imbecilic.

"I have a travel grant," she continues, suddenly afraid he knows everything. Sees paper with her father's handwriting on his desk. Crazy fatman. Padded walls. Must get out. "They're paying all my expenses; two-week Mediterranean cruise; may get a role in super Franco-Italian production on the island of Naxos. Will read all the psychoanalytic literature on the subject for my part. What does Freud say about the myth of the minotaur?"

He tells her in tears and with wild gesticulations the things that went on in her house in Budapest between her father and mother, the terrible, horrible, outrageous things. She feels along the quilted padding of the wall for the door. Knows all about that. Not a child. Knows what she's doing.

"Must repeat my mother's life," she insists gravely. "No other alternative. The only true atonement. Follow in her footsteps—wherever it leads—nothing can stop me."

"But it's not at all the same, what you are doing, terribly, terribly mistaken," he sobs. So winningly emotional. Has even a touch of Ezra. She blushes, suddenly ashamed; possibility all this is being televised. "Not at all the same situation, totally different from your mother—no similarity, terribly deceived my poor child."

She refuses to discuss it with him. None of his business, her life. Will not be deterred by consideration of family, doesn't care what consequences to them herself, once in her life will obey heart's desire, be her true self. She laughs majestically in the doorway. Takes a bunch of peacock feathers from a vase and throws one at him graciously...

WAKING up in bed on a Wednesday morning, actually closer to noon, Sophie Blind lay staring dumbly at her familiar room. Ivan's old raincoat still tacked on the window frame, and all around her reminders of lost joys, planted everywhere like Easter eggs, hatch vainly. The pains of waking are unmistakable. In dreams there is not this sense of idleness, staring at your hands surrounded by mute objects. In dreams something must always happen; a bird appears on the window sill...

For a little while longer she tried to understand what induced her to abandon a more exciting, important pursuit for just lying in bed in this room, till she realized it was not a considered choice. She blundered into awakening. If she is still baffled, and even while getting on her feet with relative ease, struggles to recall by what tremendous effort she flung herself or was cast out of sleep, if this Wednesday morning seems so odd in its banality and part of her mind continues to dive for some deep reason it's because in the dreamer's world it had to make sense. Dream has its own time. While one is dreaming one does not know this of course; that it will end. In dreaming one assumes it will go on indefinitely, as in living—a reasonable delusion based on life experience: life goes on indefinitely until one is dead. Only dreams end. And in this respect loves and plays and stories are like dreams: they end.

Books were better than dreams or life. A book ended not like life, abruptly; not like a dream, with a clumsy struggle and sense of deception; but gracefully and knowingly, preparing you for the final period. Between life and dream there was not much difference really, however the two wrangled, struggled, played tricks on each other. A book was something really different. To begin with, you know where you are: you're in a book, and whether the setting is Paris or New York or the moon or not specified at all, you know you're in a book. Perhaps you're on a plane, perhaps you're in a village in the Balkans reading a book in a hotel room, reading or writing, in someone else's room, or your own kitchen when the children are asleep. You can be dreaming and not know it. You can be awake and wonder if it's a dream and not believe it. But a book is simply and always a book—you can be sure of that. And with a book, whether you're reading it or writing it, you are awake. The question does not pose itself. Writing a book appealed to Sophie on all these grounds. In a book she knew where she was. Because, however baffling and blundering and ambiguous, a book was a book.

TWO

A FEW YEARS before the outbreak of the First World War, the son of the chief rabbi of Budapest and the grandson of the famed Rabbi Simon of Nyitra chose as his bride a woman of dubious background and gifts. Rosa Ripper, a brewer's daughter (in student circles called the Rosa Luxemburg of Budapest), was a communist agitator with degrees in mathematics and medicine, a disciple of Freud and beautiful besides. Rudolf Landsmann met Rosa at the Galilei Club, the gathering place of students, socialists, avant-garde artists and intellectuals, which they both attended regularly. Little is known of the background of the brewer and his wife. Jews of a sort, for generations outside the Jewish community, assimilated, intermarried, with relations in Odessa and Constantinople—a case could be made for Khazar origins. In the eyes of the Landsmann family, they were riffraff. In 1912 Rudolf joined the psychoanalytic movement. At the medical school where he was studying brain histology, Freud's theory was jokingly spoken of as the "technique grown-up men use to talk to juvenile girls about dirty things."

Around this time a Transylvanian count who could trace his ancestry to the conquest sought in vain the favor of the same Jewish brewer's younger daughter, Kamilla. The noble family ruined, bankrupt, mostly drunkards, Count Csaba-Csaba went to Budapest to study law so that he might raise his kin from poverty. No longer a youth, he occasionally attended the Galilei Club in an effort to catch up with the times. Futurism, Symbolism, Marxism, Freud, Esperanto—he lacked enthusiasm for these things. But from the day the blond, almond-eyed sister of Rudolf Landsmann's fiancée came to the Galilei Club, the count's attendance became regular. Kamilla, who began to accompany her sister to the club at the age of fourteen, mostly to escape from the house, was not interested in these issues either. After two years of mute adoration on the count's part, they left the meeting and walked along the *corso* in the moonlight.

Count Csaba-Csaba did not know that such women still existed. A true goddess, who could inspire a man to adore without permitting him to rape. Not the words in which the count expressed his wonder, infatuation, his feelings, his ideal, he had poetic phrases at his disposal; part of the national tradition. The times were much too out of joint to remark the fact that his dream found its incarnation in a Jewish brewer's daughter.

War broke out in 1914. The following year Rudolf Landsmann, army doctor in his emperor's service, received the crushing letter from his fiancée while he was at a military hospital in Serbia: She had decided to marry Franz Gerechter, one of the communist leaders; the revolution was imminent; the cause came first; their engagement was broken. On a week's leave in Budapest that Christmas, Rudolf, still heartbroken, went back to the Ripper house. Rosa was already married to Franz Gerechter and Rudolf's return visit to the house, by his own account, was purely sentimental. "It had become a habit," he said; for ten years the Ripper house had been his second home. He was received by the almond-eyed little sister, now almost sixteen, whom he had often held in his lap and helped with her Latin lessons, and promptly became engaged to her.

A few months later, back at the Serbian front, Rudolf received a letter from his sister Lea in which she mentioned among other gossip items that she saw Kamilla Ripper walking arm in arm with Count Csaba-Csaba in the moonlight on the Fisher's Bastion. Rudolf wrote Kamilla that their engagement was broken and not to bother to write to him again. He was through with the Ripper girls. In his sister's next letter he learned of Kamilla's marriage to the count.

Perhaps it was all for the best. Rudolf distinguished himself as a military doctor: he succeeded in enforcing anti-epidemic measures among backward peasants where others had failed. In particular,

Moslem women and nuns resisted delousing, but the young doctor attended to these matters personally and with success. He became a favorite of the Trappist monks, who were eager to recommend him for the chair in psychiatry at the Royal Hungarian Academy in Budapest. He was further promised a post as director of a newly founded psychiatric institute in Sarajevo, assuming that the Dynasty won the war. Both positions required celibacy and conversion to the Catholic faith. Did Rudolf seriously consider?

The Dynasty did not win. The defeated emperor's troops were caught in the Serbian uprising. Somehow Rudolf Landsmann found his way back to Budapest. There he found chaos. His four years' army pay which he had sent home to his parents to save was worth the price of a shirt.

A succession of short-lived revolutionary regimes was terminated by a three-year period of counterrevolutionary terror. Rosa Ripper, who had been one of the leading members of the communist Bela Kun regime, escaped execution by fleeing from the capital barefoot in a nightgown and jumping on a moving train. The count and his Jewish wife had survived the communist regime with no greater incident than Rosa's demanding that sister Kamilla hand over to her all her clothes and linen for the poor. Some years later under the counterrevolutionary regime when the police who knocked on her door one dark night asked why she attended the Galilei Club, Kamilla knew how to lower her eyes and say, "To catch a husband," with just a trace of a lisp that would convince the gendarme of any party. "And did you?" the gendarme asked. Kamilla stuck her index finger in her mouth and nodded with a silent giggle. Which husband? It wasn't clear from Kamilla's account. When this incident took place she was Rudolf Landsmann's wife. For in the course of these political upheavals Countess Csaba-Csaba and Rudolf Landsmann seemed to have met—one of those incredible chance encounters, as Kamilla told the story later—met in front of a small corner *tabac;* she was just about to enter the store as he came out. They discovered it was true love after all. Kamilla's marriage to the count was annulled—a simple procedure, as Rudolf told the story later: The count, a gentleman to the last and moreover a lawyer, produced a false birth certificate for Kamilla which made her a minor at the time she married. Neither Rudolf nor Kamilla remembered the year of their wedding forty years later. A passport issued to Mrs. Rudolf Landsmann for travel to Austria for purposes of health, and bearing Kamilla's picture, dated the marriage to before March, 1921.

In Budapest the first years of the twenties witnessed, besides the continuation of postwar chaos, the Treaty of Trianon and the setting up of a reactionary state. During the winter of 1921 a series of mass executions took place. Hundreds of politically undesirable citizens—communists, Marxists, socialists, leftists of all varieties—were sent sprawling in the grass, snow, then mud of the famous Bloodmeadow where, not so long before, politically undesirable citizens of another hue had been disposed of similarly. More, it seems, were on the list than were effectively eliminated. Rudolf Landsmann, for one, received an order to appear before government authorities. When he did he noticed some familiar faces among small crowds in the waiting room. The government official informed him that they had records of his former membership in the Galilei Club, the hotbed of revolutionaries. Admitting this, Rudolf Landsmann pleaded that he was never a member of the communist party, or a Marxist for that matter, and that he had faithfully served his country in the war as an officer of the royal Imperial Army. After a brief interrogation as regarded his occupation, marital status, present employment, he was laconically dismissed. Some fifty of the unknown number called to report that morning were shot the same afternoon.

Rudolf Landsmann at the time believed the new government spared his life because they needed doctors. Another explanation came to light some years later when he learned that in fact he had been on another blacklist—that of the communist party, which had slated him to be shot in the previous year, 1920. The list comprised former members of the Galilei Club who, being liberal but not Marxist, were the first to be eliminated if order was to be established. This list had been submitted to a high communist official who had frequented the Galilei Club in his student days, and had lain in his desk drawer awaiting his signature. The high official, as it turned out, did not get around to signing this piece of paper. Nobody was pressing for the signature and executions were being conducted in such mass and haste that a half a dozen missing corpses easily went unnoticed. The list that included Rudolf's name remained in the high official's drawer; perhaps he was simply putting it off for tomorrow or the next day, or telling himself that he was only putting it off; he had enjoyed some pleasant evenings at the Galilei Club with Rudolf Landsmann; they had played soccer together, in fact they had been friends; still, he was a high official in the new communist regime. The story told to Rudolf years later in Vienna by the former high official was that he couldn't do it; the day he received the slip he folded it with no intention of ever signing it, and laid it in his desk drawer. There it remained even after the regime fell and he fled to Vienna; there the police of the new government found it in 1921. It was fortunate for Rudolf Landsmann that he had been on the blacklist of the communist party in 1920. As a former member of the Galilei Club, he was politically undesirable; but the fact that the communists had wanted to get rid of him made the authorities reconsider. And besides, there was a shortage of doctors. At the time he was called in for questioning, Rudolf Landsmann worked at two hospitals during the day besides six hours every night in the clinic. How did he do it? He had to. It was the time of the Great Depression. The brewer went bankrupt and moved to a sorry little flat which he and his wife now shared with his daughter Kamilla and her husband who paid the rent. Rudolf was lucky to have three jobs.

In the depression of 1922 he lost two of his jobs. His father was ill, his mother complained, his father-in-law went insane, Hermann, the one brother he loved, emigrated to Canada, his marriage wasn't working out. One morning in 1922 he went to the American consulate and signed up for a visa. And having nothing else to do till noon, he went to seven other consulates and applied for visas to Egypt, Australia, Palestine, Canada, Argentina, Honduras, and Tanganyika.

When, four weeks later, he received a letter from the U.S. consulate informing him that he had been granted an immigration visa, valid for two months from the day of issue, everything was up in the air. He had a half dozen private patients, he was being considered for a part-time post at the city insane asylum, he was completing a book which he believed would win him recognition, and his wife seemed more reasonable after a fortnight's stay with her sister. Furthermore, she informed him that she was pregnant. It was not the moment to pick up and go—and under the circumstances, with everything up in the air, two months was simply not enough time to make such an important decision. The day he applied for a visa to America he thought of leaving everything behind. He intended to go alone. He didn't imagine going with a wife, let alone a pregnant wife. He put the letter from the consulate in a drawer and continued working on his book, which as he anticipated won him immediate recognition. Soon he moved to an apartment where he could have his own office and in another two years he had a ten-room apartment in one of the finest parts of Pest a few streets from the Parliament.

To the Landsmann family, Rudolf's marriage to one of the "Ripper girls" (and the lesser, at that), a girl who was a divorcée at the time of the marriage, who they suspected was *schmatte;* this was a great disappointment. The years following the end of the war brought many disappointments to the family; and worse than disappointment, shame and grief brought on by a son who stole money and ran away, another who turned into a good-for-nothing (a football player), a third who killed himself. The shame and grief over these and other sons and daughters known to live unhappy, insufficient lives was acknowledged in silence. There was no helping the death of a son, or the unhappiness of a daughter married to an orthodox rabbi with two children. Rudolf's marriage, however, they could not accept. This misfortune was unnecessary. He was not happy; his wife made difficulties for him and she did not give him a child.

Kamilla, taking all rumors into account, seems to have divided her time between consulting the best practitioners of the new science to cure her of her follies, and abandoning herself to them. Her follies included carrying on nineteenth-century-style romances (in the Austrian corruption of the Russian manner) mostly with military men; displaying herself in public in the most extreme, provocative and bare fashions of the day; and catastrophic ventures in the worlds of finance and the arts.

Madame Landsmann's affairs were objectionable to her husband and to her in-laws on diverse grounds. That the wife of Rudolf Landsmann should be unfaithful was so shocking more need not be said, his mother and sisters felt. As Olga Landsmann, Rudolf's more worldly sister-in-law, told the story later, Kamilla's lack of discretion was offensive. In short, she was stupid. "The point is not what Kamilla does," Olga had tried to argue with Rudolf, "but why do I have to hear about it? And why does it have to come to the ears of your poor mother?" Rudolf agreed that this was just the point. It wasn't serious, Kamilla's affairs. The point was the public display, public adoration; how could he explain to Olga, who hadn't read Freud, that his wife wasn't really unfaithful (a point which didn't seem to concern his sister-in-law either), that it was her neurosis, she couldn't help it—hopefully she would get over it after some years of analysis. The style in which she conducted her affairs, the costumes, settings, her choice of conspicuous military men, public figures, artists, etc., belonged to the pattern of her neurosis. Flaunting herself, not to hurt or disgrace him, no—Rudolf insisted, seeing his sister-in-law's eyes pop, knowing she thought him a fool, "...the agonies of guilt that poor woman suffered!"

"A bitch," she claimed, "women like that existed before Freud and all this fancy talk with complexes and compulsions. It's nothing new; a spoiled woman, a vain woman, a selfish woman, using a man, making a fool of him; there's nothing original about your Kamilla."

"It's a sickness," he pleaded, "I didn't say she was original. There are thousands of cases. All humanity is sick. She is a classic case."

"I say she is a bitch."

"We analysts call it a sickness."

The family continued to bewail the pity and shame of Rudolf's childless marriage the more vehemently as he grew more esteemed and prosperous. Divorce her. Let her have a child, they nagged. In due time there was both a child and a divorce.

When Kamilla announced, for the seventh time in the last ten years, that she was in the blessed state, the family was skeptical. Six weeks pregnant and not turning green? In the eighth week of Kamilla's pregnancy events took a precipitous turn. Rabbi Moses, who had been ailing since the war, was approaching his end. The signs were clear even though it was only a light bronchitis that brought the Rabbi to bed: all male members of the Landsmann clan went wrong in the head shortly before the angel of death called.

"It is very strange," the Rabbi remarked one day at meal. "I eat and eat and nothing comes out." For a fortnight now, he claimed it had been thus with him.

The next day his youngest son, a medical student, insisted on accompanying him into the water closet. It was a Sabbath afternoon and the Rabbi's wife sat with her daughters-in-law; Kamilla in a fashionable maternity garb, although Grandmother Landsmann, feeling boldly her belly, found scarcely a bulge. The ladies saw the door open and the Rabbi pass through the room toward his study sighing, "I eat and eat and nothing comes out," and young Benji holding a clump of excrement in each hand and crying, "But Papa, Papa, look!"

At the end of the week he came down with a fever and within ten days he died. So it was with all male Landsmanns.

Now everything turned on whether the wife of the favorite son of Rabbi Moses would produce a boy to bear his name.

Five months pregnant, Kamilla was received with excitement by the Rabbi's widow and her sisters-in-law. The child's sex was a decided matter. "How is little Moses?" Grandmother would ask, embracing her daughter-in-law with more than usual affection.

By Olga Landsman's account, a nurse reported that Rudolf Landsmann burst into the hospital crying, "My son! Where is my son!" Shown a swaddled infant, he rushed to the phone booth.

Olga, Rudolf's sister-in-law, summoned to the scene by the jubilant phone call, looked hard at the bright-eyed, rosy-cheeked infant who was wearing a kerchief on its head, a curious detail, perhaps to protect its ears from the draft; several nurses, and then the aunt, remarked its resemblance to a peasant girl. The sister-in-law raised her eyebrows. "Who said it was a boy?" she asked and proceeded to remove not the infant's kerchief but its diaper and, after a significant pause, repeated before the abashed father and nurses, "Who said it was a boy?"

According to the same aunt, Rudolf Landsmann turned white then purple. "It's not possible," he muttered and ran out of the room. In less than half an hour, however, he returned to his natural color and headed straight to the crib without a glance at his sister-in-law or anyone. He lifted the infant and, pressing it to his bosom, cooed to it and rocked it, oblivious to all. When his sister-in-law was about to leave, he looked up, "Mama knows already—"

Whether Kamilla was more relieved than disappointed by the birth of a daughter must be left to conjecture. The regret she expressed three decades later at not having produced three daughters to her one daughter is difficult to reconcile with fact. If motherhood did not improve Kamilla's character or, in Rudolf Landsmann's terminology, cure her of her neurosis, the Landsmann family may have been partly to blame.

"The very image of her father!" "A true Landsmann!" they cooed, gathering around the infant's crib, and appropriated it by the bent of its nose, the shape of its mouth, and any sound or movement it made. As for Kamilla, she acted the part assigned to her in the family scenario. She delivered a child. Now she was no longer needed. Rudi had his sweetheart. She would have her sweethearts.

The family drama reached its denouement in the spring of 1938: Kamilla announced her decision to marry a young journalist, Zoltan Vithezy; Rudolf agreed to the divorce. On March 12, Hitler marched into Austria. When Isidor and Olga Landsmann saw the Nazi flag waving from the Austrian embassy from their apartment window across the street, they made their decision to emigrate to America and persuaded Rudolf, along with his ten-year-old daughter, to join them.

It was a long journey for Rudolf Landsmann from the orthodox synagogue in Galanta to a three-story frame house in Garfield, New York. The narrator must pause. A wing of the newly erected psychiatric center is to be dedicated to her father, and she must fly to Garfield to attend the unveiling ceremonies and the formal dinner in his honor. He has asked her to come a day before and to stay over the weekend. How can she refuse?

He calls to confirm the time of her arrival, anxious and apologetic, "I realize it is a burden and a nuisance," he says. "You know how I feel about public occasions. Sometimes one must conform to other people's weaknesses . . ." She assures him there is no need for him to worry, even if in every other respect he could not count on her as a daughter, she understands what is required of her on public occasions. Not to be present at this event would be unthinkable. "That's what I think, too," he says with satisfaction. "Did you get my letter?" he asks, "I wrote you a long letter in answer to your questions. You should get it tomorrow. Why are you suddenly interested in these things? . . . I could tell so much more. But you will be here soon."

... YOU ASK how did my mother manage in Galanta. She had twelve children. Two died. She was either pregnant or breastfed the babies. Therefore she hardly had menstruations. Mother did not stay in bed more than a day after delivery. She got up and worked. When visitors came she jumped quickly into bed to be congratulated.

THE APPLE SCENE

Mother prepared our school lunch. We were at the exit door to leave for school. Before me were two or three brothers. Mother handed our bags to us. I was the last in line. Mother stood near me and gave me an apple, what the others did not get. (Fruit was a rare thing.) The others noticed this, Mother and I were embarrassed. All my brothers—in front of me—hated me, though they didn't show this. Only by innuendos. I was in the middle. The elders wanted to rule over me, the youngers to exploit me. All were in my way. I fought against both sides. I was isolated, but I was the stronger. ("*Der Starke ist am mächtigsten allein*"—Freud about himself, quoted Goethe.)

LITTLE SAMUEL'S DEATH

I could have been two or three years old. I had a little charming brother whom I loved more than anything else. He got sick. At that time, we did not have any serum against diphtheria, whooping cough; no antibiotics. He was dying. He was put in the studio in a wooden crib. People gathered in the studio. They were reciting (as is customary) psalms. My mother and two sisters were standing by, close to each other. The life of Samuel (it means "the name of God") was close to the end. An elderly Jew held a goose feather in hand to see when the breathing of Samuel did not move the feather any more. Suddenly he cried out the S'ma Yisrael (Harken Israel), which meant that my brother expired. And I was there, unnoticed, observing. I felt that life is utterly impossible, bitter, the dangers are tremendous; that these people should be able to do better and not to let my little, beloved brother die.

I spent my life with the other boys in the yard of the synagogue where our family lived. I went twice daily to service. In the synagogue there was burning the eternal light. The light flickered. I was told that the spirits of the dead are dwelling there and when the living come in for the service, the spirits of the dead have to be reminded that the living are coming in for the service and the spirits have to leave. One was supposed not to meet them. So I followed the *shamesz*, the man who had, among many other things, the duty to open the door of the synagogue. There was a thick and heavy door. The man had a big key. He knocked on the door with this heavy key, reminding, urging the spirits to leave. There was already a considerable hole due to previous knocking on the door. In the synagogue, there was a sort of chair on which the circumcision took place. The removed foreskins were collected in a box attached to the back part of the chair. With several boys we once raided this chair and dispersed the dried-up foreskins on the floor.

HOW OLD WOMEN URINATED IN GALANTA ON THE STREET

I often witnessed the following scene. (There wasn't a possibility in Galanta to find a facility for urination, besides at home.) It was always with two women together; they met and chatted. When they left, I found a puddle at the place where they were standing. It was dry before. Later on as a medical student, I understood that in old women there is a possibility to accomplish this without (much) soiling themselves. (Women wore long dresses.)

FATHER'S WALK FROM THE HOUSE TO THE SYNAGOGUE

He started to pray the moment he left the house for the synagogue. And he did so until he reached his prominent place in the synagogue. Nobody would have disturbed him. Leaving the synagogue, he stopped for a few minutes to talk to a member. It was like when a king would do such a thing. (Today a rabbi of a reform congregation would stop and tell even a dirty joke to a member.)

GRANDFATHER, THE FAMED REB SIMON OF NYITRA

I did not know him; he died shortly after I was born.

He didn't leave behind any writings, but the following *hochmes* (wise sayings) were often repeated in our house. When disciples came to ask him what a man needed in order to be happy he answered, "*A yid soll man sein und appetit soll man haben.*" (One should be a Jew and one should have a good appetite.) He used to say that he couldn't understand how a *goy* can be happy: he does not eat kosher food and does not apply *tefillin* (phylacteries).

He didn't understand birds. From his study window he would see a bird fly from one branch to the next, rest a while and fly on to another branch. Why couldn't the bird stay where it was, why did it fly to another branch?

BACK TO PRIVATE CONVERSATION

Around the age of eight. A small group of boys talked about whether sexual intercourse exists between our parents or not. We decided that the parents of the boys present did not have sex in order to produce us, all the others' parents did.

MY FIRST PENNIES

It was when I was four or five that his father let me work in the lumberyard to put in order shingles. I got *three* pennies. I bought with one penny a flute, painted red, made out of sugar, wrapped in fine thin paper, held together with a ring. I put away the paper, put the ring on my finger, played the flute, and consumed it. With the second penny I bought at the market a fist-size canteloupe, ate it secretly. The third penny I saved for the future.

WHY THEY PERSECUTED MY FATHER

The Galanta congregation resented my father's vernacular learning. They were savages. They claimed that he was not a real rabbi because he read the newspaper. They held against him that on a visit to Vienna he had gone to the theater and seen a play by Schiller. Once I asked him how he liked the play, he answered with a shrug, "*M'lacht...*"

BUDAPEST

I was ten and a half when my father was invited to become the rabbi of one of the greatest congregations of Europe. We moved to Budapest and my life and outlook changed completely. I became a college boy and then a medical student. With all the enthusiasm of a young man, I got acquainted with the new discoveries of chemistry, physics, with the literary geniuses of that time, with sociological theories, with new trends in art and finally, with Sigmund Freud's writings. When his *Totem and Taboo* was published I briefed my father about the main content; namely that, according to Freud, God is our projected conscience and not what religion says; that conscience is the introjected God. He was silent. When I urged him to make a comment he said: "You are *meshuga*" (crazy). This was the first and the last time that I talked to my father about psychoanalysis.

At the age of eighteen I left the home of my parents. I made myself independent. But I stayed a devoted son. As long as I lived in my parents' home, I participated in the performance of several rituals. My father knew how I felt about them. Later on, as an analyst, I wrote several papers on Jewish rituals and have shown that every ritual was a tremendous step forward in harnessing antisocial drives; but that now we can know their meaning and have control by knowing what they are. I do not oppose those who observe them, who obey.

FIRST IMPRESSIONS OF THE HUNGARIAN CAPITAL

Glorious entry into Budapest. We were traveling in first-class coach (I had never been in before—with red beautiful cover) and a terrible thing happened. My sister Lea wet herself. A large wet spot on the red plush. Terrible embarrassment. A delegation received us with music. We were taken to our apartment in *fiakkers* (carriages with two horses). The first time I saw water coming from the wall, at my will, toilet with flush (in Galanta we had outdoor *Abort*), houses with many flats, streetcars. Very soon I walked to the Danube. Later on I walked up to Buda. I was fascinated by the Royal Palace. No way to get in. Only to the gates. But I could get in to a museum at the side of the palace with relics to honor the memory of Empress and Queen Elizabeth (a real and legendary beauty who was killed in Luzern by an anarchist). I never missed to stand on the line on the street when Emperor and King Franz Josef (Ferencz Jozsef) came for a few days or weeks to his palace in Buda. It happened that I was (pretty often and always alone) near the guard horse who, when the king or prince came, drew arms to honor them, and see myself standing there, again alone, nobody bothering to ask me what I am doing there. I felt—like

Kafka—that I would never get in. But I did, I did. The Hapsburg Dynasty perished and the palace was taken over by the revolutionary government of the radical (not communist) party and also later by the Hapsburg communists too, and offices were set up. I walked in the beautiful corridors, saw the wonderful doors, wallpapers, all with great art, and I wasn't sure who would take care of all these precious things. The palace was destroyed when in 1945 the Germans withdrew from Budapest. Now the palace is restored. I do not know what happened inside.

MY "PRIMAL SCENE"

(Observance of parental intercourse, directly or indirectly.)

Age twelve to thirteen. Father went very early to the synagogue. The moment he was out of the house, I went furtively (others should not notice it) in the bed of my father. His nightshirt was there. It had a special smell. My mother's nightshirt smell was different. When I perceived that the two smells were mixed, I drew my conclusion. Since then my olfactory orientation enables me to "put my nose into everything" when an explanation is missing. It helps me to discover the hidden.

MY FIRST INCOME FROM "PSYCHOTHERAPY"

I was about fifteen. It was in Budapest.

My father called me and my older brother Hermann into his studio. There was standing a short, thin man, showing on his face great distress. Father explained to us that this man made a vow that he cannot fulfill and that this man needs an absolution from his vow. According to Jewish tradition three Jews over the age of thirteen can create a court, a *Beth Din*, and absolve him from the obligation he committed himself to in innocence.

MY MOTHER'S DREAM A MONTH AFTER MY FATHER'S DEATH

She was at a ball and a man with a wooden leg asked her to dance. They danced for a long time and, she added, it felt so good.

Interpretation: To "dance" means to enjoy intercourse. She missed having intercourse with Father. The wooden leg signified her dead husband. She was dancing with her dead husband in the dream. It was the first and last time that my mother asked me about a psychoanalytic interpretation.

SHE WALKS up the porch steps of her father's house. The front door is open; he is with a patient in his office upstairs. She is to wait for him downstairs. Nothing has changed since she left for college, except that the dining-room table where she used to do her homework is now entirely covered with his papers, piles of mail and medical journals. The black air-raid shades from the forties are still on all the windows behind the regular yellow shades; both drawn three-fourths down during the day. At night he pulls them all the way down, going from room to room, and in the morning hoists them one-fourth up, meticulously. When the house is dark during the day, he puts on the dim little wall lights.

Her father had furnished the house to suit his own needs: the living room was where he made his telephone calls; the dining room, where he answered his mail; a table with six chairs and a buffet, the set bought second-hand for a hundred and ten dollars, filled the space. A room needed furniture, but he hadn't arranged his house for entertaining, or even casual sitting around. Women friends and his sister-in-law Olga were always offering to fix up the house for him, but he wouldn't hear of it. "Busybodies!" he told his daughter. He knew he could afford finer materials, custom-made furniture, "But what for?" The chest of drawers he bought for eight dollars served perfectly well; and the curtains that were hanging on the windows when he bought the house didn't bother him. That such things should bother his daughter when she lived with him was always a source of grief. "You'll be leaving anyway in a few years," he used to answer her complaints.

She hears the patient come down the carpeted stairs, the front door open and close, and soon after, her father's heavy tread that makes the woodwork creak. He stands smiling, arms thrown apart, as he had done when she was a small child. It would be wonderful if she could run into his arms like then, run and be lifted in the air; but on her long legs she stands three paces from him, too near to run; she walks two steps and they embrace, the old bear hug.

"Well, at last! At last!" His raspy voice welcomes her, his voice like his grip on her arm, proprietary. To his child, who will always belong to him, he repeats with relish, "At last you're here. It's right. Come," he says and she follows him into the kitchen. "We have many things to discuss. But we have time." He shows her there's everything in the icebox; a roast turkey, bread, butter, cake, eggs, salami, ham. "We will eat, but not yet. We will take our usual evening walk." But first he must draw down the shades, put on the lights, wind the clocks, change his shoes. "No," he says sternly when she offers to help. He doesn't want her to touch the shades. They're old and fragile, all the fixtures in his house, only he knows how to wind his clocks properly. She follows him up the stairs; there is a clock in every room, in the upstairs and downstairs halls and on the landing. She watches him tie his shoelaces, the way he learned as a boy. Forming two loops he makes a double knot with appropriate grunts.

"Come," he says, "I want to show you..." She knows what: the envelopes with his will, with the cash, with the list of telephone numbers, instructions for his funeral. And then to the drawer with all the documents, and through all the closets, then up to the attic. On the third floor, showing her the boxes of reprints of his articles, copies of *Imago*, her childhood things, drawings, notebooks; a box where he put wedding presents for her from his friends in Garfield: Paul Revere pots and pans, and more of those meaningless pairs of silver candlesticks.

"What will you do with all this when I die?" he asks anxiously. "Do you want this? Shall I give it away? I don't want you to be burdened with such details. Everything should be in order when I die."

Ever since they had lived in the house he had spoken of his will, and periodically showed her where he kept the envelopes; then every time she left to play in summer stock and when she came home for vacation from college and when she visited after she was married; her father's house in Garfield was always the house to which she would have to return one day to open envelopes, meet with lawyers, real estate men; the house she would have to dispose of; the house where her father had just died and where it was frightening to hear his footsteps at night; a house where it felt strange to sit in the kitchen with her father while he read the newspaper.

She watches him, an apron around his waist, scraping leftovers into the garbage can, then wiping his plate with a Kleenex, his and her plate, before he washes them. He has never allowed her to cook in this kitchen beyond boiling eggs or wieners and always preferred to clean everything himself. Till she went to college they ate from cans. Since then a Negro woman trained to prepare Hungarian dishes, to be silent and to wash up everything before he sits down to eat, comes daily, and he washes the plate he eats on after. He has taken her cup; she hasn't finished her coffee, "Have you finished?" he asks, the cup already in his hand.

"Yes." It's all right, it doesn't matter any more.

"How will it be when the children come for Christmas," he worries; he wants to see them of course, but the disorder—"Will you cook? I won't be able to live here! I'll have to find a room in a hotel for the time . . ." he resolves mock seriously.

What will happen to them, he pursues; Joshua is almost fourteen, "When I was that age . . . The world has changed." And he carries on with a troubled insistence, in a tone of bewilderment as he asks, "Will Joshua go to college? Will Toby get married and have children? Will Jonathan be drafted if there is a war in xx years?" And in a tone of impotent resignation, "Joshua will go to college. Toby will get married. Jonathan will be drafted if there is a war. This is how it must be." But he is not reconciled. "How will it be?" he continues asking childishly. Everything should be under his control; everything should be known and settled.

"Why do you worry?" she asks.

"I don't worry; I want to know; I want everything to be in order."

He knows how alone he stands in his commitment to order; that men are irrational and violent, "You too," he observes sadly. The fact that he has failed with his own child hurts anew. "Why?" he asks, and speaks about the intrinsic tendency for order in every living cell—why not the mind? He must have a reason for the disorder of the human mind. Is there a death instinct? Is it a by-product of language?

Wouldn't it be better for him to be putting on *tefillin* and wailing in the synagogue, she wonders, instead of carrying on like this? If his father had remained in his village . . . then Sophie wouldn't exist. For an instant the world lights up in the heavenly splendor of that possibility, true and eternal as pure possibility, a world unblemished by the marriage of Rudolf Landsmann to Kamilla Ripper, and their offspring; a world where those three people living together in embarrassment didn't happen, nor the journey of the father with the daughter, terminating at this table; for a moment longer she covets that happier world in which her father would have lived the life of a provincial rabbi, and she wouldn't have been born, while he, her father, rambling on, concludes on a hopeful note, "Chemistry will provide the answer." And as they start walking toward the grocery store, his arm around her, he tells how he loved her as a child, loved, cared, provided for her; "But sometimes I feel guilty that you were born," he confesses, not for the first time; and asks her, "What do you think, am I wrong? Should I not feel guilty?"

Her silent smile, faintly amused, indifferent, secretive, answers him. The child to whom he keeps addressing his questions, *his child*, has refused to exist for him so long ago, she reflects, or rather has continued to exist only in this act of refusal.

Once again father and daughter walk arm in arm along Clinton Avenue, he speaking, she silent. It could be during the war years or when she returned from college, or after she was married; the same stories told, the same questions addressed to her, himself, to life. The same bleak parking lots and garish billboards rising over two- and three-story frame houses with cluttered shop fronts blinking their neon signs. "I saw my mother work from daybreak late into the night; working for nine children. And why? Was it worthwhile? Worthwhile to be born for this? For her? For me? I told her once when we were alone, 'You could have skipped me.' But then you wouldn't exist. And so what?"

It could be ten years ago, or fifteen. It is not now. It is in a book. Her father's conversations with himself always had the quality of some obscure rite in which she was incomprehensibly involved.

As she was walking along Clinton Avenue with her father in the evening during the war, "Can you imagine yourself," he asked, "a young girl married to a man she had not exchanged a word with till after the wedding; and then children, one after another—what would you have done?" he asked strangely. "Can you imagine yourself—" he continued about his mother, then about Sophie and her mother. Part of a long monologue which she never interrupted, not in answer to her question, growing out of some troubled preoccupation of his own: concern for his family in Budapest, his daughter's future, his fear of being forgotten by his daughter when she married; the conversation beginning or ending with Auschwitz.

From her father's rambling discourse she picked out a fairy tale: it was beautiful and mysterious, the story of the young girl married to a man chosen for her by her father, a stranger from another town; the marriage arranged on the basis of a sermon.

"It was not how he imagined it." Her father tells once more the story of how her grandfather became the chief rabbi of Budapest. "He never intended to become a rabbi. He came from a well-to-do family whose other members went into trade, finance, administration of land; he had received a secular education. It was not unusual for a young man from an orthodox Jewish family to distinguish himself in Talmudic learning and then afterward settle down in some profession."

"Why did he become a rabbi if he didn't want to?" she asks. Her father replies with a sigh and a gesture of helplessness, perhaps repeating the answer he received from his father.

Of the life his father imagined before his fateful encounter with

Simon of Nyitra, and his decision to marry Simon's daughter, her father does not speak. What he imagined on the train to Galanta, or what he imagined on the train back to his home town in Pazdics to take leave of his parents, no one shall ever know; only his disappointment. "It was not the life that he imagined," her father repeats.

Back in the house she looks through the small pile of papers her father brought down from the attic. The family tree. Yellowed newspaper clippings of Moses Landsmann's obituaries. Popular psychoanalytic articles her father wrote for Budapest newspapers on thumb-sucking, Jewish rituals, frigidity, potency. Things of no value to anyone that he had brought over the ocean, kept all these years. "For you? For my grandchildren?" he asked before going to bed. "Please decide if there is anything you want."

The story is about a marriage, she thinks, sitting in her father's consulting room. It's the story of the true marriage, as told by the son of that marriage to his adolescent daughter who always heard it with a mixture of nostalgia, resentment and indifference, thinking it had nothing to do with her, and would never happen to her and still wishing she had been born into that other world where a girl was given into marriage simply by her father, like her grandmother was; knowing she could never be that kind of woman, and angry that it was denied to her because of the way the world had changed, changed already in her father's youth before she was born, so that she was the product of that change: of a father who broke away from his parents' traditional home, to whom his own marriage was a problem or a joke; who took her to America where she could dissociate herself from her childhood in Budapest, where she would not be tied by roots to land or people, because America was just this hard pavement given to push oneself away from and create one's own truth, which was for the best, the young girl wanted to believe, since this was in fact her destiny; but still at odds with herself and always wondering as she listened to her father, what was this change, trying to grasp the awfulness that whatever her grandparents and all the generations before them experienced in their youth, giving their lives sanctity, mystery and meaning, had been irrevocably outruled and superseded in the name of Progress, Reason and Enlightenment. But what was it in fact? The reality always reduced to the streets of Garfield and her psychoanalyst father telling her about his religious childhood in Galanta and her inability to experience the world he was describing, to be touched by it, its irrelevance to her to whom he had not given such a childhood and the pointlessness of his telling her about it on Clinton Avenue.

She looks at the family tree before her now: it begins with a certain Jokab born in the village of Szered, 1730. Drawn up by various members of the Landsmann clan before the two brothers left for America in 1939, the document was recopied recently by her cousin Tibor, escaped freedom fighter, who drew the now eight generations in different colors. How strange to see the names Joshua, Toby, Jonathan, children of Sophie and Ezra, on that tree.

Counting from herself only to the seventh generation, the lives of two hundred and fifty-two individual men and women had to cross and a hundred and seventy-six nuptials had to be consummated in order for Sophie to exist. Of these hundred and seventy-six nuptials, all but one were hallowed. Whatever the individual failings of the persons involved, the stupidity or outright selfishness of the fathers who arranged these marriages, whatever the unhappiness of the couples, it was the objective validity of these marriages that impressed Sophie. As for her parents' marriage, she had never been able to think of it as a true marriage.

The story is about a marriage, she thinks, sitting in her father's consulting room: the false marriage of Rudolf Landsmann to Kamilla Ripper, as felt by the daughter, and her own marriage a few years after the end of the Second World War in New York City, which was to have been the true marriage. The marriage of Sophie Landsmann to Ezra Blind, the young rabbi and visiting scholar from Vienna, who had singled her out at a lecture, in its way as mysterious as her grandmother's: two people, practically strangers entering upon a life commitment without any romance and the usual preliminaries of courtship, without so much as a dinner, a movie date, without a word of endearment having been spoken, or any kind of intimacy between them; oddly impersonal, formal, totally unsentimental and yet curiously free and comfortable with each other; a marriage that happened on the basis of a sermon he delivered to her alone on the evening they met and the next evening when she answered his marriage proposal by asking him to deflower her, the sermon and the proposal repeated for the next six weeks, always the same sermon delivered by the young rabbi from Vienna to the psychoanalyst's daughter who argued against God and marriage, till the night she could not answer him: she wanted only to feel simple and comfortable like the night he deflowered her, she wanted all her life to be simple like that; and they became engaged. It's the story of her marriage to a man to whom it mattered that she was the granddaughter of the former chief rabbi of Budapest, she thinks, still trying to understand what that marriage was all about, looking at the telephone beside her father's chair to which he shuffled from his bed when she called at three A.M. (she didn't know what time it was), Ezra at her side urging her to make the call to Garfield after he had cabled his parents, Ezra taking the receiver from her as soon as she had stated the fact, her father brokenly gasping, "What do you mean—getting married? Who is this Ezra? You can't do this to me!..." Then Ezra's voice, equal to the occasion, "Father, if I may call you Father..." speaking now in English then in Hebrew, already the son-in-law, proud and festive, prolonging the conversation in a tone of gentle irony, soon on joking terms with his father-in-law, while she watched amazed, perhaps just awakening from a state of total amazement at what had happened to her, to the growing sense of its reality.

It was not a mistake, she thinks, contemplating the family tree on which her name, Ezra's, their children's names are registered. Ezra belongs there. And at this late hour, her father snoring deeply in the next room, she can smile over Sophie Landsmann's attempt to find decency through her marriage to Ezra Blind.

The toasts and speeches in honor of her father, in the Regency Penthouse of the Sheraton Plaza, confer meaning on what was hitherto a dreary, incoherent limbo of her years of growing up in Garfield. It had this purpose, sense and direction, culminating in the creation of faculties and buildings in the presence of these people from Ohio, Connecticut, Maryland, Wisconsin, Canada and Australia who, as they stress in their speeches, would not be here if Rudolf Landsmann had not made up his mind to settle in Garfield, N.Y., at a time when there was no analyst in the state of New York outside of New York City; if Rudolf Landsmann had not fought single-handed and against opposition ... She remembers the morning they arrived in Garfield; her father joked, "We must have got off at the wrong stop."

"A Godforsaken place," he kept repeating the first time they walked down the main street, and when their walk brought them before a tavern displaying a picture of DER FUEHRER between two Nazi flags (which wasn't removed till the day after America declared war on Germany), by then everything wrong seemed right; they laughed hardest at the inevitable climax. Later, passing the frame house of the county insane asylum on her way to school, what always struck her was that the people sitting on the porch were weird in the same way as the people sitting on every other porch in Garfield; it was the same stark look of isolation frozen on all the faces that had stunned them both on their first walk through the town. Her father's decision to settle in Garfield was something she could never understand, never accept. She listens to her father conclude his speech thanking his colleagues, dignified, humorous, at ease, a few sardonic remarks to clear the air of any trace of hypocrisy; she is proud of him; she just wasn't cut out to be the daughter of an apostle to Garfield.

Her presence at the banquet is one of those felicitous deceptions of a few days. "When I arrived twenty years ago with my daughter, who sits at my right ...," he had begun his speech; she had materialized to please her father.

"Well, it's something," he says when they're alone in the taxi. "Even if you see me as an old fuddy-duddy and consider Freud rubbish, it's something. It doesn't really make a difference to you whether your father is a distinguished psychiatrist or a grocer, does it? And why should it? You're absolutely right. Still, I'm happy you came."

They have made most of their duty calls. "People want to see you," he had said apologetically. "They always ask, 'Dr. Landsmann, how is your beautiful daughter?' Are you beautiful?" he had asked with mock severity.

"Of course I'm beautiful," she told him. Now it's a relief to be back in the house. People tire him, he complains to his daughter.

"Is it true that you are writing a novel," he asks, frowning, his tone troubled as he touches on the old issue.

"What sort of book are you writing? And do you know why you are writing it? We analysts..."

"We," he used to say when they first walked together in Garfield. "We are different. We don't like foolish chatter, frills, extravagance, display of feelings. We are thinkers." Both he and she were different from her mother in Budapest, who lived on flatteries, who dressed extravagantly, who was always preoccupied with her emotions. They were different from his family, different from anybody he could think of because practically all other people were vain, foolish, hypocritical. "We are different," he said. His daughter detected a tinge of sadness and irritation—as if he were questioning why this was so, troubled by the fact that they were different—which offended her pride and created a distance between them. She wanted to remain apart, to be left alone. Paternal approval gave her certain liberties: an aloof man, an aloof daughter. But he was also a father: he worried why she didn't care for her appearance, spent all her time alone, why didn't she have a boyfriend? Why wasn't she like other girls?—like the grocer's red-haired daughter showing off her breasts, she would catch a man for sure before she was seventeen; or like the reform rabbi's daughter who was high-minded, a brilliant student—but all in the service of femininity. He cited others, sometimes he was joking; he wouldn't seriously want her to be like the receptionist at the hospital, with her perfect manicure, hair set and doll smile, sitting there just to attract a man. And certainly not like one of his patients he was describing. He didn't want her to be like his mother and sisters. The world had changed. He didn't know. He really didn't know himself what was demanded of a woman in this new and changing world; what a woman should be, and his daughter in particular. It was a question on his mind he was asking himself and his daughter. Perhaps because she took too long to answer, he went on citing cases; or perhaps it was to relieve her, or simply because he was accustomed to her silence and accustomed to answering the questions addressed to her. Occasionally she spoke, and she startled him by her answers; so perhaps to spare himself her answers he went on thinking out loud about what a woman's life used to be and what it could be under the present circumstances—a question that he could not bring to either theoretical or practical resolution. He always concluded by returning to his daughter approvingly, praising her seriousness, her kind of beauty which was not cheap or worldly. "We are different," he always concluded, sometimes with a touch of theatricality, fusing pathos and irony in the sweep of a gesture, putting his arm around her shoulder as they walked.

They were different in different ways. Sophie still hadn't found any way to disagree with her father openly, except to blurt out her feelings like a child. This did not work. In her father's universe, emotion, tears, rage discredited you. She retreated into silence. There was only one course left to her, refusal to enter into argument. His premises may be fine for his patients. She had others. No, she was not interested in what motivated people. She didn't "reject" Freud. She just did not find it as interesting as works of literature. No, she was not interested in explaining people or anything. He persisted in questioning her about her interests, aims, ambitions. She answered evasively.

It was as painful for him to disavow her as for her to be disavowed. He tried to cover up; but he couldn't yield his position.

For the next years they had to live with this: she was different from him.

He presented her with options of the ways she might be different, supported by data he had on her as a child. He offered her several ways of being different; he wanted her to be different in a way he could accept, understand; he even pulled out a sympathetic portrait of her mother. She saw in his eyes veiled condescension, disavowal. She didn't trust him. She wanted to be different her own way, which he couldn't understand or accept. "We . . ." Rudolf Landsmann would say, speaking to his daughter on their evening walks in Garfield during the war.

"We analysts..." he began to say after a while. And she walked beside him thinking her own thoughts, not listening. Every so often she would hear his phrase, "...we analysts," reassuring her that they lived in different worlds.

Occasionally he might ask a question that startled her. On their evening walks during the war her father would ask, "Do you sometimes think of your mother?"

The picture of her mother Sophie carried with her to the New World was lost. She did not have it when she arrived in Pittsburgh with her father. The locket did not close well; her mother observed the fact when she showed it to her, and Sophie recalled that they had stopped by a jeweler to fix it the last afternoon she and her mother spent together. Her mother spoke sharply to the jeweler who as a matter of courtesy was profusely apologetic, but between ritual apologies and promises stated more than once that it was an old locket—the two sides didn't fit. Perhaps it was just as well that the picture fell out. It hadn't helped her to remember her mother. She couldn't conjure up her mother's face. Perhaps she had never had a clear image of her mother's face, even in Budapest; but it was only some time after the train pulled out of the station that this had struck her, perhaps because she knew she would not see her mother for a long time, perhaps never again. She was bound for another continent, an ocean would separate them. In the train to Paris and at various points of the journey she would suddenly realize that she couldn't recall her mother's face, then open the locket to study the photograph and close it with the feeling that her mother was just one of those beautiful faces one saw in magazines. She didn't ask herself if this was a new feeling, or the way she had always felt about her mother. She had no memory of her. It was as a picture she thought of her, therefore it was just as well the photograph was lost. She did not need it. She remembered the face in a grave pose, the wide mouth and faultless arc of penciled brows.

Her father's periodic question, "Do you sometimes think of your mother?" found her unprepared, at a loss. It was impossible to remember her mother. An image, simplified and idealized, had replaced all memories, yet she had a more real sense of her mother than before: a woman who still walked through the streets of Budapest where Sophie couldn't go, an elegantly dressed woman in a beautiful city; a lady married to a tall blond man, kind and well-mannered, very different from her father; a woman who had been married to a true nobleman before Sophie was born; a strange, beautiful, mysterious woman who had never really seemed like her mother. She was pained by her father's question, which may not have been addressed to her at all.

There was no picture of her mother in the house. It was strange to Sophie that her father should be concerned about the woman who was now another man's wife, should reminisce to his daughter about her little habits, her problems; worry about what she was doing at present, whether she had all that she needed; then return to speaking about her talents, her mistakes. Perhaps his daughter's silence prompted him after a while to make some concluding remark like, "She is your mother, after all."

"Do you sometimes think of your mother?" Rudolf Landsmann began his ruminations on his former wife. Perhaps she didn't. Perhaps she did, but the fact that he did not allow her time to answer made her believe that she didn't. And after 1941 when communication was broken by America's entry into the war—and now when her father asked the question he expressed his fear that she might be dead or in a concentration camp, or hiding, starving, one didn't know, it was terrible, terrible—perhaps Sophie still saw her mother as a beautiful woman walking through a city whose charm was enhanced by bombings, made more beautiful by disaster.

In 1951 her mother came to settle in America, perhaps hoping for a reconciliation with her former husband. Nothing of the sort materialized. Her father, while solicitous for her welfare, could not tolerate her manner, and she in turn could not take his chronic annoyance and picking her apart. He did not permit her to visit him in Garfield.

Ritual meetings, and then only long-distance calls once or twice a year, were still maintained. But he was pained by the estrangement between mother and daughter. He was anxious that Sophie be on at least civil terms with her mother.

"Do you see Mother sometimes? Are you in contact with her at least?" he asks worriedly.

"She came to see the children on Thanksgiving. She is fine."

He is reassured and does not pursue the subject further.

On their evening walks he speaks about his experiences as a soldier. She listens enviously. It's the only period of his life he really likes to talk about.

"You had a great time in the war," she points out to him.

"It's true," he admits, "but I did not kill."

He condemns violence. Once more he raises the old question, "Is war necessary? Will mankind find other ways for their aggressions? Unlikely," he muses aloud, and entertains the possible destruction of mankind with a certain satisfaction. "The Lord made a great mistake; he should have stopped after he created plants..." Evangelical, and with compassion for God whose grief over the bungled experiment must infinitely exceed his own, he praises the trees.

Sitting in his consulting room later in the evening, they look through old photographs he keeps in a silver box. There are over a hundred, some taken on the Serbian front, some in the Budapest baths, on the street, in restaurants, rooms and gardens in Budapest, Vienna, Paris, New York; family pictures, the oldest taken *ca.* 1860, shows Simon of Nyitra, regal in his fur kaftan and collar, his fine, forked beard, seated in the pose of a Renaissance prince, his hand rests on the large tome in his lap, the face with its haughty slanted brows and cheekbones emerges absolute, unconditioned, from the dark background. Another, taken fifty years later, shows Moses Landsmann sitting at his desk in his Budapest apartment in a gray suit and tie, his fair beard trimmed short, blond, blue-eyed, blandly handsome, the benign expression on his face, with a suggestion of a pained smile, conveys official serenity. Pictures of her father as a moustached, swaggering provincial, young soldier, cynical analyst, happy grandfather;

her mother in a variety of seductive poses; beautiful Rachel, regal in high lace collar with her two daughters, who perished in Auschwitz. Uncle Joske (the bum) in Vienna, standing stiffly in a striped suit, looks like a Chicago gangster. More pictures of dreamy young girls in the romantic manner.

"Is that Mother?" she asks with surprise; the picture with her mother's name written on the back shows a shy young girl with long hair, seated in a pensive pose.

"Yes, she looked like that," her father affirms with unexpected feeling, "That's what she looked like when I married her," he sighs, and puts the photograph back in the box hastily; she is disappointed that he refuses to reminisce about her mother when he loved her, before she turned into the would-be *femme fatale* of the later photographs.

"And what happened?" she asks.

"She became totally different," he says, in a tone of incomprehension. "She changed—" and decides not to pursue this painful subject.

It's ten-thirty, he notes; time for his nightcap.

She watches him check the icebox, make up the grocery list for tomorrow. "Will you stay downstairs?" he asks. He would like to put out all the lights before retiring. "What will you do?" he asks. "If you use the kitchen—"

"You're a tyrant," she says. "Do you know that?"

"I know," he smiles, "I'm pleased you realize at last..." he adds, leaving.

If he had had a son, it would have made him into a different man; the fathers of daughters, not of sons, turn into petulant Lears, and Prosperos. If he had had a son... she reflects.

The house oppresses, its ghost surrounds her, settles on her with increasing weight; she dissolves into the ghost. Herself, as a young girl in her father's house? But she doesn't feel like a young girl at all. The phantom is her absent mother, whose place she must fill. The absent mother whose absence was never discussed.

It's her mother's ghost that haunts this house: the young woman her mother was before Sophie was born, whose life she was reliving, put in the same circumstance, a young woman living with a man who had no time for her, who did not take her seriously, who joked about sex and insulted her with his indifference. The phantom presence of the woman of whom her father disapproved, the wife who failed and lost her place, was more potent than anything the young girl could remember of her mother or imagine as her mother's present reality; the phantom was more powerful than the young girl. It was her mother's phantom, not she, who lived in her father's house in Garfield, oppressed and fearful and in secret, concealed behind the mask of the young girl.

They walk along Clinton Avenue. She is leaving this afternoon; he is gloomy, complains about her lack of interest in psychoanalysis, and of how little he sees her. "I have lost a daughter," he says to himself.

"As an analyst you should understand," she tries to argue; he shakes his head. His look says everything.

"I'm here; I came," she tries again; the feebleness of her protest dismays her. They walk in silence back to the house. She has decided to abandon her chronicle. Reb Simon of Nyitra watching the birds, young Moses Landsmann on the train to Pazdics to tell his parents, couples strolling down the *corso* before she was born, Rosa and Rudolf, Kamilla and Count Csaba-Csaba, they are story people from a lost book of which only a few random pages remain. And father and daughter walking side by side, their words and silences caught in some dead space, they are story people too.

"What kind of book are you writing?" he asks her at the airport. They have arrived an hour early; she has checked her suitcase, filled mostly with fine Paul Revere pots and pans, the wedding presents he kept for her while she was traveling. They stroll along the hall to the gate and back to the lobby; "It's not really fiction," she is trying to explain to him, "it should please you—" But he hasn't the patience to listen and interrupts to tell a story by the Hungarian humorist Karinthy. He shrugs and they laugh.

"You were crazy about me when you were three years old," he says unexpectedly; "Do you remember that?"

Her admission does not relieve him. It's too late to comfort him, his hand clutching hers insists, as he recalls those happy days when she was three years old. "And it was pure sex," he adds, "Do you know that?"

"I know." She laughs, but he hasn't heard, or felt her kiss. He stands alone before the gate, his eyes grieving, unreconciled to the ancient loss; he sets his mouth bitterly, bravely.

She cannot please her father; perhaps no person had or could ever please him. He is a priest after all.

"What kind of book are you writing?" he asks, as they continue walking. "Can you explain to me what kind of book this is?"

(*The courtroom is filled with orthodox Hungarian rabbis and their families.* EZRA, *a skullcap lying insecurely on unruly hair, stands by the Judge's table with his father-in-law,* RUDOLF LANDSMANN. LANDSMANN *is wearing a gray fedora. A rabbi is delivering vehement invectives in Hebrew. The* CROWD *roars in approval.*)

LANDSMANN. Why are they screaming? The place stinks. My God! Dissolve the marriage!

EZRA. They're your people, Landsmann, these Hungarian fanatics. In Poland we called them Calvinists.

LANDSMANN. (*Sighing*) It's true. The disciples of my grandfather, the holy Reb Smuel of Nyitra. We called them the Dushensky gang. My beautiful sister married to one of those brutes, gassed in Auschwitz. She is there, I see all of them: Papa, Mama, Grandfather. But why do they want my daughter?

EZRA. They want your daughter because she is the great granddaughter of the holy Reb Smuel, your mother's father.

LANDSMANN. But why? What has she done? What are they screaming? I don't understand. What! They charge her with uncleanness, holding heretical doctrines, practicing abominations, loathsome and abominable forms of copulation. (*He laughs*) My daughter? Ezra, did you know about this? Are we back in the Middle Ages? My daughter practicing loathsome and abominable forms of copulation? With you perhaps!

EZRA. *Narrischkeit.* The point is your wife—I mean my wife, your daughter—has no legal status. (*Furiously*) These people mean

133

business, Landsmann. If you had listened to me we wouldn't be in this mess.

LANDSMANN. (*Offended; bitterly*) You're crazy. Everybody is *meshuga*. I'm taking my daughter out of here. All I need is the signature of two analysts to have her declared insane and placed under our professional custody.

EZRA. Landsmann, you agree the most important thing is the marriage.

LANDSMANN. The marriage must be saved. That's why I insist on having her under my custody. A divorce at such a moment! It's terrible. I refuse to be present at marital squabbles. I am not going to listen to any more "he says" and "she says"—I can't stand it. All my life, in my marriage, in your marriage, in my consulting room, in fifty years of analytic practice that's all I hear. People should learn to live with each other and devote themselves to science.

EZRA. Landsmann, where did your daughter get money to run away with the children?

LANDSMANN. I didn't approve of what she was doing.

EZRA. You can't handle her.

LANDSMANN. She married you without my approval—I'll never forget that three A.M. long-distance call confronted with a *fait accompli*.

EZRA. There you have it. And I took a plane to visit you the same week. Alone. Your daughter was in a play, you recall? And did I get her out of the theater?

LANDSMANN. You did.

EZRA. And did I see that she finished college? And got a doctorate? Did I show her half the world? And did I give her children?

LANDSMANN. With my money.

EZRA. Landsmann, you didn't know what to do with your daughter or your money.

(*The coffin is brought in*)

LANDSMANN. Oh my God...

(*They remove the lid.* SOPHIE, *in a white gown, stands up in the coffin*)

EZRA. You have to admit she looks good. Fifteen years married to me; you can't say she isn't well preserved. As good as the day I married her. How many husbands do you think—

LANDSMANN. (*Weeping*) My beautiful daughter. The tragedy! She is my daughter.

RABBIS. We want her.

(*Everybody approaches the coffin. There is a commotion as KA-MILLA DE VITHEZY, Sophie's mother, enters, making her way to the coffin carrying a fur coat on each arm. Everyone is scandalized. The rabbis and their wives jeer with disgust at her perfume, jewelry and the fur coats.*)

KAMILLA. I have come to take my daughter home. My poor darling! Why do I always find her in a rag! Sophie, aren't you going to kiss me!

EZRA. For this I'm not responsible. Whatever you might blame me for, Landsmann, I am not responsible for your ex-wife.

LANDSMANN. We all make mistakes.

KAMILLA. Aren't you glad to see me? Look, I brought you my three best fur coats and my swan feather wrap. I saved them for you through the Nazi occupation and the Russian occupation. (SOPHIE *tries on the wrap*) Sophie, have you no feeling for your mother!

(*She bursts into tears and runs out screaming.* SOPHIE *scandalizes rabbis with obscene gestures and postures, showing her naked behind, etc.* RABBIS *spit and jeer.*)

RABBIS. Witch. Whore. Jezebel. Babylon. *Mitzraim.*

EZRA. (*Sighing*) She doesn't know how.

LANDSMANN. Please Sophie, that's your uncle, the chief rabbi of Transylvania—

SOPHIE. A sanctimonious bastard! He led his congregation to death trains, torture, gas chamber, typhus. His own wife and daughters. They could have saved themselves. A fanatical brute. A murderer. Burn him!

EZRA. *Na ja.* They did.

LANDSMANN. Can't this be stopped? Where is the judge? This is terrible.

EZRA. Well do something!

SOPHIE. My father do something!

(*She laughs sarcastically*)

LANDSMANN. That's right. I failed you. (*To* EZRA) She has never forgiven me for not shooting down the biggest bear in the Budapest amusement park when she was five years old. We know what that means. (*Recalls Lear*) "A serpent's sting is not sharper than a daughter's ingratitude."

SOPHIE. Have you ever thought of becoming a character actor in Hollywood?

CLERK. (*Announces*) Blind vs. Blind. Lawyer for the prosecution: Bloom. Lawyer for the defense: Miss Evelyn von Koenighof. Silence in the courtroom.

(*The members of the jury enter and take their places. The* LAWYERS *enter, followed by the* JUDGE.)

JUDGE. The court is in session. Will Mr. Bloom present the case for the prosecution.

RABBIS. We claim the deceased. We protest this trial.

EZRA. She is mine. My legal wife. You have no case.

RABBIS. She is a whore. We declare her unworthy of the honor of bearing her husband's name. You have no case.

EZRA. As her husband I protest the charge that my wife was unchaste. I have brought fifty witnesses to testify to my wife's chastity. They are all young men of high standing. Native Americans, my best students. All have at some time tried to seduce my wife and failed. (*The fifty young men rise*) Your Honor, in view of limitations of time, ask any one of them to testify in behalf of all.

RABBIS. We protest. They're his disciples. They swear by him. Their testimony cannot be accepted as valid.

EZRA. Your Honor, I object. I may teach my disciples that love transcends the law. But not perjury!

(*The rabbis move up and surround the coffin*)

RABBIS. We charge you with acts of sacrilege, blasphemy, uncleanness and with practicing sodomy, buggery and other forms of loathsome and unnatural copulation.

SOPHIE. It's true.

EZRA. I protest. My wife is very naive.

SOPHIE. I'm sick of all this fuss. Go ahead, you dodoes, and condemn me for eating fried octopus, cock sucking, animal worship. I touched the mezuzah when I was menstruating, put that down. I confess to all your charges. I recommend to all Jewish women semen drunk straight or mixed with beef blood. Now feed me to the dogs as is your custom. (*She lies down in the coffin and invokes the gods of the deep*) Gorgons, my sisters. Poseidon, where are you? Homer, Heraclitus, Nietzsche, Joyce, comfort me! I am on fire Apollo, come!

EZRA. (*To* LANDSMANN) *Na ja*. You told me she was *meshuga*. I didn't believe you.

RABBIS. She has condemned herself by her own mouth.

JUDGE. (*Bangs*) Overruled. Her confession cannot be accepted. The death certificate presented at our preliminary hearing was shown to be invalid. Since then the court has had no further proof of her death, nor any evidence for her existence.

RABBIS. We are not impressed by your sophistries. The marriage is void. We take her.

EZRA. Then take us both.

(*He steps into the coffin*)

SOPHIE. If you don't get out of my coffin this instant, I'll tell them everything. I'll tell them with all the details.

(JUDGE *bangs for order*)

EZRA. My wife is distraught. I appeal to the rabbis. The great granddaughter of Reb Smuel deserves a fair trial. Sophie was raised by an atheist father. She read the books of Moses for the first time in a literature course at Bryn Mawr. When I met her she had left college to be an actress. She lived on tea bags and Ritz crackers in a confused revolt against the hollowness of the secular world. She was a virgin. I read to her the book of prophets Hosea: the parable of the sacred marriage between God and Israel, spoke of the sanctification of life, explained to her the paradox of the law *Credo quia absurdum*. Sophie Landsmann took the leap into Judaism when she became engaged to me. I promised her an orthodox Jewish wedding with fiddlers and dancing and the ceremony of the bride walking around the groom seven times—she insisted on all the archaic details. But I couldn't go through with it in this age of ambiguity and the eclipse of God. I short-changed her on the wedding: I arranged a mishmash compromise package at the Jewish Theological Seminary. She had to listen to an anthropological lecture on the smashing of the wine goblet by the groom—the one traditional element I managed to sneak in. The reception was a banal cocktail party with cheese sandwiches from a kosher caterer. (*He weeps, then collects himself*) I am not ashamed to confess. I am prepared to take the witness stand and speak under oath. The court must wonder what abominable acts my wife performed. It's . . .

MISS KOENIGHOF. As Ezra Blind's lawyer, I protest.

EZRA. Please, Evelyn, let me . . .

JUDGE. Protest overruled.

MISS KOENIGHOF. I urge that the jury take note that sodomy and buggery do not constitute grounds for divorce except in the state of Virginia.

EZRA. It's all written in sacred texts (from which all pornographic handbooks are copied). It is depicted in the masterpieces of Hieronymus Bosch. I asked her to assume obscene postures. To crawl on all fours and lift her leg like a dog pissing; to bark, moo, bray, bleet, hoot—I wanted her to howl like a demon. I wanted her to be a sacred whore. She was magnificent in her moments of complete abasement. I confess I was not equal to the highest sacrilege. One night when she was performing the sacred office of fellatio I ordered her to say the Pater Noster in my arse hole. Or a Hail Mary at least. Instead she started bellowing the S'ma Yisrael up my bowels. I couldn't go through with it. "Shame on you," she said, "doing sacrilege with other people's religion. Isn't yours holy enough?" She was a great woman. Sophie Blind remains my wife till the Messiah comes. Brothers, sons of the Torah, we are all awaiting the day of Judgment, united in the hope of the coming of the Messiah. We are children of calamity. What has been joined in this world cannot be sundered in heaven or hell before the coming of the Messiah and Judgment.

(*The* RABBIS *signify their agreement with Ezra. The men put on prayer shawls, phylacteries; a Messianic psalm is sung. Everybody embraces. Rabbis and their families exeunt dancing, singing. The* JUDGE *calls for a short intermission.*)

SOPHIE. (*Aside to Ezra*) You miserable ideologue! You know I never swallowed that rot about redemption through sin. Your arse hole was the cleanest part of you, if you must know…
LANDSMANN. At last I can have a cigaret.
EZRA. Well, Landsmann, did I—?

(*Exeunt Ezra, Landsmann, et al. Sophie's three children run into the courtroom. They clamber into the coffin and huddle beside her, Jonathan and Toby in a fit of giggles.*)

JOSHUA. If you babies could control yourself a little.

SOPHIE. Children!

JOSHUA. Are you having a good time? Come on, Mum, you can tell me the truth. You're not really dead are you? You know there was this woman who pretended to be a ghost in a TV show—

TOBY. Please don't move. I'm trying to keep covered.

JONATHAN. Please hide us!

SOPHIE. What's the matter?

TOBY. Aunt Renata wants to take us to some crappy children's theater. We want to stay home and see the four o'clock show on TV.

JONATHAN. Why can't we stay with you?

JOSHUA. Remember when we all used to take a bath together—

TOBY. And the great pillow fight—

SOPHIE. We can't talk here; everything is taped. Quick, just tell me how you are.

JOSHUA. The skiing is great—

TOBY. I have a talking doll. If only we didn't have to go to the synagogue.

JONATHAN. I like going to the synagogue. (*He pulls out an embroidered skullcap*) Daddy's student is teaching me to pray; he says I'm going to be a rabbi.

JOSHUA. Oh really! He doesn't even know the Hebrew alphabet.

SOPHIE. Children, listen—

(*The children are all talking at once*)

TOBY. You put the record in the doll's side and she does multiplication and spelling—

JONATHAN. It's beautiful when they take out the Torah—

JOSHUA. I think children have a right to know. It's really unfair—

SOPHIE. Children, listen.

JOSHUA. Hey, what time is it? (*He looks at her wristwatch*) C'mon Toby—we got to run.

JONATHAN. I don't watch TV. I'm going to the synagogue to pray with Grandpa.

(*They kiss her hurriedly and scramble out*)

JONATHAN. But I don't believe everything they tell me. I don't think God loves only people who pray to him in Hebrew and (*He whispers in her ear*) I like Jesus, too. Don't tell Grandpa.

(*Exeunt children. Enter* EZRA, LANDSMANN, JURY, LAW-YERS *and* JUDGE.)

JUDGE. May I remind the jury once more in our final session that we are dealing with several actions on which you will decide separately. (*He reads*) Ezra Blind, in behalf of children, suing Icelandic Airlines. We are awaiting further evidence. Ezra Blind sues morgue of rue Bobillot for false death certificate. Insanity charge submitted by Dr. Rudolf Landsmann. Sophie Blind divorce action against Ezra Blind. Proceed with your first witness.

BLOOM. Will Mrs. Lily Bodola please take the witness stand. (*A pale, emaciated, once beautiful redhead in her forties, wearing a stark black dress and a wide-rimmed black hat with a veil, is led to the witness stand by a uniformed nurse, and sworn in*) Is it true that you are a widow presently convalescing at a rest home?

BODOLA. He ruined me. But I'll pay him back. If it takes all what's left of my three million dollars. He will bleed. Pus will run out of his ears, his tongue will fall out.

(*She composes herself*)

BLOOM. We realize how painful it must be for you. We regret to have to put you through this. Could you tell the court about your relationship to Ezra Blind?

BODOLA. He seduced me by lies. In the seven years I am widowed I have never had relations with a married man. Never. It was strictly against my principles. But I believed the stories he told me about his insane wife, breaking his spirit, resorting to every vicious means of holding on to him. (*She rises, screaming at Ezra*) You lied to me! You lied to me!

EZRA. But sweetheart, you wouldn't sleep with me otherwise.

BODOLA. We were going to settle in Rio after I arranged your Mexican divorce. We were going to travel around the world. (*To the court*) In Montreux we talked about settling in Paris. In Paris we talked about running away to India. I bought a house in the Black Forest. For two years I had lawyers working for him on three continents so that we would be free to marry; I told him I couldn't go on with these clandestine meetings. For two years he had me running around in circles till he told me he was really in love with his wife all the time. He was distraught that his wife had left him. What can he do? How can he save his marriage? With the same sublime sincerity as when he seduced me. In my opinion this man should be institutionalized.

BLOOM. Thank you, Mrs. Bodola.

(*She is led out of the courtroom by the nurse*)

EZRA. (*Shaking his head*) Menopause crisis. Such a fine person. A pity.

JUDGE. Next witness.

BLOOM. Mrs. Elaine Singer. (*A pretty, pregnant young woman is sworn in and takes the witness stand*) Mrs. Singer. You live in Larchmont with your husband, and have a two-year-old daughter.

SINGER. That's right.

BLOOM. When did you meet Ezra Blind?

SINGER. Eight years ago. I was seventeen.

BLOOM. What was your relationship to Ezra Blind?

SINGER. He deflowered me. I used to baby-sit for his children. It was one of the most beautiful experiences in my life. I was worried about how his wife would feel. But he said it was a marriage of love.

BLOOM. Could you describe how it happened.

SINGER. It just happened. One day he came into the bathroom when I was sitting on the toilet—the lock didn't close well; I was a little embarrassed, but he smiled and came right in and said he was delightfully surprised to find me on the toilet. He said to the clean all things are clean—and he did it too. He pissed. Then he told me he could see that I was a virgin and that I was ready to become a woman. And we went to bed. I remember I was very happy.

JUDGE. Next witness.

(MISS RUTH EMORY, *a smiling gray-haired woman in a tweed suit, is sworn in*)

BLOOM. Miss Emory I understand you work with the Women's Interfaith Union in Milton, New Jersey.

EMORY. I am the head of Personal Relations.

BLOOM. When did you meet Ezra Blind?

EMORY. Three years ago. I went to a lecture he was giving on "Agapic and Erotic Theology in Judaism" at the local chapter of the interfaith union and we talked afterwards.

BLOOM. What was your relationship to Ezra Blind?

EMORY. We only spent one evening together but I really enjoyed it. I didn't know about cunnilingus and other Jewish customs before; I believe we Americans have something to learn from all peoples.

BLOOM. Thank you Miss Emory. (BETTINA HERTZ, *a plump, blond, heavily made-up woman in a blue taffeta suit is sworn in*) When did you meet Ezra Blind?

HERTZ. We've known each other for over ten years.

BLOOM. What is your relationship to Ezra Blind?

HERTZ. We've been friends, colleagues. We've discussed, collaborating on a book on...

BLOOM. Nothing beyond that?

HERTZ. I would like to help out my friend Sophie. I realize she's been wanting this divorce for a long time, but actually...well I find this is in very bad taste but since I've been subpoenaed and you say I'm under oath...well, if you insist—I can think of one occasion which you might interpret...I am not familiar with legal terminology.

BLOOM. Could you simply tell the court what happened.

HERTZ. Well, I don't know.

EZRA. May I testify to save Miss Hertz the embarrassment? During Christmas week two years ago when she so kindly put me up in her apartment in Paris, I knocked on her bedroom door some time after midnight. I have the greatest admiration for Miss Hertz's sensibility. I have always regarded her a most extraordinary and attractive woman. I was dazzled by her sensibility and I wished to know her—biblically, I mean—I knocked on her bedroom door in the hope of carnal pleasure. I found her most alluring in her nightgown; I must confess, however, to my own deficiency. My only explanation for it is that Miss Hertz's pubic hair was the same shade as my mother's hair—a reddish blond—and incest fear prevented me from consummating the carnal act. It was the only time I disappointed a woman.

JUDGE. Will the parents testify?

LANDSMANN. I can only speak as a psychoanalyst. From a Freudian point of view I find the procedure of this trial very painful. How can a jury evaluate my daughter's character without even touching on the crucial factors of her infantile sexual development? The fact is that a woman's success as a wife depends entirely on how she has resolved her oedipal conflicts. I have no further statement to make.

JUDGE. Thank you Dr. Landsmann. Is her mother present?

EZRA. She came and left. But we have teletyped an interview.

(*Video screen shows* KAMILLA *sunbathing on the lawn*)

KAMILLA. I never understood how my daughter could live the life of an ordinary housewife. She gave up a theatrical career—sacrificed herself for a boor like Ezra Blind. A *grobbianer*, a peasant. It breaks my heart. If she would have had some lovers at least. But she never listened to me. I wanted my daughter to have a different life, to dress in style, go out to concerts, balls, the theater, to travel. I wanted her to be surrounded by rich admirers and have great love affairs. Instead when I think of the kitchen smells, stinking diapers, the children screaming and that brute of a husband of hers... (*She weeps*) Everywhere I visited her the house reminded me of a gypsy camp. She looked like she'd never been to a coiffeur and the way she dressed... I've never seen anything like that except in movies. It's hard for a mother. She comes from a good house. I saved all my expensive fur coats for her from the Nazis and the Russians. She wouldn't even...

JUDGE. Enough! Court rules: No injunction to return wife to husband or to release her to rabbis since it has not been proven that she is dead. Her divorce is granted, whether she is alive or dead.

(*The coffin is turned upright.* SOPHIE *is presented with a Bill of Divorce.*)

EZRA. I protest the ruling of the court. My wife objects. We had a Catholic marriage. (*Addressing* SOPHIE, *who is about to walk out*) Sophie, quick—you must protest. We're married, tell them we're married! Look, I gave the confession, risked my public reputation, to get you out of a mess—save you from the rabbis; you're not going to act like a bitch and take advantage of me? (EZRA *tries to snatch the Bill of Divorce away from her*) You can't do this to me. I didn't marry a bitch. (SOPHIE *tosses him a peacock feather and walks out*) Stop her! I protest. My wife was drugged. The verdict is illegal. I want to testify. What about her insanity? I demand to be heard.

JUDGE. The court has been adjourned for the summer. No further hearings till after Labor Day.

EZRA. This is unheard of. I won't accept. I will take this case to—

JUDGE. (*Amiably*) You can always marry your former wife again. It's no problem.

EZRA. (*Weeping*) I could believe anything, but not that my wife is a bitch.

WAKING up with Ezra in a small *rive gauche* hotel room; shades drawn. Back in Paris? They say you relive your entire life in the instant of death. Unpacked suitcase, his things strewn over the bed on top of her. He paces and rants. "I saved you from the loony bin and what thanks—"

He taunts her with the divorce bill, rolling it up, wags it obscenely like a penis. "So now you've got a divorce. So now what have you got. Look at me when I talk to you. *Schweinehund. Drecksau.* Look at me. Say something, idiot. Why don't you say something?"

Would he treat her better if she had big tits and a giant bum? No. Yes. Could mistreat her better. More in his style.

"Lost your chance. For the rest of your life..." he is threatening her. Tears. "Had enough of your emotionalism," he pursues. In transport of tears, hear German words like cracks of a whip. Not sure if he's pulled off the sheet. Is he beating her? Is she giggling, dancing? Cynical, a nihilist. Writhing with uncontrollable laughter.

"Sophie, don't leave me like this. Sophie!" he sobs.

Some way to comfort him? Can't speak. Water rising warm around chin, back of my neck. Oh, Ezra I shall never be able to explain to you. Proof or no proof I'm afraid I'm really dead. Stopped breathing. Just like the night we got engaged. No, you wouldn't remember; we're so different.

Blaze. Cynical. Nihilist. Bitch, you call me. It's true; I can't help it—and now all this has become irrelevant.

*

Happy here swimming around in my underwater cove. A mermaid just what I wanted to be. Wishes fulfilled of the dead. Now, to find a merman.

Visitors coming? See foot kick in black shoe. Ezra? Would be greatly surprised. To the ends of the earth but not to the bottom of the sea. Has his limits. Black tie flapping. Wonder who. Anyway, don't have to worry about dressing. Just wrap fishtail around rock and sit pretty. It's Nicholas, kicking and waving his arms.

"Here, hold on to this rock so you won't be washed away." Sits legs crossed wedged in the tub, hair brushed upward by current, a weird sight—try not to giggle. Starts intoning in Greek. It's too much.

"I did not know the dead laughed," he observes bitterly. Not impressed by my hilarity; got special permit to descend; complains about the unseemliness of my death. "... I find your name under *Accidents de Route*. Why didn't you drown yourself at least? Wasn't your life wretched enough? In the fifteen years of your senseless marriage to Ezra couldn't you find an opportune moment—?"

"There wasn't enough water under the Pont de Sèvres."

"Other people seem to manage."

"You don't understand anything about a woman's life."

"Will you never accept that you're a fiction!"

"Is that all you came to tell me?"

"You look ridiculous with that fishtail. I expected you to come to my concert. I wrote you I was playing in Warsaw." He looks at his watch. "It starts in two minutes. That's all right. Let them wait." He laughs fiendishly. "Hitler always let the crowd wait at least forty minutes. Produces the proper state of hysteria. By the way, Ezra asked me to give this to you in Paris." Hands me bunch of letters. Nothing from Ivan.

"You look so disappointed," he laughs, "do you expect some important mail?"

Lost each other in the water. Just as well.

*

How funny; I heard Aunt Olga's voice. Just like on long-distance phone from Pittsburgh to New York.

"Sophie, listen to me carefully—you understand if I talk to you in Hungarian? Never forget that you're a lady and you'll be treated like a lady. I'll tell you something else: You're not an angel, no woman is. I've never done anything my husband or my children have had to be ashamed of. I'll be sixty next year and I can't swear to you that tomorrow a man can't turn my head. I don't say it can't happen to me because I don't know. And don't you ever say it couldn't have happened to you. As for your mother—forget about her. You two have nothing in common. That was a nice wedding you had and I'm glad to see you got married. The one thing I want you to remember, listen to me and you won't regret it: You can have all the fun you want with your husband once you're in bed, but never undress in his presence. I don't care if you're married ten years and have six children, you don't let him see you in a slip; you always come to bed in a nightgown—and naturally you lock the bathroom door when you brush your teeth. You follow my advice and you won't regret it—and of course none of this nonsense of your taking a shower while he shaves—I'm telling you, I've been married almost forty years now and I don't lie to you that I'm a virtuous woman ... And never forget that if you ever need me, if ever you're in trouble, you call me wherever you are—reverse the charges if you haven't got cash. All you have to do is call and say 'Aunt Olga, I need you' and I come with the next bus. And promise me you'll always keep your nails clean ..."

Yes, I know, I believe you Aunt Olga. I know you'd come and I know you're right. It's because I didn't lock the bathroom that everything went wrong. I know you love me and you're so right about everything. A nail file won't save me now. Let's see what's in the mail. A German stamp. Wonder who? Heinrich Dieter Uhl: "... looked you up in Paris and was sorry to learn ... If this reaches you ..." He should have carried me away from Ezra ten years ago! Bank wants my Social Security number; fifth request ... If I'd be interested in doing a book on contemporary religious sects in America ... More rubbish ... Renata sends photograph of the children. Dressed like for the synagogue. Boys in white shirt and tie; hair slicked back. Toby in expensively dreary wool dress; the bored expression on their faces. Makes me sick. Must find some way to see them. I suppose I should sit on a rock and sing.

The telephone again.

"Ivan—How are you? Yes I'm quite awake ... At three you say? Yes, I'm in."

Drop in. Just like that! Ringing me up after months of silence as if nothing's happened. It's unnerving. What does he really want? We've had our funeral.

Two minutes left to prepare. Decide how to look, what to feel, what to say.

He appears three on the dot. Punctual as always. Very grave in his this-winter-we-take-Moscow coat. Strange look on his face. Out of his mind? Dead? Questions one doesn't ask. Seems not to recognize me. The old pose. Turning himself into stone to prove I'm Medusa. Try to start up a conversation.

"Is it very cold out?"

"No," he says. "I'm sick. My throat."

"Oh. Have you tried honey? Let me make you some tea."

"It's not important," he says. His coat is torn he notices as he unbuttons slowly. "I had an awful time getting here. But you're looking well." Brought me the papers I left in his closet.

"You're moving, you say?"

"I have never seen you look so well," he says, "The sea seems to agree with you."

"Oh I like it here at the bottom of the sea."

"I came to tell you that I'm getting married."

Telling me in that dreary voice just when I'm pouring the tea. Maybe he thinks the dead must be addressed in a special funereal tone. Congratulate him anyway?

"You're getting married?"

"It looks like it. I haven't told anyone yet, but it's decided. Everything points that way. I mean, it's just the obvious step. I can't go on with the life I've been living... I suppose I'm going into it like every other idiot..."

How he goes on. Reminds me of the letter Nicholas wrote me the day before his wedding: "... going the way of all flesh," "... caught in the inescapable net of fate."

"Whom are you going to marry?"

"Not someone you know..."

Can't say a really nice thing about the poor girl. Protecting her from my jealousy, I suppose. Still, why so dreary about it all? If you're worried about the propriety of our meeting under water—but it's a fish pool now, my lap. Besides, we're just having tea.

"The time has come," he says, "I can't say no to a risk. You look so shocked. But you should understand. You took this risk. I know it's no answer..."

So that's what you really wanted all the time. Get married. Can't think all that weight of years I just threw off. How terrifying it must be for you.

"This is excellent tea. I think I'll have some more. Is your watch right? I must be somewhere at five. You're so silent. I can't blame you for thinking... It's too late to begin to explain..."

"I wish you all the happiness." Suddenly everything is clear. I see you stand before me in your coat, ten of you, cardboard flat, each differently intriguing. Love, I can't put you together again. You will join the happy people in Father Time's family album.

You must be leaving; of course. I watch you button up gravely. A nice stranger, you ask about my work. Now that I'm dead I can write my autobiography at last. Of course I'm not serious.

"But you should," he says. "I'm sorry I can't stay longer. But I hope..." You look at me kindly, in a shy new way. Have I changed into someone else? You look lost. I'll go with you part of the way if you like. Yes, I have time, all the time in the world. And I've been wanting to see the Statue of Liberty.

"Come," you say and take my arm. It's all right now that we are strangers. My love is as secret as on the day I flew out of Idlewild thinking I'd never see you again. It's perfectly all right to adore your profile; you should be dictator. Did I tell you about my crush on Mussolini? Il Duce, Count Ciano...What beautiful names they had. I don't see the Statue of Liberty, do you? Missed it again. You walk so fast, it feels like flying. No, I don't mind. I love it. Where are you taking me? You realize I'm only a child. Kidnap—that's an American word. Are you Lindbergh? White skies over skyscrapers like in a movie, are we really flying?

As soon as this dream is over I'll jump out of bed and get under the cold shower, so help me God.

A cup of coffee? Sure, why not. This is where we had breakfast the morning I left for Paris. I remember your look of triumph that said: Ezra was slain, and smiling at you with amused complicity. Why should I have told you it wasn't Ezra you slew but the old dream lover conceived long ago behind black air-raid curtains in my father's house, to whom I turned unfaithfully with Ezra, with you—dreams are invincible. Still, you chopped off at least one of his heads. And does it now sit on you? Alas. My greed for reality that winter in Paris, if you can forgive...

"The book I'm working on? Yes, I've begun..." Reading love sonnets on the plane; of course I didn't miss you. "It's about a dead woman."

"I remember, you wrote me about it from Paris."

"This is something else. It's told by the dead woman."

"You would do something like that," he laughs.

"It's not so easy. You can't remember a dream till you awake."

"How will you do that?"

"You wake up when you have to."

"You must know."

How very well I look, you say for the hundredth time, saying good-bye before the subway station. Just now when you smiled a storeroom of plaster casts exploded into powder. Thank God for all this wind blowing. You kissed me so fast I didn't know it happened till I saw you step off the curb, you will take a taxi downtown after all. Queer to be standing on Broadway in the daylight. Stroll down the street, stare at mannikins in new spring shades, wander into discount stores. Bedspreads on sale. See what's playing at the New Yorker. If anyone asks how I came, what I'm doing here, who I am— nobody asks, this is America.

IT IS AT a calamitous moment that the past opens into view. A block of high apartment buildings raised in fifteen years of marriage has been bombed away, revealing a long-forgotten landscape which lay hidden behind the walls. The clearing of the wreckage must wait. As for the price or damage to body, soul and mind of fifteen years of her life blanked out—or is it more?

The sensation of forgetting comes back first, how one walked through years sealed in oblivion. It was a substance with its own weight and density, without color, texture or taste, like some abstract Newtonian matter, the unremembered past. The first crossing by boat to America putting an ocean full of mines and roving submarines between her and her childhood in Budapest, a sea voyage, a world war, another country, another language—distances which cannot be measured in miles or years—may have helped to cancel the first decade. Growing up in America during the war, the ten years she lived as a child in Budapest broke off. As for the years in America from 1939 to 1947, they were disowned when she married Ezra.

The next crossing, covering a negligible distance by taxi from the hotel to the synagogue where she was to be married to Ezra Blind; up some stairs; in and out of rooms to sign papers; then walking from a side door to the center of the room under the canopy—pointless to count out the steps of what in one step had to annul the preceding years of her life.

The process of annulment, begun the night of her engagement to Ezra Blind, was completed in the public wedding ceremony; it was like being hollowed out—thankful to know that one was only a mold—and being filled very slowly with some thin even fluid that would slowly harden.

At the reception after the wedding she showed superior indifference to all the people wishing her happiness; and hordes of men, young and old, taking advantage of this day to kiss her, some boldly on the mouth, she received with equal pride. Invulnerable to personal insult or happiness, she accepted everything jarring or simply irritating that happened that day as contributing to her transformation, her triumph over past selves. The sense of triumph gave her strength to put up with what was unpleasantness and delay and hide her impatience, her wanting this day to be over, the congratulating, she needed all this to seal and bind so she could begin her new life.

Thinking back after fifteen years to that day, she recalls the sense of annulment, already in effect as she walked under the canopy, like some bleach it permeated through every pore of her eighteen years. This dominated over her disappointment with the indifferent room, a library or classroom where a canopy and chairs had been set up; straining to hear the music. Mrs. Brensky was playing the piece on the piano in the next room, too far to hear. She was reluctant to enter, when they said *now*, she was waiting to hear the music, the wedding march. She is playing in another room, they explained, and then she began walking but she heard no music even inside. And of the hours preceding, the mind retains only the inessentials: in a hotel facing the park, the night before, Aunt Olga's voice saying: "Don't put your hair in pins, it will press at night and give you a headache." The drive uptown in a taxi through Central Park on a June day. She shut her eyes and looked and shut her eyes again on the green they were passing; because it was not like an ordinary drive through the park; nor was it like passing through the city for the last time before leaving; it was not like anything she had experienced before; for each annulment is new and disturbing in its own way.

She believed she had brought all her possessions, what she wanted and in the shape that she wanted it, into the marriage. It seemed she would lose everything. But she lost only what was packed in that trunk.

And now it is very strange, this new sense of the present, of a street in New York more like she experienced it as a girl than in the more recent decade of her marriage. As if a middle segment of a bone had been cut out, and the end sections joined.

It worries her off and on—will the juncture hold? Sometimes she feels a painful crack. How fast our little props wear out their charm. These Italian sunglasses carried her through the week; but now it's time for a new purchase.

One walks more lightly, easily distracted by street sights, pursuing now a fantasy, now fabrics in shop windows; long-forgotten desires and interests resume their power. How odd to be thinking of Barry back in high school. The class had them practically engaged in spite of the fact that he was a shameless fairy. Still, the only boy in school who wasn't frightened off either by Dr. Landsmann or his daughter, and courted her teasingly. She remembers the first time he came to the house; when her father appeared he put on a hilarious faggot act, at first declining to shake hands, "Oh Dr. Landsmann, don't you come near me, I'm so ticklish," he giggled, twitching all over. "Oh my goodness, you watch out, Dr. Landsmann, I know you're a bug doctor!" He was so crazy and handsome and corrupt. And then he went into the navy and she never saw him again. Right now she feels like having a cup of coffee with Barry. Is she back where she was fifteen years ago?

She has never walked so lightly, not as a girl. The breeze was never so fresh. It's the gratuity of the present and the sense of this great continent where by historical accident she was taken as a child, but where she never really lived. Though she went to school, married and worked in America, she never really got off the boat in 1939, and now as it dawns on her she isn't at all certain whether this time she has really arrived; and yet finding herself in New York, ridiculously stranded, seems to make some weird sense.

Years that do not belong to one's life. Pittsburgh, 1939–1942, impossible to recall with clarity as it was at the time impossible for a child to perceive with clarity. Blocks of smoke-blackened houses with their rickety porches and grimly jutting fire escapes. Cars, billboards, soot, stench, litter, a lot of noise and no place to go except the movies. Walking down the street in outgrown dresses from Budapest or in strange ladies' garments from the Jewish Welfare Agency, she thought: It is not I. Seeing too many movies, shoplifting from the five-and-ten, daydreaming in class, reading comics, screen romances and crime magazines from the drugstore rack, forging sick notes for the teacher in her aunt's name; it was America, nightmare, trash, vacuity, stupor. From the year she came to America for the next eight years in Pittsburgh then Garfield then Bryn Mawr College till the year she married, she tried in vain to grasp the meaninglessness of every room and street corner, her inability to experience the rooms and streets as a moment in her life. In America the sky was not sky, the grass was not grass, Sophie Landsmann was not Sophie Landsmann. But America was America.

A child of ten getting on the boat with her father and her uncle's family in 1939 was immune to the sorrow of leaving everything behind and fears about the years ahead of them in a new country. The grown-ups had decided to make the step that would change their lives because they feared Hitler would occupy Hungary. They left to escape the terrible fate Jews would suffer; it was of this that they spoke, and of the hardships awaiting them in America. In the train from Budapest, before crossing the Austrian border, the Hungarian passport official had said to her aunt in beautiful country dialect, "Good woman, why are you taking these three beautiful children out of the country?"

"Because they're Jewish children," Aunt Olga said, "if I don't take them out of the country the Nazis will kill them."

"We're all Hungarians," the passport official said with feeling. "Jewish or Christian Hungarians, it's the same thing. We Hungarians will not let the Germans harm the children on our soil."

"They are Jewish children," Aunt Olga repeated and the passport official protested again that they were Hungarian children.

She sat, her eyes nailed to the floor in mortified rage. It was over, it would have nothing to do with her in her new life. She stopped being Hungarian when she got on the train. From the day they boarded the *S.S. Aquitania* she wrote only in English, even though she had to look up most of the words in the Hungarian-English dictionary.

The grown-ups' reasons for leaving were their business; she had to hold on to the meaning this voyage had for her, the fulfillment of longings and presentiments that had begun to stir some years ago of a great event that would change her life.

Sailing across the Atlantic on the *S.S. Aquitania*, Sophie was too caught up in the wonder and excitement of the voyage to think about past or future. The *S.S. Aquitania* not only had everything—shops, bars, restaurants, ballrooms, studies, game rooms, swimming pool, gym, movies, promenade decks—it had it three times; the three classes like interlocking cities of a floating island. She dressed up very nicely and practiced her English with stewards, deckhands and nice old gentlemen in the first-class bar. When she said she came from Budapest, eyes twinkled; many had been there, remembered the baths and the *corso* lit up at night. Tea every afternoon. It was not just the tea and cookies but the ceremonial way the steward poured it, asking how she liked her tea as if she were a real first-class passenger and as politely as he did for an older person. There was a beautiful wood-paneled study with leatherbound books in glass cases and writing desks with many drawers and slots full of different kinds of stationery. She would have been happy to spend the rest of her life on the boat.

She wanted to love America. The Twentieth Century Fox newsreel played behind the word, coming on with loud music, the pictures changing so fast and more happening than one could take in—ladies playing tennis in white shorts, airplanes, a boxing match, a burning zeppelin, a parade, someone doing a backdive, exploding oilwells, bathing beauties, tanks. She thought of the twentieth century not just as the continuation of the nineteenth, but as something incredible that happened, as surprisingly and mysteriously as the newsreel turning on in the dark cinema, and it happened in America more than anywhere else. America was the twentieth century.

Sitting at one of the desks of the wood-paneled library, she began writing in her new language. She had to construct the sentences slowly, a Hungarian-English dictionary at her side—often prompting her to make up something she hadn't intended just so as to possess on her page an exotic word glimpsed at random in the dictionary.

The sun was beginning to set when land came into view. A flat coast, low brownish rocks. A man pointing in the direction of the sun said soon they would see the Statue of Liberty; he told her it was a gift from France. But before she saw the statue she had to go inside and wait in the tourist-class smoker for customs officials. Every so often she got up and peered through a porthole, but there was nothing to be seen except people moving or the side of another boat. It was dark when the boat docked; they passed over the ramp with the crowd into a narrow passageway that seemed a continuation of the ramp, through a small doorway into an enormous hall where trunks were being pushed under the various letters of the alphabet.

"Are we still on the boat?" her little cousin kept asking.

There had been the excitement of a week's boat trip; one day in a big New York hotel where the children raced each other up and down thirty floors on the stairways and the elevators; another day's journey to Pittsburgh, emptying the great bags of sandwiches, potato chips, all varieties of candies and soda pop their American uncle gave them; suddenly, it seemed, they got out of a car on a littered sidewalk and quickly, with only a glimpse of people sitting on the stoop, through a narrow doorway and up four flights of stairs; then Uncle Dave said, "This is home," and they walked into a one-room furnished apartment, each of them overcome by the sudden shock of loss which had to be hidden.

Every night through that first long summer she listened to the grown-ups' low, anguished voices and went to sleep believing they would go back. Only after war broke out in September did everyone fully grasp that the voyage to America was final. They could never return to Hungary. When Hungary joined the Nazi powers it ceased to be their country. From that time on Sophie wasn't sure that her Hungarian past had anything to do with her at all. She stopped thinking of Budapest. The person she had been there ended there.

Chance memories of any particular place or moment blurred instantly into shame and confusion. After living in Pittsburgh for a year she could not have said what she missed in America; she missed her father, of course, who had left for New York. But she never thought that she missed things she had been used to in Budapest.

They lived in one of a long row of identical houses forming part of the Jewish ghetto; a block further along the same street was the Irish ghetto; at the next intersection began the Italian ghetto. The children of the three ghettoes did not speak to each other except to heckle. It was weird to land in a Jewish ghetto in America where being Jewish was an issue between people in a way she never experienced it in Budapest. She was accepted on the block when they arrived because she was a "Yid" and they were constantly after her to make her more their kind of "Yid," telling her with whom she might or might not associate; teaching her Yiddish. The shopkeepers teased her for refusing to pronounce English with a strong Yiddish accent. The children on the block harassed her as the word got around that she went to the house of an Irish Catholic girl.

In school there were the noisy classrooms, angry teachers trying to maintain order by yelling and hitting; the scuffles in the corridor between classes. Often she didn't know whether the kids who heckled her or wouldn't associate with her were from the Jewish ghetto or the "others."

There was the corner drugstore where the big kids hung out and where every lollypop- and ice cream–licking child aspired one day to spoon the sundae or banana split whose giant images were plastered on its windows. There was East Liberty with its three five-and-ten-cent stores, twelve movie houses, its soda fountains and slot machine joints, its stench of exhaust gas mingled with the smell of popcorn and sweet carbonated drinks, where everyone from the surrounding slums flocked evenings and weekends. And towering over the store windows and movie marquees, the giant cereal boxes, tires, tubes of toothpaste and the silly smiling faces of beer-drinking, soup-gobbling, car-satisfied men, women and children, the gods of America.

There was downtown Pittsburgh, a bigger East Liberty, more

ponderous and somber, where the movies, department stores and soda fountains were more expensive.

There was nothing you couldn't get in America, her uncle said. He was a well-to-do businessman who came to America before the First World War, and boasted about his Buick and his fine brick house in the best residential part of Pittsburgh. His street was cleaner, the houses bigger than where she lived and there was a bit of lawn between the porch and the sidewalk, but it wasn't really different. It was near her uncle's house, the day after they arrived in America, that she heard for the first time a boy yell "shaddup!" with that ugly snarl that she would hear everywhere around her, in her uncle's voice telling how he rose from being a salesman to a floor manager. "... in this country if you've got what it takes, you can get anything you want," he said, his mouth twisted in a snarl as he talked of America's wealth and opportunities. "But you gotta work for it," he said, "you gotta forget the old life, you can't sit around in a café here, you gotta work or you're nobody..." Her uncle talked just like the shopkeepers in the ghetto, only meaner.

When people asked her how she liked America it was simply to hear her say how much better it was here than in the old country; whether it was a kid on her block or her uncle's boss who drove a Cadillac, they wanted the same answer. Nobody wanted to hear about "over there"; they told you that "over there" you didn't have things like you did in America, and telling them about the baths in Budapest or maintaining that one did have telephones there, only invited the phrase, "Then why don't you go back where you came from."

"You're lucky to be here," people told her. To be in Europe now would be terrible, her family, as well as everyone else, kept saying. Every hour from seven in the morning her aunt listened to the news broadcast—the occupation of the Lowlands, Norway, the fall of France, Dunkirk, the Blitz. She tried to make herself indifferent to historic events from which she had been excluded, which it was impossible to grasp, living in Pittsburgh. She went to the movies every day in the summer, movie people filled her mind, she lived in the many movie worlds of prison breaks, spy rings, navy battles, historical romances, love, horror and cowboy movies. The reality of the war in Europe came across most in the daily greeting of the shopkeepers, "Aren't you glad you're not over there now!"

Being in America at this time didn't make the terrible things happening in Europe less terrible. One heard about deportations already in Budapest; in Pittsburgh one continued hearing about death trains, mass exterminations, conditions in the camps. What was happening far away was closer than the streets in Pittsburgh; the death camps were closer and more real than the drugstores she passed which mocked her with the colored pictures of giant candy bars and ice cream sodas; perhaps she herself was on a death train; perhaps a machine-gun bullet just pierced her throat; the streets she roamed between her block and East Liberty became an unmapped limbo while she rejoined her real or phantom self that remained on the other side. Week after week on her way to East Liberty she made her journey to the camps, unable to obtain her death from the thin-lipped, white-smocked Nazi doctors of her fantasies and unable to think herself anywhere else. Herself, walking along the street in Pittsburgh, had no reality at all.

Then there were the hours she spent writing; after everyone went to sleep, the words came to life, absorbed with their shapes and hues she was in an enchanted forest, hunting treasures far from the world where words were ugly sounds coming out of people's mouths. It was only words from a dictionary; this happiness had nothing to do with her, she realized; moreover she stood in its way. Sophie Landsman was an obstruction that wanted to be expunged.

In the summer of 1942 getting out of a car in New York before the Hotel Park Plaza where her father lived, the nightmare ended. The three years in Pittsburgh were just a bad dream that had nothing to do with her as they walked down toward Central Park West in the evening breeze and the city felt alive and festive. Elegantly dressed people getting in and out of cabs, and poor people on Columbus Avenue had a liveliness she had forgotten.

"Is it true that you flunked all your classes?" her father asked, laughing; "Olga wrote that you did it just to spite her."

They had dinner with friends, a seven-course feast in a little Hungarian restaurant, all for seventy-five cents; afterward her father read to her from her last letter, "... I'll live on bread and water, just let me come."

Life was beautiful in New York. While her father worked she went to the Museum of Natural History across the street or walked up and down Amsterdam Avenue looking into antique shops and hardware stores. At night they opened the folding cot where she slept and put a screen before it. Free all day, she could write anytime she wished in the hotel lounge, which even provided paper. It was as nice as living on a ship. When people asked how she liked America, she told them that she loved New York.

From the Pittsburgh slums to New York—a brief six weeks' holiday till her father passed his medical examinations and once more they got on a train. Garfield, New York, where her father set up his office and she went to high school; small towns in New England where she played in summer theater, Bryn Mawr College; in that eerie, shallow present, her personal past discarded, she began her journey to past and imaginary worlds. While she tried to escape from America in books, the stage, dreams or sheer blankness, not really living in Garfield or the many New England towns she passed through playing in summer stock, whose names she forgot or never knew, while she fled or simply ignored America, America changed her.

SOPHIE Landsmann, arriving in Budapest in August, 1947, saw no corpses floating in the Danube nor any traces of blood on the cobbles. Two years had elapsed since the last Nazis had fled Budapest, blowing up the bridges and leaving some three thousand corpses strewn in the streets. No one was safe; but, their time being short, the Nazis concentrated on Jews already assembled in large numbers at orphanages and in nursing homes, as well as in the central ghetto. Those who actually lived and survived these times of terror walked along the *corso* with a nonchalance that awed the American visitor. Business was lively in the shopping section even though the upper stories of the houses had been bombed away. A covered scaffold had been raised over the sidewalks to protect the populace from falling rubble. A thin drizzle of plaster rained on pedestrians, nevertheless. A nuisance . . .

Fashionably dressed women sporting fancy hairdos, emerging out of scarred passageways, picked their way through rubble and broken pavement on elegant thin heels. Their laughter and fragrance mixed with reflections in the river on this bright summer day. To one who was not present at the scene of the disaster, who left too soon, arrived too late, these incongruities had a special harmoniousness.

Sophie had not planned this visit to Budapest. In the summer of 1947 Hungary was closed to American tourists. Having left Europe on one of the last westbound crossings of the *S.S. Aquitania* in 1939, it seemed appropriate that she return on one of the first boats making the eastbound trip—a still unconverted military troop ship with hammocks—from New York to Liverpool.

But the object of a trip to Europe had not been entirely clear to

Sophie. What could she go back for? Or back to? Growing up in America during the war years, she wished at times that she had never left Europe, or dreamed of returning to live in Europe as though she had never left it. But she didn't seriously believe in this. Europe was only a lost dream. In any event, her father wouldn't hear of a trip. More of his daughter's craziness, like becoming an actress and studying philosophy. Go to Europe in 1946? Go to Europe after Auschwitz? Europe was rotten, centuries of rottenness behind a facade of impressive architecture, outward graces. Nothing but lies and rottenness. "Culture!" her father said scornfully. He didn't want to hear of Europe or of his daughter's visiting Europe. It was pointless for her to mention Hiroshima or argue that America had some responsibility in Hitler's rise to power when her father spoke from the bitterness of what he experienced, bitterness and disgust with Europe that reconciled him to life in America. She had no political point to make nor any dream to oppose to his acceptance of life in America. She had on her side only the fact that she was not reconciled, for which maladjustment was the word, which spoke against her. Therefore she never pressed the issue.

A trip to Europe nevertheless materialized upon the persuasion of friends. Sophie's roommate in college, Jessica Lipsky, complained of suffocating in American materialism and soullessness. Her mother, in whose Manhattan townhouse Sophie spent many weekends, similarly deplored the philistinism of the land. Of Europe as the fountain of art and culture, Mrs. Lipsky spoke rhapsodically to both "daughters" (having some time ago adopted Sophie as her spiritual child). "There are no good men in America," lamented her friend Jessica. "America is hopeless." Sophie agreed, even if she couldn't share her friend's idealism about Europe. Her sense of the matter was that things were generally hopeless and that there was no place for her anywhere: the world in which she would have wanted to live had ended—before Hiroshima, before Auschwitz. Just when the first trumpet blew that sent the four horsemen of the Apocalypse galloping across the sky, she did not know. But a trip to Europe, any long trip, appealed to Sophie. Time was oppressive, superfluous. And time passed more easily when one traveled.

"America is no place for two such young women as Jessica and Sophie," Mrs. Lipsky pleaded tearfully with Sophie's father and added, "Rudolf, you're a boor. I cannot change that but you cannot be so selfish. We cannot deny our children the profound spiritual nourishment of..."

Rudolf Landsmann agreed to finance his daughter's trip to study at the University of Geneva for a year. At this time Kamilla de Vithezy, his former wife, had been making plans to leave Hungary and emigrate to London where her sister lived. It was finally arranged that Sophie, instead of leaving with her friend in the fall, would go to London in the summer to see her mother. When she arrived in Liverpool at the end of June, Sophie found only her Aunt Rosa at the pier and learned that her mother was not allowed to leave the country. Kamilla, though in possession of a dearly purchased exit permit as well as an English visa, had been detained at the airport. A recent shake-up in government made her exit permit, issued by the ousted party, invalid. New rulings were not yet in effect.

There followed a month of frantic correspondence, tearful long-distance calls, ending in resignation. Sophie would spend the summer in London with her aunt and proceed to Geneva in the fall as planned.

In the third week of August, however, a friend brought to the aunt's attention an ad in a small Hungarian paper for the Industrial Fair. Representatives of American business firms would be granted a week's visiting visa to Hungary. Within forty-eight hours Sophie's passport was stamped with a special visa for the Industrial Fair and her flight was booked to Budapest via Prague. Arriving at the airport in Prague at noon, she found out that her connecting flight to Budapest would be delayed. There was no cause to worry, two cheery, blue-eyed Czechs assured her, driving her into Prague in a dusty light-blue car; the plane was scheduled to depart at six A.M. the following morning. They dropped her at a hotel facing a river. She would have her meals there, they explained, all at the airline's expense; and promising to return to drive her to the airport at four A.M. the following morning, they drove off. And what if they didn't, Sophie thought, strolling dreamily through Prague's old streets and over its delicate bridges. Perhaps she never expected to leave Kafka's city. She couldn't believe she would actually arrive in Budapest. And when the two men arrived at four in the morning, all during the ride they joked that they were kidnapping her, of course; she noticed it was a different car—she was wishing it might be true.

"They wouldn't let me out with an English visa and an exit permit, but they let you in. I really have a clever daughter," her mother exclaimed jokingly.

"Perhaps fraudulent papers worked better. It was a matter of luck," her daughter shrugged modestly.

A group was taken to the Industrial Fair where her passport was stamped.

Walking through the streets of the city she left in April, 1939, she was most struck by the ruins, a long-familiar sight for her mother who had been in Budapest all the time, all during the German occupation, the siege, the Russian liberation. She laughed about that, the so-called liberation. "You can't imagine—nobody can imagine," she was telling her daughter as they hastened toward the shopping district—they had so little time. "We didn't believe it while it was happening—naked corpses piled along the *corso*, neatly like sacks of potatoes except they stank. In the winter the bodies froze to the pavement, we had to scrape them off. Corpses everywhere, in doorways and the gutters, corpses floated in the Danube. Nobody believed it of course. Then the American planes—" she shook her head incredulously and shrugged. "I never went to a shelter. Most of the people hid in cellars and we had the hotel all to ourselves. No electricity or water, of course—the top three stories were bombed away—still, we somehow managed. But when the Russians came—" she would tell her about that later, not on the street. "You never know." And they walked into a shop where Sophie would have some pretty dresses made before she continued to Geneva.

For Sophie, the changed aspect of the city was perceived under the emotions of homecoming, however unappropriate. It was impossible not to be stricken before the sunken chain bridge that she had crossed so often as a child. It was also difficult to grasp that she was really walking in an occupied city. Russian soldiers loitering at street corners, conversing freely in their native tongue, continued to amaze her. "Behind-the-Iron-Curtain country" or "Soviet satellite" were the phrases commonly used in America; but to Sophie "occupation" was the term known from history books: there had been the Turkish occupation, the Hapsburg oppression, and more recently, the German occupation. And now, walking on Russian-occupied ground—even for ten days to the Industrial Fair with a special visa extended to representatives of American business firms, which Sophie Landsmann was not—all this heightened the sense of unreality to an outsider of a city not quite real to itself.

It's amazing to see her mother so youthful and unscarred; she had had her personal misfortunes—her third marriage over in less than a year, the affair with the painter that was a long tragic story. But when she is asked how she managed, her face turns blank, she shrugs: "I never went to register; I don't know, I never read the notices. Most of my friends were not Jewish, it was no problem. When the bombardment began—I suppose it's because I'm so neurotic," she says cheerfully, "it didn't bother me. I slept like a bear."

Her mother is surprised that Sophie arrives from America like a poor relative—one suitcase with some cotton dresses and underwear, an old raincoat and not a single item with chic. "A young girl of eighteen!" she repeats with incomprehension and then apologizes to her dressmaker for her daughter's shapeless, tasteless cotton dress. She left in such a hurry, she didn't have time to shop in America. Yes, it's her daughter from America, her beautiful daughter. She wants the nicest silk or chiffon. There is none in all of Budapest. Not even the black market. But this rayon is almost like silk.

"Budapest has changed," Kamilla sighs. It was another life now with the new wage and working laws that favored the working class. "The plebes, the proletariats fill the restaurants," she complained. The Russian soldiers, it would appear from Kamilla's account, hadn't washed for some time; many of them were unfamiliar with modern plumbing, drank from the toilet bowl, unscrewed the faucets fancying it was silver, didn't know the use of toilet paper—but the burden of her complaint was the theft of the best fur coats, some ten she was saving for her daughter; the Russians left her three. And her journals—some thirty-eight volumes she had kept for twenty years—stolen. Of what possible use could they be to the Russians!

"You're here for only ten days. I would like to keep you all to myself and hear about everything—everything, your life, your feelings, your dreams, your father, etc., etc. But I promised the family, Omama of course. I said you weren't arriving till the day after tomorrow or we would have had to rush to her from the airport. You will have to visit Omama and Uncle Benji and Aunt Lea and Mitzi and her husband—they have a baby, you know. My family isn't a problem. My brother Emil will drop in for a few minutes, just wants to see you. I haven't seen Jani or Marta—you know about my poor brother Fritz—the Nazis shot him, he provoked them; it was completely unnecessary, he was such a crazy man. But I have a very nice surprise for you. Do you remember the little boy you used to play with when he lived on Pasaréti út, Peter?" Of course she remembers. "Well, he has grown into a fine young man. We met maybe twice in the past six years. And can you imagine, the day after I received the cable that you were coming, I met him by chance at the ballet. I told him you were coming in four days; he walked me home and I showed him your photograph. He was enchanted—neither of us could believe it of course, that it's the little girl we knew, or that we'd see the young lady with the long hair and the Mona Lisa smile. (Really, my dear, nobody would guess that you're American except for your figure—is it really fashionable to be so slender? I mean if you're not a movie star or a model—do the men find it attractive?) Peter asked if he could take you out, so I said he must ask you. I invited him for tea Thursday after you visit the family and you decide."

For Uncle Benji, a physician, times have improved: the sick receive care and medication regardless of income. Of course, if the Russians withhold penicillin..."When you left, Budapest was Eastern Europe. Now it's Western Russia. Nothing has changed."

Uncle Benji jokes and talks about his niece from America as if she were part of a dream and in the tone appropriate for a little niece he joked with years ago in Budapest. "Did the American young lady think about her Uncle Benji in Budapest?" What should one say to Uncle Benji, who has come back from Buchenwald an old man? Should one mention dead members of the family? Those who died on their way to Auschwitz? They question her greedily about America, about her father's house in Garfield, like little children who don't know what to do with answers. They just want to go on saying, "Incredible, incredible—can you imagine?"

"When will we see you again!" Aunt Lea exclaims with emotion. "I'll visit you in America, what will you say to that?" Uncle Benji laughs and pursues his fantasy. "We don't know what will happen to us," Aunt Lea sighs.

Cousin Mitzi greets her in a fancy pink negligee. She doesn't fit into any of her dresses since the baby and everything is brought into the perspective of Mitzi's good-humored, sexy vulgarity. She is blond, glamorous and gay; her tiny apartment has the look of an expensive boudoir: everything carpeted, curtained, spread in velvety pale pastel colors. No rude or naked object in sight, even the baby's bottle has its pretty ruffled mit. She is married to a factory manager. Her small baby boy is named after her dead father—"missing," she says, "but you know..." and, sending her brother down to the patisserie with a tray, assures Sophie that the pastry is still first class. Mitzi hasn't changed—talking about her figure. Wasn't it disgusting how she has spread since the baby? But her platinum blond hair, of which her mother disapproved, it was to please her husband. "But tell us about America, your father."

As for what they lived through—always the same words: "You can't imagine; you were lucky." "And we were lucky," Mitzi says with a significant look at her mother.

"Lucky to be alive," Aunt Lea agrees without expression.

Should one ask or wait for them to tell their story? Isn't it un-natural not to ask? "Were you in Budapest all the time?" Sophie asks Mitzi. No, they had fled; they went to the country; peasants hid them. She and her brother and grandmother together, she says looking in her lap—it was a long story.

"It's better forgotten," Aunt Lea says quickly, and they each say something in turn about how terrible it was for Grandmother. "Imag-ine, she had to eat non-kosher food. We hid as servants in different houses; we had to assume false names; we had to pretend we didn't know each other," Aunt Lea says with sudden emotion. Mitzi tells the story of how she and her mother had secretly arranged to meet at the market once a day and as they passed each other one whispered, "Mitzi" and the other, "Mother."

Then as Mitzi, in her fancy pink negligee, walked her to the door: "There were things I didn't want to talk about in front of my husband and my mother especially," she tells Sophie in the hall. "He knows, of course, and she was present when he raped me but she can't bear the thought, she still hasn't gotten over it. I have," Mitzi says gaily. "I adore my husband and my baby, why should I be unhappy?" and kisses Sophie good-bye.

Grandmother Landsmann is past eighty and blind; she isn't wear-ing her ritual wig. A strong, impatient, angry woman, she pushes the hand that would guide her to the granddaughter from America. "Rudi's daughter," she says, feeling her hands and hair. She heard young girls painted themselves in America. "But you don't," she confirms with satisfaction. "So you have come, they said you were coming, you know what happened here, you know what they've done to . . ." It's told by a raging old woman; no one can stop her. She swats at them if they try to fix her kerchief. It's told in the pure bitterness of a personal loss: a wrong done to her, her children, grandchildren murdered, Nazi brutes did it, the enormity of evil measured in her personal loss, not in millions. Her lament as bitter for what they made her do as for what they did to her. What they've done to an old woman who was pious all her life. They made her remove her ritual wig and now she doesn't care if the kerchief slides off. "Look what you have made me!" her scorn lashes indiscriminately at the whole world, her own life, those around her, the Nazi brutes, God.

"Will I see you again?" she asked anxiously after each visit.

On Sophie's last visit, she cried bitterly in a terrible shameless way. "I'll never see you again; I'll be dead. And your father, why didn't he come? Why didn't he come to see me? Why didn't you bring your father?" she continued wailing.

"You must feel very strange being back," Peter says. "Do you remember that statue?" he asks her. And, after a pause, just as she is about to guess: "Please don't say yes," he says, "it's the monument of Liberation built by the Russians. A bronze lady with drapery—maybe they had the Statue of Liberty in mind. She is offering a laurel. And note the pack of Russian soldiers with machine guns huddled around her to emphasize the peace motif."

At a sidewalk patisserie a waitress laughs a deep vibrant laugh, rich and scornful, as she serves them. "A former countess," Peter explained. He seemed on most intimate or just informal terms with the woman, perhaps slept with her. It was exciting for some of these noblewomen to leave their shuttered rooms and become waitresses, hairdressers in the capital, he told her. "No, you would not have wanted to be here," he kept saying. "All the girls became prostitutes—and it wasn't the nice ones who survived. But how old were you then? No, you wouldn't have had a chance. I worked with the resistance—spy work—since my family is Catholic, so I saw what was going on. No, I'm glad you weren't here. I suppose you could call it a time of terrible ironies," he said facetiously with a tired smile. It was difficult to believe he was only nineteen. He told her some of the stories. Jewish boys went around at night in arrow-cross uniforms to make a bid for the poor dogs the Nazis were picking up—just to play with them. The victim might still get his arm broken—but still. A friend of his, a Jew and Latin scholar, hid camouflaged as a priest for a poor working-class community whose priest joined the Jews in their death march. He learned the whole Mass overnight. Her companion laughed, so she smiled her weary smile. She didn't know what to say.

"You're so serious," he observes. Her mother had told him she was studying philosophy and writing and theater. "I wonder, I wonder," he keeps saying. "What you will become in the end—" And taking her arm, "How come you're so shy?" he asks. "Tell me, are you a virgin?" Amazing. He didn't think there were virgins over fifteen in America. There certainly weren't any in Budapest. "But what would you like to do?"

He is waiting for his exit permit—it would come through eventually. He has a job in London beginning January and wants to practice his English with Sophie. "I don't quite believe it myself as I look at you that you're here, that I am looking at Sophie Landsmann. And you still speak Hungarian. We were playmates when you were six and I was five—do you remember that?" He speaks now in English, now in Hungarian, and keeps offering her American cigarets. "We have Scotch too in Budapest if you like. I know where to get the best black-market Scotch—or don't you drink?" He laughs when she confesses her preference for vodka. "Here we have only red vodka," he jokes and asks about life in America, what she did, is she liked to dance, liked jazz. There were two or three first-class night clubs, maybe not as good as in America, or would she rather see the old sights, the baths—an excursion to Castle Hill. She said she liked gypsy music. If it was true gypsy music. Then she was ashamed. Most of the gypsies they knew were exterminated or sterilized. She was ashamed to have asked if some were left to entertain her. But Peter finds it amusing. "So you like gypsy music. I have a weakness for it myself." He knows the one place that is open till dawn; you just bribed the gendarme. But they still had all afternoon—didn't she want to walk across the bridge to Buda to see her old house?

They stood before the tall padlocked iron gate; she took a brief look at the red stucco house set in the hillside at the end of an alley of walnut trees, then stared at his hands that gripped the iron bars; she didn't touch it. He was giving her a history of the different occupants since she left. Government people owned it now. She expected to be disappointed, or a little moved, but felt nothing. The house she noticed was squeezed behind a great old mansion surrounded by bushes on the left and flanked by a smaller house with a tall apartment building behind it on the other side; they obtruded on her view of the house now so oppressively, it was surprising that she had entirely forgotten them.

On their way back to Pest, walking past the Field of Blood toward the new bridge, Peter kept saying how odd it was the way they played as children; they spent so much time together without knowing each other at all.

"Children can play together for months and have absolutely no relationship to each other," he said, "don't you think that's true?"

She wasn't sure what he meant; she remembered that the little boy Petie was very important to the little girl she was. His face hadn't changed much; the same skinny boy grown very tall; she is still surprised by the wide shoulders and his big feet; he is another person now and just like any other young man with whom she does not know what she feels or should feel. The same strangeness with Peter as with every other man, waiting for something to happen, to change in her, or change between them; never having known any other feeling; asking herself, "Can I love this man?" waiting for some impossible revelation or simply for a man to take hold of her and make her will-less.

They danced around the deserted square in the early dawn after the tavern closed, a little drunk; he told her, "I hope we'll meet in London." He was just breaking off a very complicated affair with an older woman and he was very impressed by someone like Sophie, so serious and a virgin—she must forgive him, this was a crazy place— he was hoping they'd meet when he wasn't in this crazy place. "I can't believe anything will ever make sense; but I'm going to London and who knows..."

The ten days over, on the night train to Geneva, the numbness that had settled on her in Budapest begins to lift. She recalls the flight from Prague: ten days ago, early in the morning, as the plane crossed over the foothills of the Carpathians where the Danube bends south, seeing the Danube loop, the sense of homecoming swept over her; she stared through the thick slab of glass, resisting the onslaught of sensations, of summer days of long ago, unprepared for tears. It was not the moment in her life to remember the smell of the Danube across Visograd; and she walked through ten days guardedly, as in a dream where it is useless to pick up gold coins scattered over the street because you wake up in a room in another country without those lovely coins, feeling terribly deceived.

"I DON'T know why I'm sitting here," Kamilla says. "We have nothing to do with each other, do we?"

"You called," she reminds her mother breezily, starting to prepare tea.

"I called you because father asked me on the phone if I know how you are. I didn't even know you were back in New York. You don't write me. We haven't been on speaking terms for years. I have accepted that I don't have a daughter. But your father is a funny man. It worries him that we are not in contact. I don't understand and the truth is that we have no relationship. Why am I sitting here? You are a stranger to me. I am a stranger to you."

"Because father wants it. It's very simple. You have just explained: you came to please father. He does the same to me. Every time he calls he asks me, 'Have you spoken to your mother?' 'Do you know how she is?' We're sitting here together to please father. So let's have a cup of tea and a nice conversation."

"What funny people you both are! You and your father!" she laughs, wagging her head. "I'm going to have tea with my daughter," she intones theatrically. "We'll pretend to enjoy each other's company." She goes on while Sophie serves her, asking how she liked her tea, if she cared for toast or cookies—some brandy perhaps?

"No, no," Kamilla protests. "I'm not used to being treated so well. I am very comfortable, thank you. But sit down, my dear. I am a lucky mother to have such a nice daughter. I'm serious, my dear. I really appreciate your kindness. But you should be more kind to your father, poor man," she sighs, pulling out a jewel-studded antique cigaret case. "I don't understand what has changed him so. I remember how different he was in Budapest. And now...what a sad, strange, lonely life he has been living in that big house by himself. I have become resigned to the injustice of fate that I have no place in the family, but your father really deserved better. Ever since you were born he has lived only for you. It's his great tragedy that the only creature he loves gives him no affection. Poor lonely man."

"But mother, you left him."

"I left him?" Kamilla repeats incredulously. "What are you talking about? You mean the divorce?"

"That's right. You divorced him and married Zoltan."

"The divorce," she laughs. "I wanted to make it easier for your father when you decided to go to America. It was to make everybody happy. How unjust everybody is! My dear, I never did anything to hurt your father. I had been going out with Zoltan for the past five years; it was how Father wanted it; he didn't have time for me so he asked Zoltan to take me out for concerts and dancing and vacations. Your father wasn't interested in these things, he only cared about his work and you, but he wanted me to enjoy myself. To say that I was unfaithful to him, when he asked Zoltan! He and Zoltan were best friends. Of course the whole town knew about it. Zoltan didn't like the situation; he wanted to marry me. But your father just laughed and said he could have me any time. He didn't want a divorce because of you. Then finally when he decided to go to America, I told him I wanted a divorce to make the decision easier for him. I knew that he and you would be happier without me. I married Zoltan so that you and your father could leave for America with a free conscience. The truth is," she concluded tearfully, "that I really love your father. I am the only one who really loved and understood him."

"Then you should have stayed with him."

"No, he didn't want my love. My love was only a burden for him. It was your love he wanted. That's how people are, they want what they can't have," she sighs philosophically, her eyes fixed on her daughter with a strange, sorrowful look. Pity for her who was born to be the cruel daughter?

"Didn't you have affairs before Zoltan? Before I was born?"

"Really, my dear, you make me laugh!"

"You mean all the stories I heard about you aren't true?"

"I don't know what stories you've heard. Naturally I had many affairs. But it was all right, your father wanted it."

"That's very strange."

"I'm serious. He encouraged me. I hope you will forgive me for saying that your father was a little neurotic. The first-generation Freudians, you know, were not properly analyzed. It gave him pleasure that I had affairs. He wanted to be the husband of the woman who had the most admirers."

"And you?"

"I couldn't help it, my dear," Kamilla tells her sadly. "I went to the best psychoanalysts in Budapest and they told me that I had to have affairs to prove to my mother that I could have all the men. When I was a child my mother told me that I was so ugly no man would want me; therefore, you see, I had to make every man desire me, even though I had the most wonderful husband. This was the tragedy of my life. You can't imagine how much I suffered. I was in analysis for fourteen years. We can't change our nature," she sighs. "People are the way they are. You too, my dear. You can't help that you are unkind to your parents. It's useless to fight our nature. So now I live alone in my little cottage in New Jersey. I see no one; I speak to no one and you know something? I am happy for the first time in my life! But tell me something about your life," she asks wistfully. "I have no idea what you're doing since you went to Europe five years ago. You have left that awful man—Father told me. And are you finally divorced? Well, thank God that's over. How could you stand to live with . . . But let's not talk about Ezra. Tell me about yourself. I think the last time we talked was when you were in Budapest in 1947, you were interested only in metaphysical ideas. I remember how sweet you were trying to explain to me . . . You know when I came to America in 1952, you were like another person. It was impossible to talk with Ezra around and then the children. I am so glad they're in a good school. And now we can talk. Tell me about yourself. I want to know everything you are doing, thinking, feeling, everything about your life, your work, your ideas interests me."

"I am writing a novel."

"My daughter is writing a novel!" she repeats grandiosely. "How wonderful! But tell me is it mainly romantic, or something philosophical or psychology? Father told me that you have asked him for material about the family for your new book. Is it that? I could tell you so many stories ... But tell me," she ventures shyly with childish eagerness in her eyes, "do you have someone, a lover? You have a lover!" she exclaims.

"It's a secret."

"Oh, that's wonderful. It's the most important thing, my dear. I won't tell anyone, you can be sure. Can I meet him someday? You wouldn't have to introduce me as your mother," Kamilla pursues, "in fact, it would be much more interesting for me if I would meet him as ... No?" she laughs. "Oh, I understand perfectly, my dear. But if you told me when you are having dinner with him in a certain restaurant, I could see him without his knowing, I'm so curious. But, you're right my dear. I am so glad you have a true romantic relationship at last. I hope you don't intend to get married. Believe me, marriage ruins every happy relationship. It's the little irritations of daily life—he sees your hairbrush on the table or you see him cutting his nails and the beauty goes. You are very wise to live apart. To share only the beautiful things. I know. Zoltan and I were the happiest lovers for five years and then as soon as we married ... I don't even want to talk about it. He wanted a mother substitute, a nurse, one of those classical neurotic types ... but it really isn't interesting. What you have with this young man is the ideal relationship. You should keep it that way. Even if he should want to get married, you know, men sometimes ... You mustn't do it. I am so happy for you, and perhaps now we shall see each other more often. And maybe you will come and visit me in New Jersey. It's only an hour by bus. I have a cottage by the lake. It's so peaceful. You should really come in the summer."

Getting off the Greyhound bus at Meadow Lake station, Sophie doesn't recognize her mother right away. She looks for her in one of the parked cars dimly aware of a hippy woman in a dirndl-style summer dress standing at the other end of the platform. Is this her mother? Her mother, with her face oddly as if someone had screwed chin and head between two boards and pressed slightly. She wears a dog collar of studded bamboo stalks. Suddenly she beams, grinning from ear to ear. It is her mother.

"Sophie," she gushes. "Has my little girl come? I was watching the people get off the bus, asking myself where is my daughter? Where is my daughter? And here you are!" She is without her car. She was too nervous to drive today, she explains, and they take a taxi.

They enter the cottage, the gilded mirror and the old antique divan stare her in the face like from an old photograph. The familiar furniture is depressingly out of place in the little low-ceilinged bungalow with its unelegant square windows looking out on the asphalt road of a New Jersey pike and some more tasteless one-story cottages like the one they're in mounted on scrappy lawns. They settle in the air-conditioned kitchen where the only trace of another era is a framed poem in Hungarian hanging on the wall: a child's fancy calligraphy in red, black and silver ink, with illustrated capitals. Glimpsing it as they entered, Sophie read, "For my dear mother's birthday," and passed on, not daring to read further.

They sit drinking tea. "Sophie dear," Kamilla begins in her little-girl voice. "May I ask you something? You won't get angry? Because there is something I would like to understand—and perhaps now that we're on better terms you can explain to me something that has always puzzled me about you. How can you live with yourself? Have you no pangs of conscience?..." It's from an old soundtrack. Sophie hears out the record to its end and says, "All right, I was a terrible child, but you know I had difficult parents."

"You—" Kamilla gasps, "you had the most wonderful parents in the world!" and launches into a new torrent of speech.

"But the divorce—" Sophie interrupts her mother's paean to the ideal parents, but Kamilla is going full steam. "The divorce! It was the most beautiful divorce!" she exclaims with deep pathos. "There couldn't be two people more loving and considerate to each other than your father and I—we laughed about the whole thing, we couldn't decide about the dishes and the furniture. He wanted me to have everything, I wanted him to have it; no, my dear, you have a completely wrong idea, this wasn't like the usual divorce, we cried and embraced and comforted each other; there couldn't have been a more beautiful divorce and it didn't mean that we stopped caring for each other; on the contrary. It was just a divorce of convenience. Everything would stay the same—who could imagine that you would go to America, or the war! Surely I am not responsible for that! Had I known that you would go to America, I would never have agreed to the divorce. Never! I thought the divorce would ease the tension and everything would continue as before. But to be separated from those I loved by an ocean, I have no other family than you and your father," she weeps. "Sometimes I think that the whole thing was a plot against me. I don't think Rudi would deceive me; we were both kept in the dark. The family waited till after the divorce before persuading your father. He had always been against the divorce and I would never have consented had I known. And now we are here, each of us living alone with our problems, your father alone in Garfield, you alone in New York and I alone here in New Jersey."

"Can we go to the living room?" Sophie suggests after a pause. "It's freezing here." She stops on her way out to read the poem she wrote for her mother's birthday in March, 1939, in which she wishes health and happiness to her beloved mother and regrets that she will not be with her on future birthdays. "Forgive me, dear Mother, that I won't be at your side but I must follow the irresistible call to adventure to far and foreign places, to cross the wide ocean, etc." The child managed to make all this rhyme, if somewhat clumsily. The calligraphy is still impressive...

They sit in the living room which has too many doors and windows, which for this and many other reasons, the mirror with the gilded baroque frame and the divan do not dominate on this sticky summer day in New Jersey's nowhere.

"Mother," she ventures gaily. "You never told me about your first marriage to Count Csaba-Csaba."

"My marriage to Count Csaba-Csaba?" she echoes, wide-eyed. "Oh, that was nothing, my dear. He came from one of those very old noble Hungarian families in Transylvania. They were completely ruined under the Hapsburgs, mostly drunkards; he came to Budapest to study law. But I tell you, it was nothing. We weren't married even a year. I was only fifteen..."

Once more the story of the broken engagement is told. Kamilla tells it as the little sister; an old lady now looks at her daughter with the eternal girlish eyes that captured Csaba-Csaba and Landsmann. Her sister's decision still rocks her. "...I couldn't understand how Rosa could do it. They were the ideal couple. There was simply no comparison between your father and Gerechter. But I never held it against her. My sister and your father are the two people who have meant the most to me in my life...those were different times... actually Csaba-Csaba behaved very decently in the end. He attended to the legalities of the annulment himself so it didn't cost us anything."

"...And then you married Father?"

"Yes," she says slowly, her face assumes a mask of childish perplexity. She doesn't know what her story is in all this. She can't recall what year she married Landsmann, and when her daughter asks how they lived just after they married, Kamilla dwells nostalgically on their blissful honeymoon on Lake Balaton. All she remembers is the ceiling. "For a month I didn't leave the room. I can't tell you how beautiful it was those first years. We were so in love; we couldn't be separated for a minute. People called us love birds."

"And then?"

She sighs, her face saddens. "And then," she says very softly and timidly, "you were born and it was over." The memory of the old hurt brings tears to her eyes. "He fell in love with you, you know the story. He gave you all his love, he took from me the little words of endearment and gave them to you, my little fish, my canary—" She pauses, for a moment the room resolves into that imaginary interior where a woman stands stripped of her satin ribbons that a man with talcum-powdered face and slicked-down hair hangs over an infant's crib; then changes back into the cottage where an old lady weeps over her ribbons. "And the rest you know," Kamilla resumes with a philosophic gesture. "Then you went to America with your father. No one is responsible for his nature. I don't blame you ... I am happy since I learned to live with myself. My one dream is to have one or two women friends like myself to talk to; analyze our nature. Understand what makes us do what we do."

"Why do you live out in New Jersey?"

"That's such a strange story you won't believe it. But I'll tell you if you really want to hear. It's a true story. You know how troubled and full of disasters my life has been with you and your father, then Zoltan and the war, the affair with the painter and a lot of things you don't know about—and then at last I met a man with whom I had a beautiful and harmonious relationship. You remember Eva? She called one day—a week or so after I told her about the way it ended with that impossible accountant your Ezra found for me. She has a proposition to make to me; she has an acquaintance, a fine man, in his early fifties, attractive, very wealthy, who travels a great deal and is looking for a woman about my age, cultivated, intelligent, for companionship when he was in New York; someone who would share his interest in concerts, opera, good dinners; would I be interested in meeting him. I said yes, I didn't really believe the whole thing, it is rare that a man seeks friendship. 'There is one condition,' Eva said, 'he insists on this. You must not ask him any personal questions as regards his family, his work, where he is coming and going. You will know him by the name of Alex Bondy, the name he gave me—it's not his real name; you're not to inquire about the life he lives when he is not with you. Before he meets you he wants to be sure you agree to this.' Well we met, and discovered that we were truly kindred spirits."

"Didn't the conditions bother you?"

"Look, it is what a man is in relation to me that matters to me, not what he is with his wife or mother or any other woman. Every man I have ever been with has told me the same thing: that I'm the first woman with whom they can be completely themselves. Alex, like the others. In a way our relationship was the purer in that he never compared it to others he had. I was happy to be with him. I did not care what place I had in his life and when he confessed to me that, in fact, I had moved to a central place I was rather surprised and somewhat apprehensive. I was afraid he would propose marriage. But Alex was really marvelous. We were closer than I had even imagined. He said that while he could not marry me, he wanted me to have a house built on some beautiful spot—the love of beauty united us— designed and furnished to my taste, which he would consider as his 'home' whenever he was free to come to me. Money was no consideration—an hour's drive from New York. I found the perfect spot. It was a dream; completely isolated, overlooking a lake. I inquired and it was for sale. When Alex came again we drove out. He was enchanted; it was exactly what he wanted and he made a deposit toward the purchase of the grounds. I spent the next weeks in feverish planning, contracting architects, making estimates. I realized I would have to supervise the building so Alex bought a two-room bungalow across the lake where I would live temporarily. Yes, this, where I live now. We were going over the blueprints and I confessed to him that I was worried—the house seemed a great responsibility—couldn't he make an exception and give me an address where I could contact him in case of need. In answer he pulled out wads of money from his briefcase—the full amount for the purchase of the land, which he wanted in my name. I should make a contract with the architect and in a week he would be back with ten thousand dollars cash to start construction. Then he didn't come. No letter, no telephone call, nothing. I waited another week then I called Eva, to ask whether she had heard from Alex. 'Forgive me for not calling you,' she said, 'I couldn't bring myself to it. He had a heart attack ten days ago and died. I was hoping he had left instructions that you be notified. I just didn't dare to call you.' So here I was with the plot, and this bungalow. I didn't have the strength to move. And that's how I got involved in the real estate business."

"Did you ever find out who he really was?"

"Some details, but it's of no importance as I told you . . . My life is a novel," she concludes, "somebody should write it. Why don't you? I am sure you could make a lot of money with it. If the Russians hadn't stolen my journals . . . thirty volumes from 1920 to 1945. In 1937 —— wanted to publish it. I had to refuse of course. I was still married to your father at the time and it contained things . . . I would never do anything that might harm his reputation. To begin all over again now? I tried a few times, with a tape recorder in Hungarian, but to find somebody to translate it. It's impossible for me in English. But you," she smiles, looking coyly at her daughter, "you write in English, it's easy, all you have to do is write it in good English, the story is all there and you could make money with it."

IT IS STRANGE even in a dream to find yourself in the country of your childhood; she had been traveling up the Costa Brava bound for Italy when suddenly the railway tracks stopped in the middle of a marshy meadow. The fields were flooded throughout the north of Spain, the Barcelona radio had announced—or was that in another dream? For here she is greeted by a group of Hungarian peasants who insist that this muddy swamp is the Danube. They invite her to a meal in the kitchen of a farmhouse whose low curved ceiling is as sooty as the inside of an oven; she speaks guardedly: Will they recognize by her accent that she is a foreigner? Why are they so friendly? One of the kerchiefed women looks like Aunt Lea from Budapest. Do they know that she left for America before the war? Is this a trap to punish for deserting? For she did not plan this visit. She came to Europe to make a tour of Spain and Italy: there was a fresco of the Last Judgment in Pisa she was supposed to see before continuing to Naples, and the geographic as well as political boundaries of Europe had been drastically rearranged so she'd be caught in the Hungarian plains.

Dreams have their own topography and it is to the country of childhood she returned, sometimes as a traveling scholar; or slyly substituting the child, dressed in regulation sailor blouse, navy pleated skirt and high-laced shoes, she descended the wide stairs of a vaulted building with a group of schoolchildren. It is the entrance to the baths of St. Gellert with its bubbling pool ringed by marble columns. The cavelike walls are hewn out of the mountain. At its peak, far above the Danube, is the statue of a martyr saint holding up the apostolic cross. The entrance forms part of an old basilica: its walls are hung with notices, like in French village churches, announcing weddings, births, baptisms, funerals, current cinema showings, books, either approved or banned by ecclesiastical authorities. As the line moves ahead the child edges toward the wall and tries to make out the writing which becomes more blurred as she comes close while, three thousand miles and three decades away from the scene, the dreamer, impatient for the information, whispers with awe, "These are the most ancient archives of memory..." The child can just barely distinguish the white square of the bulletin from the darker wall. The child, unable to make out a message, disappears. The dreamer awakes.

Some minutes are necessary to overcome the frustration of not having glimpsed a single word of the message, while in the window frame the laddered water tanks at various rooftop levels come into focus in the early morning Hudson River light. Breakfast must be prolonged to recover from the deception, the shame of having once more been so seduced. Finally, the bed made, the boots on, the coat belted and the day begun, dropping three nickels in the coin box of the Eighty-sixth Street crosstown bus, it is disconcerting to have to acknowledge that Hungary is a real place on the map of Europe and not the private property of the dreamer. That its capital, though heavily bombed in the last years of the Second World War, has not been utterly destroyed like Lidice, but restored to its former architectural splendor, and competes for tourist trade, besides carrying on its daily business. That in fact, as a stroll along Second Avenue in the November drizzle confirms, travel agencies advertise package jet flights for the Christmas holidays. Two weeks round trip for only $288. Spend Christmas with your family, the hand-lettered posters urge in Hungarian. Causing her to draw in her breath. Christmas in Budapest conjured candy stores. First the flash of tinsel wrappers, the red, the green, the silver and the gold. Next the taste of that wonderful inferior chocolate which went into little animals, sheep, donkeys, dogs, birds, and into larger hollow Santa Clauses that were hung on trees—a taste which good Swiss and Dutch chocolates couldn't compare with, and not even the worst American chocolate. It was very special. The shape entered into the taste, as the child's tongue traced the legs, ears and tail of a lamb or cracked the hollow skull of old Santa before chocolate melted, while it was hard and dry; and the taste did not interfere, a muted hard stale, faintly sweet, faintly bitter taste.

Inside dingy darkish office which one suspects doubles for money exchange, credit and clerical services of another financial era, unimaginable to a present-day New Yorker, a sad and ferreted face greets her in the most courteous Hungarian. Her request, in the friendliest English, for Hungarian travel folders, brings color to the yellow cheekbones. Lady wishes to travel! "The owner will be back shortly," he promises excitedly. "The manager will be delighted to ..." The lady, fearful that "shortly" may mean any length of time which she would rather not spend in company of seedy clerk whose eyebrows are too mobile, even more fearful of meeting the manager; she imagines a two-hundred-pound Hungarian who might actually persuade her to book for a real trip—the lady regrets but she is in a hurry. Once more she inquires if by chance he has a folder —The manager knows where everything is, the clerk cries in despair. Just a folder with a map of Budapest, she pleads. He withdraws to back room where other people are working. Communists? Anarchists? she wonders. Fund-raisers for regaining the Crown of St. Stephen? The clerk returns with two travel folders, one pink, the other, an old photograph green. The colors remotely relating to dominant colors of Hungarian flag. Apologetic and downcast, beseeching to be reassured that she will return when manager is in the office, he hands them to her. She will drop by later, she promises noncommittally, as clerk holds the door and she walks out on Second Avenue.

"Visit Budapest, the Pearl of the Danube," the green travel folder invites the American traveler. "With its history spanning a period of two thousand years, the city has preserved a number of historical monuments and artistic relics ..." The pink folder, issued by Ibusz (what the Ugric tongue has retained from the Latin *omnibus*), offers "WINGED HUNGARIAN HOSPITALITY" aboard Malev planes scheduled to twenty-three European and Near Eastern cities. For information, ticketing, booking: 3 Vaci Utca, Budapest, V. Telephone: 134–034. It lists under its sightseeing program a tour of Buda castle twice a week at 10:45 every Wednesday: "The motor-coach will leave Roosevelt ter and make for the Parliament, accompanied by a guide. The visit to the interior of the Parliament is accompanied by special guide. From here, the coach will go over Margaret Bridge, Martirok utja, Moszkva ter up to Castle Hill, to the terminus of the microbus. Here the visitors change over to the microbus, the guide takes his seat at the microphone, and explains the interesting spots on Castle Hill on the route that takes about forty-five minutes. From here the visitors will be taken back to Roosevelt ter, crossing the Danube on the Chain Bridge."

There is a small Hungarian bookstore across the street that might have a map. The front is cluttered with souvenirs, shepherd dolls, peasant lace, pipes, embroidery, folk-song records. The tastefully dressed lady in her fifties, by a small table, writing on stationery paper, is presumably the owner. She could be a friend, neighbor, relation of the owner, she has such a pleasant air of indifference, of coming from somewhere else, of being at home anywhere. She gives Sophie a brief look, a friendly nod of acknowledgment, it could be to her sister or daughter coming home from work, to whom it is not necessary to speak. A map of Budapest? She thinks she has one upstairs. The customer isn't in a hurry, is she? There are some Hungarian books in the back, she is welcome to browse around. She must go upstairs anyway in a little while to put the roast in the oven, she'll look for it then.

Foreign novels—American, German, French—translated into Hungarian fill most of the shelves. But there are some items of interest. A bound volume of the weekly illustrated *Vilag*, or World, the Hungarian counterpart of *Life* or *Paris Match* for the years 1921–1922, catches her eye—unfortunately buried under a huge, dusty and precarious jumble of journals, pamphlets, as well as heavier untitled volumes. That's just as well. Now is not the moment to look into the twenties. It's the volume of the First World War years Sophie would like to see, that she leafed through so often as a child. There was one in her father's waiting room and at her grandmother's. Almost every house had it. It was a big book bound in red, with the picture of the Assassination of the Archduke Francis Ferdinand in Sarajevo on the first page, followed by pictures of members of the Hapsburg family, beautiful young men and women, the sad old Kaiser Franz Josef and Kaiser Wilhelm in his pointed helmet. The next page showed jubilant crowds dancing in the street, hats thrown in the air, hands waving bottles: the crowds celebrating the news of the outbreak of the war in Paris, London, Vienna, Berlin, Budapest. The rest of the book was war pictures. The same pictures, page after page, of soldiers, men going into battle, marching, retreating; men in trenches drinking from tin cups, grinning men with bandaged heads and limbs; dead or wounded men carried on stretchers, dead soldiers strewn or in a heap on the ground; or just one dead man's face, the empty stare of dead eyes that made her silent inside. She would like to see the First World War volume and the volumes for the issues between 1936 and 1939; where she saw in the single issues as they came out once a week pictures of the things happening in the world right then, in Germany, Italy, England and France. Those soft, flappy pliant single issues you could roll up, lying about on tables and chairs, which did not have the weight, permanence and reality of the bound World War volume. They contained the events of the week about which there was always so much discussion, where she saw pictures of Stalin, Mussolini, Hitler in the last years of the thirties. But it was in America, after the Second World War, that she looked at length at those pictures of the thirties.

The proprietress of the shop returns with a large, twenty-five-cent folding map of Budapest and its outskirts. She is taking it of course, it's exactly what she needs but she wants to buy something more. That large new *Legends of the Magyars* for children, with illustrations, appeals at first, but in English it has lost its flavor. On another shelf, however, she has just spotted a schoolbook-size volume badly printed in Argentina, appropriately titled *A Multunk* (Our Past), with a picture of the white-haired lady who wants Hungarians wherever they happen to be to remember their past. It's all there, from the legend of the golden stag that lured Nimrod's sons to the promised land: a bird flies from branch to branch, a song flies from mouth to mouth.

It's all there. She remembers looking at the same picture in her schoolbook. It was an elementary school primer for the second to the fourth grades, in which ancient legends, stories of historic battles and kings, were oddly mixed with contemporary sketches of little Gyuri's visit to Fiume, how silver is mined, and timeless lyrics on the beauty of wildflowers.

Leafing through, it's a shock to experience that none of this has become foreign to her. A language and stories she left behind, shed, some twenty-five years ago, read like yesterday, or simply now. As if nothing has changed, neither the reader nor the book. Sophie's school-child's feelings about Attila, the kings and legends of Hungary, have been preserved, fresh in their original color, and stored away inside her, differently, more mysteriously than in the book: the images evoked by the text and line drawings have that sudden, unexpected power, of sound that is not in the notation of the score. It is clear also that whatever more sophisticated perspectives, judgments, or suspensions of judgment subsequent study of history might produce in her, she can have no other feelings about Attila and the kings of the house of Arpad than the feelings that continue to haunt and sound from images formed in the first grades.

She is looking for a picture, but she doesn't find it in this book: the scene of the people gathered on the frozen Danube to proclaim Matthias king while he was prisoner in Prague. She realizes, having leafed through chapters on the glorious renaissance of Hungary, the picture she thought she remembered from her elementary school primer vivid and throbbing with life is missing. Finally, from another book, or perhaps from the fleeting memory of a poem learned in class she remembers: It is the picture of a woman in a room, the mother of the future King Matthias, a writing stand with quill beside her; she stands by the window, her arm outstretched, her face lifted to the black raven who has just flown off with her letter to her son, prisoner of Frederick III in Prague.

The elementary school book of Hungarian history ends with the battle of Mohacs: 1526. Now Sophie understands why the stretch from the sixteenth to the twentieth century has to this day been a misty, insubstantial rift, a gap in time. It explains why important facts and dates she learned in school—Napoleon, the French Revolution, Cromwell, Bismarck, the Boston Tea Party and the Victorian Age—though dutifully copied from blackboard to notebook, and passing obediently from notebook to examination papers, never took root in her mind where three centuries were a swamp: endless massacres, mud, misery under Turkish hooves, Hapsburg heels. She returns the book to the shelf.

She reads, in a volume of ballads by Arany Janos, opened at random, poems she read as a child. She reads like a child: the poem walks away with her, like a man dancing with a small child, so tall she can't see his head. She knows it's not for real, she does not understand the power moving her, the movement stronger than emotion or meaning. This poem is silent, holding its breath, stepping like a thief or a fugitive. The poem about the woman washing a bloody sheet in the brook does not move at all. In the last stanza as in the first, she washes the torn rags, her hair gray, her knees frozen into the ice, still she washes the thin rag that the brook is still playfully snatching from hand but cannot relieve her of. The story in the middle, of her imprisonment, trial, acquittal, serves to make the single image larger and stronger, to prepare for the last stanza that turns the key once more in the lock.

She is startled to find herself in a bookstore, tall and bulky in her coat, looking out on Second Avenue, as she raises her eyes from the book.

THREE

PAPI LIKED to talk about things Sophie did when they lived in an apartment building on the other side of the river in Pest. But she herself didn't remember before she was five years old living in the house in Buda. She remembered the day they finished building it, and very dimly the earlier stages of its being built. There was a celebration, a wooden scaffolding tied with colored ribbons was torn down and burnt. The house was not ready to move into, there were still piles of brick, mountains of sand and gravel, troughs with cement and a lot of mud all around. But it was all built. She remembered the scaffolding coming down like a tree from the sky, the conflagration, people standing around, workmen and others, dressed nicely, clustering about the terrace and the stone steps because of the mud, but she didn't remember herself at the celebration or remember the house she went back to, anything at all about the house, or moving out or moving in.

There was the Danube and the Parliament, apartment houses, stairways, streets, trees and trolleys. There were rooms and scenes dimly remembered, but she was absent from them, or another person; like in her dreams, she wasn't really herself. She didn't remember her parents before they lived in Buda or any other person, with the exception of Grandfather Ripper, her mother's father, who died when she was three. He had a foxy pointed face and pale eyes. She remembered him in a dingy room with yellowed walls. He ran around in a loose white nightgown. They treated him like a naughty child, coaxing him to get back into bed, and he'd pop out again and rush to the table. He covered sheets of paper with marks that formed narrow columns. Then he folded a long strip of paper very small, made a few cuts with scissors and when she unfolded it, it was a row of bandy-legged clowns holding hands. Later her father explained he went wrong in the head when he lost his fortune.

She remembered that a glass door led from the room to a terrace which ran along the four walls of an inner court. There was an iron railing. Afraid to lean over, she looked down through the lattice on the cobbles below and remembered her stomach rise as it registered the depth.

"Do you remember?" Papi asked on their Sunday walks, and told her about things she did or said, and that they two did together when they lived on the other side of the river and she was three years old, or just a baby.

"Don't you remember," he said, "you had two enormous teddy bears when you were three years old. I must have paid fifty pengos for the pair."

"What happened to them?" she asked.

"You threw them out the window! Don't you remember?"

"Why?" she asked.

"You said you did it to punish them."

"Why didn't you go down and get them?" she asked.

"I was in my office with a patient. We lived on the fifth floor. By the time the maid went down, they were gone. Somebody walked off with them. Two beautiful teddy bears!"

What he said about her and what she really remembered belonged in two different boxes. Except she wasn't sure what was really her own, it was mixed up with other people's things: what they were telling her, Papi and Omama and her many aunts and uncles. She really needed a drawer where she could put away their things.

Papi claimed that she smeared her excrements on the wall. He enjoyed telling it to her. It proved his theory. Why didn't the govern-ess stop her? she wanted to know. But the governess had strict instruc-tions not to interfere; in fact, she was told to call him from his consulting room should Sophie . . . She had confirmed his theory. He wanted to see it with his own eyes. There was nothing so thrilling as science. He predicted she might become a painter. He was full of theories about children; there were essentially three types: head-bangers, masturbators and rockers. She was a rocker. When she was two and a half years old she hit another child over the head with her shovel because he came to watch her dig and build in the sand. When Papi came in her room to give her a kiss, she pushed him away.

She also said a lot of things he thought very clever, which he put in his book. That, at least, she didn't have to remember.

At Grandmother's there were always strange fat women and funny men who pushed their grinning faces close to her and asked, "Do you remember your Aunt Piri who gave you a box of chocolates?" or "Do you remember your favorite uncle?" She knew she was expected to say, "You are my Aunt Piri," or "You are my favorite uncle." But maybe it was a trick, she wasn't really sure. They also remembered things about her they thought clever or funny that Sophie didn't remember. Aunt Lea prepared chicken paprikas for her because she remembered how much Sophie liked it, when Sophie didn't.

Omama Landsmann held her pressed against her belly, rocking to and fro, and in a singsong voice told her what she must always remember: She was the daughter of the most wonderful man, a very great man. She would make up for all the wrongs he suffered and she would never be like her mother, she would be a good Jewish daughter, and God-fearing, and learn Hebrew so she could read the Holy Scriptures where it said . . .

Omama pronounced the Hebrew words one by one, her mouth shaping them, her widened eyes helping to define their outline, then translated it for her, bending down, making their foreheads touch; strange disconnected phrases about women who were a snare and a misfortune, beautiful wicked women whom God punished. But she was her father's daughter and the granddaughter of the chief rabbi of Budapest and the great granddaughter of a very famous rabbi; she would always be a joy and honor to her father.

Her mother was away most of the time: or so she was told and so it seemed. She was used to her mother's not being in the house. No-body told her when her mother was leaving or coming back; therefore it was surprising to see her in bed or in the dining room. But curiously it was her mother who expressed surprise, who behaved the more surprised of the two. She couldn't speak right away, she gasped, her eyes widened in a rigid stare as if a robber had burst into the room. "Who are you?" her mother would exclaim in a severe voice. "What are you doing here, little stranger? This isn't my little girl—" and she laughed. Was she joking or serious? Her laughter wasn't real; there was such an odd expression on her face as if she might burst into tears any minute, and her head tipping from side to side looked like a live puppet.

"I wonder if my little girl remembered to bring me a kiss," she said very softly, staring at the ceiling. She was like someone in a fairy tale making a wish.

"I might even have something pretty for her. But she must sit in my lap."

Now Sophie was curious about something pretty her mother might give her, perhaps from her own things, a scarf or a little necklace, or a gift from a foreign country.

But when Sophie sat in her lap her mother started laughing again, differently than before, her long fingers playing in her hair, stroking her cheek, "You're a funny little girl," she cackled. "Do you know why you don't love me? Because you have no heart." The smile and look of triumph remained on her face, but her tone softened. "People who don't have a heart have very unhappy lives. We are not responsible for our nature," she sighed wistfully and continued speaking strangely, perhaps just joking, saying things that couldn't be true, they were so nasty, or so sweet. When she left the room Sophie couldn't be sure of anything. Maybe her mother was right: she hadn't been away at all; Sophie was making up things and avoiding and ignoring her; or maybe it was Sophie who had gone off on a trip, leaving her mother all alone. Everyone in his own way was practicing some kind of magic on her.

Perhaps it was possible to have different parents at different times, as it was possible to move to a new house. On their Sunday afternoon walks her father pointed out some of the houses they passed. "Would you like to live in this house?" he'd ask her. Sometimes they would talk about it seriously; which room would be hers, which his, and where the governess would sleep when she had one. Her father was asking her, Do you really want it, shall I buy it? And if it was a big old-fashioned stone mansion with turrets and stone fence and iron grille she'd urge him yes to buy it now, but he'd find some small reason why not, and to placate her he'd say, We'll go in and ask how much it costs—maybe it will be terribly expensive and I won't have enough money. He looked so sad and upset she had to feel sorry for him. Still she would insist that he find out. "Should I?" he would ask. Yes, she'd dare him gravely, but he wouldn't. And in the same way he would ask, if some impressive figure passed by—a peasant in sheepskin or a cavalry officer with a plumed helmet, or a small Jew with a bushy red beard—he'd ask if she'd like him for a father. At home on following Sundays he gave imitations of the people—the peasant, the cavalry officer, the bearded Jew, pretending each was her father—so she thought it was possible to have a different father or live in a different house even though it never happened; but that was only because in the end they never asked for the price of the house, or asked the cavalry officer with the plumed helmet. He was a coward, and she too; she wouldn't ring the doorbell or run up to the cavalry officer and ask him if he would be her father. They were just a pair of cowards.

At St. Gellert's bath you saw the water fall through the air and run down the steep hillside, splitting into many streams; some got caught in moss and ran into holes; most of it came down along the middle rushing in and out of rock pools at different levels, changing shapes as it dropped from bowl to bowl down to the great basin at the bottom where people could wade. It was lovely to catch the stream that spouted from mouths of marble fish or stand under the shower coming directly from the rock, feel a thick sheet of water break on your back; when it was too much, numbing, you could stand behind it, not too long, you didn't know if you had enough air. By the rocks the stream was coming down its own many ways both hard and soft; big cold drops on the same spot; if you held out your palm, it hit with its own beat, unpredictable, alive, like someone talking to you. Four drops coming one after another and then you waited; it was busy in the moss further up, delayed in crevices, but it arrived eventually, a stately drop in her palm, very leisurely and taking its time.

She played in the outdoor pool where every half-hour for five minutes they put on artificial waves. But the fountain was more marvelous; even though she enjoyed the waves as they got bigger and bigger, other people's screaming spoiled it, even grown-up people screaming when the big waves came, she knew they weren't really scared; but that you screamed because you were having fun; she didn't understand this, it always scared her, even her own Papi, he tried to explain, but it didn't help. She was really afraid of herself, he said, she was afraid of herself screaming, he insisted; that made her even more afraid.

His skin smelled funny in the water. He smelled different wet than dry, that's what always struck her first when Papi appeared in the bath; she found him or he found her, they were always losing each other. Most of the time she was alone. But sometimes he suddenly surprised her in the water; or she found him sitting somewhere smoking a cigaret and reading the newspaper. He had a special waterproof case for money, matches, cigarets.

He talked a lot about what a great athlete he used to be, how he practiced diving when he was a young man. She wanted to see him do it. Muscles and good looks, that was all nonsense, he said, what you had in your head was the important thing.

But to please her, he would show her what he could do. She could be proud of her father. See what a father she had. Play-acting with mock seriousness, maybe imitating himself as a young man to whom a flawless dive was important, imitating himself and other people, he took up various positions on the diving board—the matinee idol, the fat middle-aged Jew deciding in turn for and against attempting the dive; he made Sophie laugh. He had a real actor's sense, her father. He could get her to laugh so hard his actual diving lost importance and when she didn't care any more whether he dived or not, then he dived very competently and did a crawl across the pool and back. He came up the ladder dripping. Sophie wanted to see him do it again. No, it was enough, he said wiping himself, careful not to get water on the newspaper and cigarets. It was enough. Ah there was a time... Then sat smoking, once more the scientist, explaining to Sophie why she enjoyed seeing him dive.

Fat women sat or squatted in the water, engaged in lively conversation, sometimes they dipped under or splashed themselves; when they stood up in their funny bathing suits that looked like underwear they were so amazingly hideous she couldn't help gaping at them. It was to hide their ugliness they stayed submerged, she thought. They looked at her so sternly when she gaped that Sophie learned to look from the side of her eye. She could look at people carefully while flopping her head as she frolicked in the water.

Her mother always stayed in the part with grass near the restaurant when she was at the baths. Most of the time she lay oiled on a beach chair with separate part for the feet that always collapsed when Sophie tried to sit on it. Her mother swam with great care for style and always asked her boyfriend afterward whether she was doing it well. She had different boyfriends. They all were very tanned and reminded her of Papi's imitations of matinee idols.

She was playing in the water most all of the time; they had to drag her out of the water when they wanted to go home. Look, everyone is going, look they're closing the pool. See the guard over there, Papi would say. She got mad when people lied to her. She didn't want to go home. Then she was very ashamed: people were staring at her because she was screaming. When she screamed she forgot that there were people around her, she wasn't screaming at her mother or Papi, people stopped existing and she was screaming all alone in the world, then suddenly she saw them and their looks, or just remembered the shocked and disapproving faces because she was running ahead to the trolley stop; she didn't want anyone to see her face. When she was running very fast it was like being partly out of the world and outside herself. Sometimes it was possible to change yourself just by pressing your cheek against the window of the trolley.

*

She would be kidnapped by gypsies or simply wake up in another house with other parents who were her real parents and forget what had been just a dream. She thought this always when she was riding on the trolley. A dirty old man got on the trolley. He had trouble picking out the fare from his torn pockets. He looked bad-smelling and his eyes rolled. Please don't let him sit down beside me, she prayed. I'll say the national anthem ten times, dear God, if you grant me this wish. The dirty old man lurched on down the aisle and slumped in a seat in the back of the trolley. Suddenly Sophie felt very bad for that poor dirty old man who was her father in another life. She regretted her wish but she kept her end of the bargain. Then while she was murmuring, "I believe in one God, I believe in one Country, I believe in one Eternal Justice, I believe in the Resurrection of Hungary," it struck her that one day she will forget Papi; she will be living another life and he will be a poor old nasty-smelling man she won't recognize and won't want to sit next to her. It made her feel very sad. She would try to be extra nice to Papi.

All the years in Budapest she thought about waking up and forgetting. It was a strange, powerful, frightening thought. However, she reflected, it was frightening only now. Once she woke up in another life she wouldn't be afraid because she wouldn't remember having been someone else before.

It was all very strange and difficult and wonderful to begin and have her own room in a nice villa with colored pencils and lots of paper. If only she could make up her mind about being in so many worlds. But she was of many minds. One mind said: I like to stay where I am. Where I am is the right place. Another mind liked to travel. It loved to be surprised; to lie down in one bed and wake up in another, in another country, another person. Or discover you're a whiskered fish swimming in the water; or look out the window and see water all around instead of trees and mountains. Or ring your grandmother's doorbell and have the trolley conductor open the door. If you put a chestnut in a box and closed it, there was no reason why it should be there half an hour later or why there couldn't be two chestnuts or a live kitten in it instead; that's how her second mind liked things to appear and vanish and change. Her third mind said you have to be careful.

At Grandmother's it was sometimes wrong to ask for paper and pencil. It was a day on which it was forbidden to draw and she saw in her grandmother's face that she had done something terribly wrong in asking, even if she couldn't understand what it was.

Sabbath wasn't like Sunday. You woke up and it was Sunday. But you had to wait all Friday for the Sabbath; nobody was sure when it began. Uncle Benji was showing her how to draw a horse. Omama said it was time to put the drawing away because of Sabbath. "Look how dark it is." It wasn't Sabbath yet, Uncle Benji said. It was a cloudy day. He looked at his watch—it's only four-thirty. "Look in the newspaper," she said.

"We still have over an hour," he said. Just a little over an hour! It was late. The table had to be set. They put away the paper and pencils hurriedly.

"Is it now?" she asked Uncle Benji. No, it was not. It was coming.

At Grandmother's house dark, glossy furniture filled the room. From morning till late afternoon there were visitors coming and going: bearded men in black with pale shiny faces, wide-rimmed hats and thick lips, their voices high-pitched and full of sudden shrieks and gurgles, to whom she served red wine and offered sweets which they always declined. They spoke excitedly in a foreign language as if they had just arrived from another country with bad news or a secret message.

She didn't like to sleep over at her grandmother's because the Sabbath was in her house. It wasn't anywhere else. She looked out the window from the dark room and saw the street lights and stores lit, cars moving, people moving about. At Grandmother's she felt like she was outside the city.

She was drawing a battle scene: a whole row of men blown into a black cloud, the last one, running, a huge bloodflower in place of his head.

It's not nice that picture, Grandmother said. Papi asked her questions and then explained the drawing to her. He spoke a foreign language, pointing to parts of his body that other people thought shameful. But she liked the story he told about Matushka the peasant boy who blew up trains with dynamite in the time of Franz Josef. She drew him very handsome with black hair to his shoulders and a red vest. What did dynamite look like, she asked Uncle Benji; he was her father's youngest brother and more like a cousin. He drew a giant candle, then a pack of candles. She copied, drawing the wicks carefully. Why was Matushka holding sticks of dynamite in a picture showing a train already blown up? Papi asked in a voice that was sure her answer would prove his point. "For the next train," she said. "He has lots," she said angrily.

She lived in a red stucco house with a garden. Her father worked all week. Sundays they spent together, going on long walks, or to the zoo, or the children's theater. Afterward, they visited at Grandmother's. Her father and she were close; they looked alike, that's what everybody said who met them on the street. She looked like him and was smart like him. Sometimes they asked about her mother. Was Kamilla still in Italy? Was she back from Austria?

Sophie was surprised if she found her mother sitting in the dining room when she entered. She was used to finding the dining room empty in the afternoons so that she could steal cookies locked in the buffet that she took with her to the meadow. Her mother wore a knitted dress and she was writing in a book, her hands seemed carved out of ivory, very beautiful, not like other people's hands. She hovered around her mother. She bounced on the upholstered chair, circled around the table, banged against her mother's chair, but didn't have the courage to push her mother's elbow; nothing made Sophie so angry as when someone pushed her arm and it ruined the page. She resolved to be so obnoxious that her mother would take her notebook into another room. She jumped from the window sill so that the chandeliers trembled.

"Can't you see how bad I am!" she cried out finally, and left the room.

The house was empty; it was all hers. Her mother was away. Sometimes she gave bridge parties in the house. That always upset Sophie, to see the quiet room filled with smoke and shrieking people; bridge tables set up and chairs from other parts of the house brought in. She came in; painted women cackled over her. Servants hurried, passing around things on trays too high for her to reach. She ran out again. While she was at kindergarten or out playing the house was transformed.

She peeked into the room on the other side of the bathroom when she woke up. Sometimes the shades were drawn, instead of the great big room there was a smaller dark bedroom. Her mother lay in a big bed. She saw her blond curls, a stocking over her eye; heard her snore and closed the door. But other mornings the sun was pouring into the room. She ran to the window overlooking the garden; she felt the soft blue velvet of the divan. She touched a gilded leaf on the mirror frame. She went to the dresser, careful not to catch a shocking reflection of herself in the mirror. She stared at the variety of flasks and jars and bowls, all the same blue crystal. She sniffed all the flasks, ran her finger over the fluted silver handles of her mother's brush, her hand mirror, the sheath of her comb. In the left-hand drawer was the little box of black beauty patches. She knew where her mother kept her jewelry, her scarves, her silk stockings, fancy evening shoes, her fine underwear and furs. When most of her things were not in the drawers, Sophie knew that her mother would be away for a long time. Some mornings she saw her mother asleep, but when she came home from school her mother's bedroom vanished; instead there was the big room which went all the way from the dumbwaiter to the divan. Sometimes the sliding doors were closed. The dining room was small. She listened. If there were voices, she went away. If it was silent, she unlocked the buffet, filled her pockets with cookies. She looked at the porcelain parrot behind the glass—did he see her steal? She went out.

If the door to her father's office was open it meant he was out. She went in, sat in his chair, bounced on the couch which was covered with a scratchy carpet. She took sheets of paper from his desk with the stationery heading: Dr. Rudolf Landsmann, Neurologist. She tried out all the buttons on the typewriter. She opened the bookcase and looked at the pictures of two-headed babies. Was it like having two eyes or like being two perfectly different people where one could have secrets from the other? If one could still be one person it might be very interesting.

Grown-ups were stupid; they hid keys where she could find them, on top.

The first year they lived in Buda she played every day with a little boy who lived in a big white house across the fields. Petie was four and a half and very skinny, with short-cropped woolly hair. It was marvelous how he peed. Very casually he pulled a slender tube of flesh from the slit in his pants that tapered like a spout of a gardening hose, and tilted the nose upward making an arc of water. They both watched the arc diminish to a dribble, then resumed playing.

They were going to run away to America. Petie's mother had an evening gown covered with diamonds; if they'd cut off just ten or twenty they would get enough money. The stones were sewn on very tightly, and they were afraid of being found in the closet so they cut strips from the gown. His mother found out. She laughed, the stones were only glass, Sophie could keep them and her father had to pay for the ruined evening gown.

They would fly to America, she told Petie. She went up on the roof with her father's big umbrella and her rain cape for their first flying lesson. After a while, Petie started to scream and the maid came running and then her father.

She was told she couldn't play with Petie any more. She was a bad influence—always getting him into trouble, tempting him to eat worms, to leap off the roof, making him steal from his parents. "They are right," her father said. She went to cry in the kitchen; she complained to the cook, a fat Slovak woman.

The cook said, "If you were a good girl they wouldn't make up stories like that about you."

All this time she was drawing pictures, always battle scenes with planes on fire and bloody heads and arms flying in the air, till school started her drawing flowers, snowmen and maps.

HER FATHER wasn't an ordinary kind of doctor. He didn't have a bag and visit sick people. He cured her cousin of stammering. When he was still a medical student he could hypnotize a frog and a chicken, sometimes even people. "It is wrong to teach a child to say thank you!" Papi always said, raising his index finger if anybody in the family or the maid or the shopkeeper asked her to say thank you. Omama was no exception. He was no exception. Sometimes Papi stopped in the middle of a sentence to correct himself, just as he stopped to correct anybody else. Papi belonged to a movement dedicated to rooting out hypocrisy and roundaboutness whose leader was a man called Freud. When you asked for something you mustn't say, "Do you have..." or "Could you give me..." or "I would like to ask you..." no, there was no getting around Papi; Sophie wouldn't get that piece of chocolate till she said, "Give me..." She couldn't; she cried. "Why is it so difficult?" Papi laughed.

"I want some chocolate," she said sullenly.

"Is that so?" Papi said and walked on, poker-faced.

The shingle on the gate said, DR. RUDOLF LANDSMANN, NEU-ROLOGIST; he was a medical doctor and a neurologist, her father explained to her, but he was really a psychoanalyst. It was a new science that a very few people really understood; it was a difficult science and a lot of people were against it, not only people who had wrong ideas about it but even his own patients; it was part of it that you didn't like it; this was called "resistance." He explained to her the Electra complex: She was really in love with him and wanted to marry him and there was no point in denying it; that was part of her Electra complex to deny it. Mostly Papi was talking to himself: he asked her a question and answered it himself. Sometimes he quoted something she said or did when she was three or four so that it seemed as if she had answered. He said she would deny this so she didn't have to bother to deny it. Her father believed that the discovery of this new science was the most important event in human history; he was doing something that would change all mankind. It was a great struggle because it involved ideas that were in conflict with people's habits and feelings. In time, however, people would accept it. All that Sophie understood of psychoanalysis was that it was a tricky doctrine which said that it was part of human nature to dislike and reject its view about human nature. You thought you were saying something against the doctrine or about human nature but in fact everything was said in the doctrine about you. She wouldn't have liked to be one of his patients but then she wasn't, she was his little girl and she liked having a powerful father with bushy black eyebrows she could play with. He could look a certain way that scared everybody, even the servants who said he was the kindest and most generous man: it made you feel he knew something about you that you didn't know, except that it was horrible; you'd die without ever finding out, or he might any moment reveal it to you and then you would die. He did it just with his look, his face perfectly still, not like when he had to muss up his hair, change his face and posture to appear like a peasant, an idiot or a beggar or a drunk. Sophie didn't let it scare her, she giggled, she pulled his jacket and climbed up his back and covered his eyes; she knew it was only her daddy. When she got mad because he really scared her doing the dead-man's face, she hit him: it was only her daddy being stupid and she refused to be scared; she was his little girl.

He made her laugh with his imitations of religious Jews in the rapture of prayer, and of different Hungarian types, people who thought themselves important—fops, dandies, hypocrites, and his crazy patients.

He addressed her the way the nobleman father and the peasant father would, all in proper Hungarian dialects; she was so enchanted she believed it. And when he became himself again—his face slackened with an expression of deprecation, almost disgust—he made what was noble appear ridiculous; it was such a disappointment. His impersonations were truly grand and he knew it. His final gesture of dropping the act, the mask softening into wistful irony, belonged to it. "I could have been a great actor," he said, throwing away his opportunity for renown.

On Sundays he belonged to her; they did wonderful things together. Going on walks was what Sophie enjoyed most, more than going to the theater or the amusement park. She pulled him or stopped him. She marveled at her power over someone so much bigger, a man who earned money, owned a house—was this what the dog felt when she took him on walks?—this mad joy in running, jumping on and off all the ledges? Why couldn't he run? The dog and she both went after his walking stick. They could ruffle him, they weren't afraid. Could he make the dog behave at least? He made solemn and threatening faces, trying to get her to listen. He wanted to show her things, explain things. She wanted to play; she didn't know what explanations did. He wanted to talk. She asked questions, why and what then and so what—made him grind out answers just to exercise power over him. Power and curiosity and wonder that this big man with a walking stick and bushy eyebrows who smoked cigarets could be pushed and pulled and made to talk and buy things for her, and she was happy till he spoiled it for her by putting it in words. "...why do you think I spend the one free afternoon of my week with you and buy you things, and why do you think I love you?" On and on about all that he did for her. And why? Why did he do all this for her? Because he was stupid. He put the words in her mouth. No, she only thought it and he said it. It was all right, he said and spoke about the laws of nature, the selfishness of children; they were all instruments of nature but he was resigned to it, he said, making it sound sad. Then she hopped and skipped and ran till she got rid of her anger.

Why did people really come to him, she asked; what was the matter with them, what did he do for them. She listened very carefully so she could avoid this happening to her. He told her about the sick people he treated: a man who hardly had any skin on his hands because he had to wash them every time he touched anything. Why did he have to? He explained but she still didn't understand why he had to. She was only a little girl and there were many things she couldn't do but there was nothing she couldn't stop doing once she decided. He told her about a man who came to see him, his head wrapped in an enormous bandage, and when he took it off there was no wound. That made Sophie laugh. People came to him just to lie down on the couch and talk. They didn't want to be seen by other sick people or anybody in the house—not even Sophie or the maid.

Each patient had his hour. They didn't want anybody to know that they came to her father, so Papi never mentioned them by name. He talked of his ten o'clock patient. In the five minutes he left free between patients he'd talk to her.

The five o'clock patient was always late. This was very significant, Papi explained to her. There was a reason why she came late. Sophie wondered why the patient couldn't stop being late—even if just to spite her father, as she herself would do, not to give him the opportunity to say, Ha! But perhaps the five o'clock patient didn't realize that her father noted this against her, how her father kept score. Perhaps he was keeping her in ignorance just to test her, as he often did with Sophie.

The six o'clock patient always came early—sometimes an hour before he was supposed to come. Papi sometimes had to hide him or tell him to go for a walk so he wouldn't collide with the five o'clock patient. He was a real problem. It would take seven years, Papi explained, before the patient could understand the reason he did this. Papi knew, but he couldn't tell him because the patient wasn't ready to accept her father's reasons. Telling him would only make him more difficult.

The last patient came after supper at nine, always on the dot. Never a half a minute late or early. When it was almost nine o'clock Papi pulled out his gold watch and they both watched the second hand make the circle. When it skipped past the half mark he raised his finger; at the three-quarter mark they both took a deep breath and when the doorbell rang, with the minute hand on twelve or just a little before or after, his finger came down and they went into stitches of suppressed laughter.

People coming daily for years and years, some of them would still be coming in seven years—how awful! These people who came to her father and told him everything, they didn't know one's secret is the most important thing. They didn't have a secret, that's why they were so miserable and had to come back to her father. Maybe they lost it with her father. She was afraid her father did something to them that made them so helpless and will-less that they had to come to him; their thoughts and lives were no longer their own. Sophie would rather be dead or any old thing, a worm or a pebble, than one of Papi's patients.

She asked her father if he ever had a patient who tried to kill him. When he answered her at length, she wondered if he read her thought behind the question: she imagined that if she were his patient that's what she'd do. His face and tone betrayed no suspicion of her motives, but perhaps he was feigning, concealing. She listened to her father explain that his patients discussed this with him—they talked about their thoughts and urges instead of doing it because they really wanted to be stopped; he told her of a patient who wanted to assassinate Admiral Horthy, and another who wanted to blow up the Parliament. He was a brilliant chemist who worked in a laboratory and had the explosives all ready. "But I stopped him," her father said with pride. She was weighing the issue, deciding how to feel about her father's power and triumph. He went on talking about Matushka, who for years blew up trains before they caught him. Papi would have liked to have a talk with him, but he never had a chance. She wanted to know more about Matushka: What did he look like? How many trains did he blow up or derail? How was he caught? Where did he come from? Did he have parents? What did he act like when he was taken prisoner? Her father answered too briefly; he didn't satisfy her curiosity, instead he explained that the dynamite and blowing up was something else—he talked about penis and orgasm, if Matushka had been his patient... She knew it was horrible to blow up a train full of people, still she admired Matushka. He laughed when he was captured. He didn't care. Someone noticed him watching from nearby with dynamite sticking out from his pocket. Matushka didn't know he was doing something horrible, he didn't know what suffering he caused, and he wasn't afraid to die. That made him like God; she couldn't help loving him, especially since she imagined him young with raven-black hair, the face of a scoundrel, wearing his hat crooked.

She didn't like to listen to Papi talk about his patients, except for the woman who came only once. That she remembered and asked him to tell to her again.

There were two women in the waiting room, her father told her, and when he asked which was the patient, one of them said, pointing to the other, "My sister thinks I am the patient." But she was quite willing to talk to him and went with him into his office.

"Why does your sister think you ought to see me?" he asked her.

"I don't understand it at all," she said. "I don't understand what makes people behave the way they do."

He asked her to talk about the sort of thing that bothered her.

"Well," she said, "it's the same every day. I get up in the morning, wash, dress, and so forth, I come into the living room, my sister says 'Good morning' and I say 'Good morning.' She asks me how I am and I say fine, and I ask her how she is and she says fine. And it goes on and on and something. I put on my coat, I go to work every day. 'Good-bye,' I say; 'Good-bye,' she says. If I meet someone I know on the street he says 'How are you?' and I say 'How are you?' and it goes on and on and something. I go into the building where I work, I meet people who work in the same office in the elevator, they greet me, I greet them and it goes on and on and something..."

Her father continued with the woman's story. She was so right, Sophie thought. But what did she mean by the "and something"? "Ah!" he exclaimed; that was the crux of it. The secret, which it seems he couldn't unravel. It was too complicated, he told Sophie. He couldn't tell her the whole thing. The woman was incurable and he sent her home.

"And it goes on and on and something," her father repeated the woman's statement and for a while they walked in silence and she contemplated the words.

HER MOTHER was back from a trip. Sophie saw her roll up the shutters and stand in the window, but her mother couldn't see her. She was in the garden, watching from behind the bushes. Later when she saw her mother coming down the stairs dressed to go out, she told her the German teacher wanted her to have a certain book. Her mother listened, laughing, her lids fluttering, her face very painted behind a veil full of velvet dots and a dress that was a coat with a fur stole in one piece. She asked her mother in a funny way, Sophie knew.

"You're a funny little girl," her mother said to her, as Sophie expected she would. She didn't know how to be any other way with her mother.

She watched for her mother and when she saw her come out the front door, pretended she was playing and didn't see her. She ran up and down the path, jumping and tossing her head with such abandon she couldn't possibly see her mother or hear her calling her. But of course she was watching carefully and planning; just before her mother reached the seventh almond tree Sophie streaked across the path, startling her and blocking her way. She was such a funny little girl, if her mother wanted it that way. Sophie didn't care as long as it was all right with her mother. And it seemed that way from her little laugh and winks of complicity.

The day before her German lesson she went to see if her mother was in the house. It was afternoon; her father was working, the door to her mother's bedroom was closed. But she heard her moving about. She knocked. "Come in," she heard her mother's voice. She went in. Her mother lay on the blue divan in black satin pants and a Japanese kimono; she put aside the book she was reading, and stared at Sophie as if she didn't believe her eyes. Was she expecting someone else?

Her amazement spread in a smile, she was seized by giggles before she could speak. "To what great event do I owe the honor of my only daughter's visit?"

Her tone was not sarcastic and the expression of her face was so strange Sophie forgot about her book. Besides, her mother gave her no time as she continued wagging her finger and laughing mysteriously. "I think I know! I think I know! And if you'll let me fix your hair, I'll tell you." Her fingers were undoing the braids the maid had braided at some aunt's command, loosening and fluffing the strands while she murmured about little secrets between mother and daughter. Sophie took off her hand angrily. Her mother smiled knowingly. "Do you know why you don't love me?" she began in an artificial tone of reflective serenity and looking witty, as if to announce something new that would amuse, edify, and reconcile them both. "I'll tell you, it's very simple."

To say something to stop her mother from continuing, Sophie said, "Because you're always away." Now she was angry at herself. She heard that from others. She had no right to say it to her mother. She was glad when her mother was away.

"Little liar. I was home all this week; did you come and say hello to me? Have you ever said a nice word to me? You come only if you want something.

That look...you should see the look in your eye..." Her laugh was taunting now and increasingly enraged as she carried on while Sophie stood still, her eyes nailed on the ground.

"...an unnatural child, from the day you were born. Already as a baby you pushed me away. All children are selfish, but it's unnatural for a child not to love its mother..." She watched her mother as she paced, declaiming, reproaching, threatening; observed the faultless lacquered nails, the reddish face with bleached fuzz, the dry, blond curls. Her arm rose from the wide sleeve of the kimono and vanished. Now as the arm extended horizontally pointing at her, the blue parrot on the sleeve appeared long enough that she saw it whole, saw the different shades of blue, some green, a touch of orange—suddenly it split and vanished into wrinkles, her mother made a sudden gesture, taking a step toward her, her arms turning like those of a circus performer doing fancy figures with a whip. The spectacle was totally absorbing: her dramatic gestures, the changing line of her mouth, the pattern of her kimono showing different colors as the folds shifted, her slippered feet stamping—at moments all these details would converge in the overpowering sensation of her beauty, majesty, ugliness. One moment, beautiful—all of her had had the beauty of her porcelain hands; at another, all of her repulsive like a wounded animal. Sophie felt herself dissolving in the violence of these sensations. Of herself only a schematic outline remained and a painful awareness of the child in the room as someone else, an undefined mass, an empty outline. Parts of the child kept appearing, dissolving, reappearing— sudden, fragmented, irritating like false images: the feet shifting weight, the hot damp skin of a face with a bone, brains, jelly eyes and darkness behind the skin; no person in the darkness, shrugging shoulders. She took a step back, saw her ugly brown laced shoes. The phantom of a child rose up, angrily protesting a storm of accusations which were not true. A child trapped in a losing battle, her self-defense provoking a more horrible judgment: annihilating. A child before whom its mother was speechless, worse than bad, unnatural, scandalous, so outrageous it was unspeakable. "... any other parents would have beaten you to a pulp," she was groaning out the words; "... it's only because you have a father ... a father who is the sweetest, kindest, most generous ... he is too good, he lets you get away with ... if it wasn't for your father ..." Sophie heard the words coming in small gasps and groans, as she stood frozen, her head bent, her back stiffened, as if anticipating a blow. She stood at once frozen and torn between fear and desire to be struck by this woman who dared not strike her only because of her father who was too good. She was at once troubled, and relieved that no injury was done to her flesh. But as the danger diminished, more troubled than relieved, because she couldn't grasp what really held her mother back. Was it really her father, preoccupied with a patient in a room in another part of the house? She wanted to picture it as something solid. The invisible wall between herself and this woman, protecting her; the invisible leash holding Mother back, allowing her to claw and spring only so far and no further, troubled Sophie, forming pictures in her mind which didn't apply.

Her mother stood by the dresser dabbing her eyes, still crying. Sophie waited till her sobs were subdued. It was hard for her not to feel sad for her mother. For now she was a very pitiful woman, crying, lost to her sadness, totally alone, oblivious of Sophie, her rage at Sophie quite forgotten. Her forlornness had both beauty and ugliness. Sophie couldn't tell whether she was more beautiful or ugly, only that she was pitiful... Sometimes while she stood thus, waiting for her mother to collect herself, afraid simply to leave the room, she had time to ask herself a host of questions she couldn't answer. Shouldn't she comfort her mother? Why couldn't she? How would she go about it if she could? But she didn't. Couldn't. Wouldn't. Shouldn't. She didn't comfort her mother. Whatever held her back said in her *mustn't* when she felt very sorry; or said *won't* or *can't* when her mother's head turned slightly and their eyes crossed; Sophie could not grasp it. It was what her mother had said of her, which was so terrifying her mother didn't have a word for it. Heartless, inhuman, unnatural— these were the words grasped merely to express her incomprehension before what she saw in her child, whose reality only she, Sophie, could grasp and feel because she embodied the unspeakable, incomprehensible evil. It didn't feel like anything. It was the feeling of her body as a lot of bones, tubes, stomach, lungs, heart, intestines all packed together.

Her mother was seated before her dresser; she pulled out all the drawers searching for something with quick nervous movements, her look preoccupied. She didn't find what she was looking for. She flung a scarf angrily on the floor.

"I am going out in the garden," Sophie said, turning to go.

Her mother looked up, holding a bunch of tangled silk hose she had just lifted from the drawer, frozen midair.

"Didn't you come to me because you wanted something—" Her voice was weighted with fatigue, indifference, only the suggestion of a taunt came through the rough edge of leftover rage.

She said the title of the book and went out.

SCHOOL gives childhood an unanticipated sanction and dignity. You enter a new existence—formal, public, regulated; here you will spend the next twelve years of your life, progressing from grade to grade. Here you wear a uniform, a sailor blouse over a pleated skirt, dark blue like all the girls of your class.

It's a magical and exalted world. The days become different under the tutelage of those big round clocks; the bells, the hours, every segment has its characteristic activity: color, bodily sensations, excitement and boredom. It's like the seasons only cut up smaller, the same sense of return, knowing that you will come back to Monday afternoon reading class next week.

Sitting in class was like being on a trolley whose route you knew, anticipating the familiar stations; a certain turn particularly thrilling, dull stretches when you can daydream. School was like that. There was the pleasure of being told what to do and then of doing it with only now and then an instant of fright which always had to do with the hand of the clock and with time moving while she stopped to think about what color to draw the roof, and the sudden realization that time moved while she stopped was like falling off a moving thing.

Silent reading always produced an acute distress. The clock ticking in a silent room, one felt the earth hurtling through space, the Chinese standing on the other side hanging upside down, one heard the blood pounding in one's ear and at different points of the body a voice that said: "Time is passing time is passing time is passing." Against such discomforts there are remedies like drawing secretly under the desk or turning pages when teacher isn't looking, or methodically studying the children's legs crossed, uncrossed, socks, shoes.

Every morning before class they stood very straight and solemn beside their desks singing the national anthem:

> I believe in one God.
> I believe in one country.
> I believe in a divine, eternal justice.
> I believe in the resurrection of Hungary.

The big flag standing in the corner was unrolled while they sang, one student kept the pole upright and another held the cloth straight. There was a gold crown embroidered on the white ground in heavy gilt thread. It roused mysterious, joyous feelings, uniting pleasures of winter and summer: snow, chocolate Santa Claus wrapped in gold paper and the fireworks on St. Stephen's Day. The map on the wall showed the greater, or resurrected Hungary, a thin black line indicating the present boundaries established after the First World War.

It was exciting drilling for air attacks, trying on gas masks. Her father said it was nonsense, propaganda. Lies. War was ugly. He had lived through a war, fighting on the side of the Dynasty. He saw the revolution and counterrevolution. It was a lot of nonsense. Stalin was important.

Everyone was sure there would be a gas war. Which country was preparing the attack wasn't clear. One of Hungary's neighbors, maybe, or was Hungary preparing a war? On the way home from school they sang, "Burn every Rumanian, hang the Czechoslovakian, drown the Yugoslavian, kick the Austrian in the pants." The kick was especially vivid because they couldn't resist trying it out on each other more or less playfully and usually landing in the mud. Who were the Rumanians? A fiction of the treaty of Versailles. Yugoslavia, Czechoslovakia—they were not real countries. Hungarians had occupied this land for over a thousand years, every Hungarian schoolchild knew.

It's not good for the Jews, she heard people saying at her grandmother's house. These Hungarian patriots would kill the Jews. Sophie said she wanted to fight for her country. They were all laughing. "They won't let you, you're a Jew." Every morning she prayed for the resurrection of Hungary.

Hungary was where you were born and really belonged; Hungary was your home, not the little red villa but a great expanse of land under the sky that went on beyond the hills of Buda. It was great mountains, lakes, forests, rivers. The Danube flowed from the Black Forest to the Black Sea. Hungary was the lowlands: the shepherd with his flock and dog. It was peasant girls wearing lace-hemmed skirts and boots, and fishermen mending nets on the shores of Lake Batalon. Shepherds, the lowlands, huts, wolves, storks, peasant girls and boys were more truly Hungarian than Budapest. All these things she saw in pictures, and drew in her class notebook with great care and love, the storks especially. Storks standing on one leg in a swamp. Stork nests on chimneys. The stork feeding its little ones. Storks in flight, that was the hardest to draw.

Fireworks on St. Stephen's Day, the celebration of the fifteenth of March when everyone wore a ruffled pin with the colors of the flag, some quite fancy with a crown in the center or the picture of the poet Petofi—all this belonged to the present together with NO, NO, NEVER stickers on every wall. Trianon was neither a place nor a treaty but an act of butchery: posters showed it clearly: a knife held in a hairy fist slicing the land. "Trianon" named the crime depicted on the poster. The answer to Trianon was: "No, no, never." Hungary was the four seasons, but mostly spring when the storks returned from Africa to build their nests; when the grass was new and very green. The red, white and green pins worn on the fifteenth of March belonged to that sense of freshness and expectation in the same way as the first snowflower. It was very hard for Sophie to imagine that it could be as truly spring anywhere else as in Hungary—because in Hungary it was already in the colors of the flag—the red, white and green in the blue sky: the red blood of soldiers who died for their country, the white for the snow and clouds, and the green for grass.

Why did she have to go to Hebrew lesson when her father didn't believe in God? One day she told her father she had had enough.

"Humanity isn't ready," he pleaded. Sophie was ready. "Shh," he said, "there is a patient in the waiting room." She took the Hebrew Old Testament from her schoolbag and flung it to the ground. It landed open, the pages all messed up near his foot just at the threshold of his office. Her father picked it up without a word. She took her schoolbag and went to her room.

.

PASSOVER was at Grandmother's, on the second floor of an apartment house in Pest, across the river. All the Landsmann family came to celebrate Passover at Grandmother's. Nobody in the family, with the exception of the aunts who married rabbis in far places, was religious. Not even Uncle Benji who lived with Omama because he was a bachelor, and worked in a hospital. He joked about religion and didn't observe the rituals outside of the house.

Religion was something old and shabby; it was a dusty ugly piece of furniture you were ashamed to have in your own house, even in the back room, but you couldn't get rid of it any more than you could get rid of Grandmother.

But there was another side to this. Religion was embarrassing; but you were proud to be a Jew. Why? Superiority of being a Jew was so obvious to everyone, her family looked dumbfounded and disapproving when Sophie asked. Jews were different from all other people, couldn't she see that? Of superior intelligence, they were too intelligent to be religious. Her father attributed his scientific mind, his atheism, to Jewishness. And conceded most reluctantly and with reservations that a non-Jew could be a truly great thinker. Specialists, technicians, artists, but when it came to facing the truth ... Nietzsche was the one exception. Her father quoted Nietzsche: "I'm not genius, I am dynamite."

It was very confusing. When she woke up in the morning or ran along the street jumping over puddles she wasn't Jewish. But at Grandmother's house you were Jewish: you did things religious Jews did. Being Landsmann and being Jewish were the same thing—that's

224 · SUSAN TAUBES

what was confusing. It was the way everybody talked, even Granny who was angry at them all, and wanted them to be different. If one of her children or grandchildren was praised voices rose, "Naturally, he is a Landsmann," or, "A Jew is always smart." A Landsmann child. A Jewish child. They meant the same. The only exception was Omama. She had her own excellence, neither Jew nor Landsmann. If anybody else in the family did something clever it was being Landsmann and Jewish. Omama made the greatest Passover feast because she was Omama.

Omama was a very angry, offended, suspicious old woman, sniffling at you from the moment you walked in, rubbing the material of your coat in her hand to assess the quality of the fabric, asking, How much did it cost? She looked you over, feeling your cheeks, arms, sides and hips like women at the butcher store buying a goose. "What's this?" she complained, shaking cousin Gabor's skinny arm. "You let him run around too much!" When Omama asked you what you did or what you ate, holding your arm, bending close over you, it wasn't in a friendly way but knowing everything without accepting it, and wanting to be able both to hate and to hope and be a little deceived, and having to pretend and preserve some humor and common sense; they should have a well-fed and well-to-do look at least, and this night they would eat her soup and matzah balls and fish and roast lamb and duck and this belonged to the excitement of Passover.

Omama knew that they weren't religious, she told them in so many words, a long speech or a scornful "Hmm!" They weren't fooling her; she knew and told every one of them, even the son who lived with her, what she knew, and as her anger mounted said it in Hebrew, short phrases, perhaps curses, spitting out each phrase. Omama's outburst was part of the Seder, with her looks of disgust and knowing and the muttering curses in Hebrew. Everyone looked down on the floor waiting for her to finish. Then the women murmured plaintively till a voice rose, her father's, to say, "You are right, Mama, we are hypocrites." Then he praised her, she was a great woman and exemplary in every way as a wife, as a mother; he recalled her acts of devotion and self-sacrifice, her service for public charity; he spoke with intensity, sometimes declaimingly but meaning it and wanting to declare and convince others. Speaking of how good she was as a mother, he was both moved and embarrassed. Then her uncle came in, bellowing, "We are not worthy," and went into a long praise of virtues in a cantor's chant. "It is true," her father put in periodically, in a low-voiced refrain. "It is true," he said with loud emphasis to terminate his brother's chant and, looking around the room at every one significantly, "We are a bunch of hypocrites. We are not worthy of Mama," he said with a sudden change of energy. The prerogative of the oldest male in the room and master of ceremonies clear in his voice: "Let's begin." There was a great commotion like backstage just before the curtain rises—Omama rushed into the kitchen; all the aunts and uncles were moving about the room to check if everything was in its place. Was the table setting exactly as it should be? Were there enough chairs? They were ordering each other around—fetch this, take away that. The children were told where to sit. Did everybody have a Haggadah? Did Gabor? Did Lizy? Did Mitzi? Did Sophie? Did Tibor? Talking too loud, all this to-do quite unnecessary, it annoyed Omama. Omama looked grieved. Papi held her hand. "Sit down," he told Uncle Isi, who gave him a hurt look. Papi adjusted his gray fedora. The men exchanged glances and started praying. Uncle Benji's hand reached across the table, trying to flap the page in Sophie's Haggadah to the right place. "Show her," Aunt Lea said to cousin Mitzi. Before she could read the translation, cousin Mitzi whispered it in her ear, in her sweet, smiley voice, her voice blond like her hair that tickled Sophie's cheek. Feelingfully taking little breaths in the tone she had for everybody that was always saying, I am the girl who makes everybody happy.

Everything about the Passover ceremony is strange: a book beside everyone's plate called the Haggadah tells about it. A picture shows how the table must be set; the text gives instructions between snatches of prayer for dipping greens, drinking wine, for breaking and eating matzah, for getting up, sitting down, for washing hands. It says what is being done and why and what it means. The youngest child is supposed to ask, Why is this night different from other nights? The question and answer are read from the Haggadah. The men sitting around the table in fedoras make it seem as if they were not really in a room; usually you did not see a man wear his hat inside the house unless he had just arrived or was just leaving. One of the men ranting and nodding at the other end of the table turns his head: it's Sophie's father and he smiles at her broadly with a wink as if they were at home, but he looks like someone else. It is her father wearing his gray-green fedora rather than the embroidered skullcap his mother gave him; he chants swaying back and forth, the expression on his face not like when he is just Papi or imitating someone else and ridiculing at the same time. Drawling, ranting, with strange jerks, he pushes the hat back on his head, his expression bored and arrogant. Now he is really a Jew praying, now he is making fun of a Jew praying. It's hard to tell, perhaps there isn't that much of a difference; perhaps that's how a Jew was meant to be praying.

The picture in the Haggadah shows a family at a Passover table: the child in the picture looks at the picture in the Haggadah of a child looking in the Haggadah. It has never been different than it is now: the family sitting around the table, the men in skullcaps, reading from the Haggadah; sometimes the matzah is round, sometimes it is square. The family sitting around the Passover table, this is what Passover is about, and God leading the Jews out of Egypt is just a story, mixed up with rules for people to argue about. Another picture shows the four sons at Passover: the wise son, the wicked son, the dumb son and the one too young to ask. There are also pictures of men in loin cloths carrying stones, and of the ten plagues.

A child easily loses its place . . .

She was bored. She looked at the pictures on the first pages as you opened the book, which was the end of the Haggadah. She stared at the picture of the Angel of Death:

> that slew the butcher, that slaughtered the ox
> that drank the water, that quenched the fire
> that burnt the stick, that beat the dog
> that bit the cat, that ate the kid

that Father bought for just two bits:
one kid, a lonely kid.

The stream of blood gushing from the throat of the ox was drawn like the water that put out the fire. The butcher's knife was bigger than the sword of the Angel of Death. The fire and water seemed wrong squeezed in the middle with cats and dogs and sticks and people. The Holy and Blessed One who smote the Angel of Death—how could that be believed, what did it mean? A hand reached over the table, the fingers turning the pages to the right page. It was her father or an uncle giving her a significant look. *"Rasha ma hu omer:* What says the wicked son?" Her uncle from Sarajevo, the rabbi with the great rectangular beard, translated in his funny Hungarian the words of the wicked son, "'Of what use is this service to you?'" To YOU and not to himself. By excluding himself from the community he has denied God, the Almighty. "Do thou, then, set his teeth on edge! Say to him: 'This is on account of what the Lord did for me when I went forth from Egypt.' For ME and not for him; had he been there, he would not have been redeemed."

A child is bound to be impressed by the passage in the Haggadah in which this cunning people predicts the deviant at every table, as if from the beginning; this too was a part of the Passover ceremony: the child who didn't see the point of it, a Jewish child, because, as the saying goes, being a bad Jew didn't make you any less of a Jew. It might very well make a child wonder what it means to be a Jew and it made Sophie, in particular, wonder if she owed the happy circumstance of being in Budapest to a chain of pious Jews beginning with some ancestor who went with Moses out of Egypt. For merely on the basis of the pictures in the Haggadah she would rather be herself than the Pharaoh's daughter. She pondered the lines said of the wicked son: Had he been in Egypt the Lord would not have delivered him. The argument which rested on the *if* broke and sent her flying in all directions. If she had been there . . . was she . . . could she have been there? Where was she at the time of the Pharaoh?

She heard a boy giggle. Her eyes fastened on the page, she sensed looks crossing the table and wondered if she was their target. But perhaps it was only to the sons all this applied. It was different for the daughters. They had no choice. One way or another they had to be good Jewish daughters. They were dark, grave and pious like her two cousins whose father was a big rabbi in Transylvania. Or they were gay, blond, pretty liars like cousin Mitzi who could hug Omama on her way to see a movie or drive in the country with her boyfriend on the Sabbath. A Jewish woman had no choice unless she was very wicked and a whore, like the women Omama warned her against, quoting from the Bible. Her mother was like that, Omama said, and there was the mother of her classmate who was married to an industrialist, the wealthiest Jew in Budapest, about whom she heard even more shocking stories. But the wicked woman, the whore, met only with disapproval, scorn and disgust. She was not utterly disowned like the wicked son.

"Why is this night different from all other nights?" the Manishtana begins, and the rest describes what is different in the table setting from other nights and from the Sabbath; it answers the first question and yet continues asking, "Why is it so?"

A legend is begun, trails off in digressions, quote within quote, commentary around commentary, with comments thrown in. Are they translating from the Hebrew? Is this irreverent remark or the joke about two Jews in a concentration camp also in the liturgy like the part about the wicked son? Off and on, a Hebrew phrase thrown in has the same ring as a cynical aside.

The men keep leaving the table to wash their hands. The women follow Grandmother into the kitchen. The children may leave their seats till the soup is served. It's all coming and going. Aunt Erzsi came by train from Transylvania with her husband and two daughters. And the man with the big gray beard came all the way from Sarajevo, which was in another country; and they would go back there and perhaps she would see them again next Passover at the same table or in Jerusalem; or perhaps they would all go to America or at least she and her father and Uncle Isidor and his family because Aunt Olga said Hitler would kill them and they had had enough. Grandmother wouldn't go. Nor Aunt Lea—her husband had a fine hardware store and they wouldn't leave that. Grandmother is hushing them, they should get on with the service, there has been enough interruption. The children will fall asleep before the meat is served if this goes on.

There comes the slow-paced chant, lovely like a long journey but again the voice breaks off—Uncle Jonas must tell an anecdote—it infuriates the child, even Grandmother is smiling. The men rise again to wash their hands. The roomful of people is transformed into those irreverent, scoffing, unruly Israelites, who grumbled against Moses for taking them out of Egypt, the land of plenty, who danced around the golden calf. Now it is Sophie's father who tells them to stop fooling around and get on with the service. They want to hear the ten o'clock news broadcast. They are rattling off the prayers fast to be finished before ten. You can get any city in the world on Uncle Benji's radio: you can hear Hitler and Mussolini, London and Tokyo: the children are very excited; they shriek out the ten plagues on Egypt.

In the spring of 1938 Passover at Grandmother's had the quality of a gathering for a massacre. And perhaps this is what being a Jew always meant. It began with slavery in Egypt and a God who led them out to be his chosen people, and then they were always strangers, wandering, remembering in the land of the stranger how God led them out; and waiting for the prophet Elijah to come through the door left open to him and drink the goblet of wine, and then he would immediately (or would they have to wait another year?) take them to Jerusalem, which was not a clear place—maybe in heaven where God was king, but also a country far away, the opposite direction from England and America, called Palestine where nobody really wanted to go; a place they joked about. It was always the strange stories and waiting for a prophet, but actually for something terrible to happen, a great punishment. The noise and confusion and joking at the table made her feel that: unruly children chasing around the apartment of the dead rabbi, both the grown-ups and the children screaming plagues of blood frogs, darkness on Egypt like in some grotesque comic opera.

THE RIPPERS were a funny, scattered family. To begin with, they didn't all have the same mother. Grandfather Ripper was married twice, they never came together as a family and Sophie wasn't quite sure how many they were; she heard stories about aunts in Serbia, Bosnia, Istanbul, and had a dim memory of seeing one or more as a small child, but it was not clear if they were her mother's half sisters or sisters of her grandfather's first or second wife. The one she heard most about was Buena Tante and probably she was her mother's and not Sophie's aunt.

The story they told about Buena Tante was that one day she got on a river ferryboat with a man without telling anyone, leaving her family just like that. Nobody knew what became of her till she wrote them a letter from Astrakhan some years later telling them she had a wonderful time going all the way to Kiev. And now she was very happy living in a fine house with someone else, a very rich man. And that's how she lived. She came to visit her family one day to show them her baby; she wasn't living with the rich man any more, she married someone else and she was very happy. Nobody ever met her husband. Nobody really knew anything about her life and perhaps when they didn't hear from her for a long time they started making up stories like she did, which may or may not have been true. But she came and visited every so often, always looking splendid and expensively dressed, even if in a somewhat funny Eastern style, and she had fine and healthy children and was always very happy. Even Papi couldn't explain Buena Tante. She was crazy, of course; the Rippers were all a bit crazy, he said, except for Rosa, and he'd talk about how old Ripper went cuckoo and how he'd driven his wife crazy and about Uncle Fritz who was a schizophrenic, and her mother—and then he'd tell the stories about Buena Tante; but when Sophie asked what was wrong with her, he shrugged, saying she had wanderlust, which didn't sound like a sickness.

Grandfather Ripper was a mean man; he loved his first wife very much and when she died he was heartbroken and married just to have someone to take care of the house and his three or four children. He didn't love his second wife; he kept her like a housekeeper and treated her worse than a servant. Grandmother Ripper suffered terribly from her husband but she was a fanatical woman and no matter how tyrannical her husband was, she outdid him in her obedience. She worked harder than even he could make her. The children wore only white and were always spotless, even if she had to wash and iron and sew night and day; and the girls were never permitted to do any manual work, to sweep the floor, or even enter the kitchen. Grandfather Ripper went cuckoo when he lost his fortune after the war. He spent all his time making complicated calculations to prove how rich he would be now if he had invested his money differently.

Aunt Rosa, her mother's older sister, was considered a great beauty; she was the woman her father ought to have married. Everyone told the story of how she escaped from Budapest at the time when they were shooting down all the communists, leaping on a moving train in her nightgown. She had lived in different countries, married to different husbands. Aunt Rosa lived in London now, she had a baby but wasn't married to anyone; she was a psychoanalyst like her father.

When Aunt Rosa came to visit them one summer with her little boy, who looked like a fat angel with blond curls and round blue eyes, and Grandmother Ripper, Sophie couldn't quite believe it. Aunt Rosa was a smiling, dark-haired woman, slightly older and shorter than her mother; she wore a suit—it was hard to imagine her as a young girl, barefoot in a nightgown and leaping on a moving train—she had become a different person and wasn't unhappy about it. It was upsetting the way Aunt Rosa and her mother hugged and kissed, her mother weeping how much it meant to her to see Rosa, how terribly she missed her, and Aunt Rosa's good-natured acceptance of her mother's adoration. She didn't understand what it meant to be sisters. And she wasn't prepared to see Grandmother Ripper, a strange, terribly bent old woman, in their house. She thought of Grandmother Ripper as always living in that shabby, yellowish apartment in Pest where Grandfather Ripper died.

They were a strange family, and real to Sophie like people in stories; these people she knew mostly from stories told about them; people who were either dead like Grandfather Ripper and his first wife; or Grandmother Ripper and Aunt Rosa who didn't live in Budapest, whom she saw only once; or the famous Buena Tante who didn't live in Hungary either, who may have been her mother's dead stepsister or her aunt, who lived in a foreign country. She remembered dimly a woman visiting from far away, dressed very fancy and colorful, laughing, with jewelry and fat arms, like she remembered things that happened before they moved to Buda.

Of her mother's two stepbrothers who lived in Budapest, Sophie mostly heard that they were small, unsuccessful, unlucky people.

Sophie saw her uncles once or twice a year. There was something special about the visits to her mother's relatives—it belonged to another life, like when she spent the day with the maid and her boyfriend. She went with her mother on the trolley; her mother was dressed more simply than usual. She had explained to Sophie before that they were going to see Uncle Jani or Uncle Emil to make them happy. They were always asking about Sophie and wanting to see her. Her mother knew it wasn't very interesting for Sophie to visit grown-ups and had made excuses for her, but she couldn't always refuse. Her mother explained it to her so nicely: The visit was a favor she was doing for her mother as well as the uncles so the uncles wouldn't be cross at her mother.

It was one of those rare occasions when she felt well with her mother. It was the way a picture in a schoolbook of a mother and her daughter in the trolley made her feel simply right and, at the same time, festive because it happened only on rare occasions. She watched her mother; and the way she chose a seat, paid for their tickets, and all her small gestures were new and different from the way she appeared to Sophie in the house. She talked nicely as if everything were always fine between them. It made Sophie feel guilty: maybe her mother was really this nice person all the time but everybody, including Sophie, was mean to her and didn't see her as she really was.

Her mother's brothers didn't act like relatives—as if she belonged to them and they were terribly important to each other. They seemed just like any other people, whom one was free to like or dislike and with whom one was naturally polite.

Uncle Jani was a small man with bushy gray hair and an old-fashioned moustache; everything about him, his shoulders and forehead, was always furrowed with worry. His wife was a very big, kindly and helpless-looking woman and it seemed especially horrible and unnatural to Sophie that a fat woman like that couldn't have children. They were really poor; they lived in one small room with a table, sofa couch, a buffet and some chairs, everything cramped and painfully neat. You had to go through the court to the toilet and Sophie didn't know if they had a kitchen. There was a bowl of fruit behind the glass of the buffet that Uncle Jani's wife put on the table, urging Sophie to take something. It was all the food they seemed to have, and they were saving it for guests. She didn't want to take it. Aunt Marta took an apple and, shining it with her sleeve, offered it to Sophie in an apologetic way—afraid Sophie really wanted something she didn't have in the house—so she took it quickly. She gave all her attention to eating the apple and showing how much she enjoyed it and not showing how awkward she felt because of the way Aunt Marta looked at her. Her mother was talking to Uncle Jani about money matters. Sophie knew she mustn't appear to be listening to them because it was embarrassing that her father was helping him out financially and Sophie shouldn't know about that. In a sense she was alone with Uncle Jani's wife looking at her with a strange helpless intensity, sad and yearning. Sophie knew she was terribly unhappy that she couldn't have a child, everybody had said it and here Sophie was, a child, not her child, eating an apple she gave her and this made Sophie feel very awkward.

Afterward when they were out in the street her mother always said they were good people, such poor people, kind people, unhappy people and thanked Sophie for behaving nicely. Then they took the trolley to one of the coffee houses by the Danube and had pastry and hot chocolate.

Uncle Emil was a bachelor and very different from the sad and timid Uncle Jani—he had a brisk manner and showed his gold teeth a lot and enjoyed talking gossip and money matters with her mother. They met in a coffee house. He had always a comfortable air about him and looked at home in the world the way he leaned back, motioned to the waiter or laughed about some rotten deal. Even if business was bad and he wasn't making out (and he didn't pretend he was a happy man or particularly enthusiastic about anything) he was still altogether at home in this world. His pale gray eyes scanned lightly or looked sharp and quick. They didn't have that trapped and baffled look of the Landsmanns. Both Uncle Jani and Uncle Emil were different from her father's brothers: they didn't try to make an important thing out of being uncles: they were probably just curious to see Sophie once or twice a year. They seemed so much like ordinary people that it was hard for Sophie to believe that they were Jewish.

Uncle Fritz, her mother's full brother, she didn't have to visit; he wasn't curious about her or interested in his family. But she knew him best of all her Ripper uncles through her father's frequent mention of him and his vivid evocation of Uncle Fritz wearing an elegant imported tweed suit, with breeches and cap, fancying himself an English duke, feigning a foreign accent, walking a wire-haired fox terrier along the *corso* on a red leash. She thought of Uncle Fritz exactly as her father pictured him to her, although she never saw him with a wire-haired fox terrier. Uncle Fritz was the incarnation of the sort of person her father found ridiculous. He couldn't even give a decent imitation of him. If Sophie wanted to have a wire-haired fox terrier, that was just like Uncle Fritz. If she said she wanted to marry Prince Peter of Yugoslavia or join the English Navy, that was like Uncle Fritz. Whenever she expressed dissatisfaction with what she found vulgar, drab, boring, ugly and meaningless, it was like Uncle Fritz and her father pulled out the picture of Uncle Fritz. Actually, he always concluded, Uncle Fritz was to be pitied. His mother dressed him like a girl with ringlets down to his waist till he was twelve—that's what made him crazy. He was a skin doctor. Her mother took her to his office one day. She had some scaly skin on her elbow and they'd ask his opinion what could be done with it. They sat in a narrow waiting room with other people. How sad it must be, Sophie thought, for a man who fancied himself an aristocrat to have to look at people's pimples and rashes. When he appeared in a white smock she saw him differently every ten seconds. A crazy man with a very triangular face and thick glasses. A youngish man with full lips. A skinny man, but with fleshy eyes and lips. The teeth, showing behind a slight sneer, reminded her of Charlie Chaplin. A man with blue eyes that didn't see her. Quick, sure hands. He was looking at her elbow in the waiting room. It was simple, he said, he could do it right now. He talked very fast with his eyes somewhere else. Her mother said they'd discuss it at home first. It was nice walking out of a doctor's office without being jabbed or burnt. And Uncle Fritz wasn't sad. He had a little sneer.

HER MOTHER never really lived in the house in Buda. It was not her real home even though she had the most beautiful room with the window overlooking the garden. The first time they knocked the walnuts off the trees, her mother wasn't there. She came and went like a visitor. Everybody was upset when she was in the house. Sophie didn't know where her mother lived when she was away but she had a glimpse of her mother's real world away from the house. It was only a glimpse of her mother with her boyfriend at the baths, the ski slope, a drive in the country, even if for a whole day's outing; still it could only be what can be glimpsed at random of a world Sophie knew didn't belong to her, which had no part for her, which, in fact, was flawed by her presence. No matter how nicely she was treated, she felt acutely both the loveliness of her mother's world and that her presence flawed it.

Glimpsed through the screen of her natural envy, loneliness, dismay, her sense of exclusion from a play for two with no part written for a daughter—none that Sophie could accept; still it was the beauty of her mother's romances Sophie experienced. The nicer her mother's suitors were, the more considerate, reserved, delicate, sensitive to the situation, the more hopelessly Sophie fell in love with them and the more she had to play at being a child.

On drives through city and country, the sights kept her busy. At the baths or ski slopes, she couldn't do the graceful things her mother could: dive, do the Australian crawl, elegant ski turns. This belonged to her mother with whom she would not compete; on the positive side, she could do more, do it longer, faster: jump from higher rocks, take icy, messy slopes that arty skiers would avoid. It was for the general good if Sophie preferred to stay in the water or on the snow while her mother and friend had refreshment or a rest. This was a kind of life she enjoyed to see her mother living, except they were too leisurely—too many breaks for tea and wine, too much lounging around. That was boring. But then she was different from her mother. But what really offended Sophie was when she saw her mother tease men who courted her, and treat them with condescension, cruelty, coyness. Men who were nice and good looking, why did she go out with them and keep on flirting if she disliked them. Was this what Grandmother meant about bad women? She would never be like that.

When her mother was happy with somebody she was so different; the whole world changed, soft and quiet and gentle. It wasn't that she was kinder or more affectionate to Sophie. No, she seemed just vaguely aware of Sophie, and sometimes she was quite oblivious of her presence, or when she noticed Sophie it was embarrassing; her voice took on a false ring. But mostly she was ignored by her mother's boyfriends and by her mother most of all. It was strange and new, both wonderful and disturbing, her mother's obliviousness and the fact that she wasn't making any demands on Sophie or blaming her. A harmoniousness that they did not normally enjoy seemed assumed by both. If her mother stroked her face or drew her in her lap casually while conversing, Sophie accepted it naturally. It wasn't like at home where her mother made it a problem. It was how Sophie liked it.

It was troubling to see her mother so changed, so much softer, more remote and really beautiful because there was that other mother she knew in the villa with her bad daughter; her husband who treated her as a joke or a case. There were other faces and voices and a different smile in other rooms. At home she watched her mother wash. She stood in silk panties, bent over the sink, splashing water on her arms, face and breasts. She recalled her father saying it was a pleasure to look at her, she had a fine torso, and her breasts were perfect hemispheres. Then her father came in, between patients. His voice shocked Sophie; it was so raspy, unmusical; it was a jesting, mock-affectionate tone with a bit of imitation peasant, the tone he used with the dog.

He said the same silly jingle he said to the dog, full of nonsense words. "On what does Pajtas fatten?" He named various foods. It ended: "Fattens most on his master's love." The dog loved it, he lay on his back, his paws in the air, drooling while Papi patted his white belly rhythmically. He did it to Sophie too, she never liked it and now he was patting her mother's buttocks like the dog's belly. She played along, then laughed at him for being such a bore. There was something very different in the ski lodge with her mother and her lover, Zoltan Vithezy; she wasn't sure what it was because it couldn't be hers, except she felt robbed of whatever it was. Her father couldn't know because he didn't have it. And her mother, who had it, always told her that her father was the sweetest and kindest man on earth. He was the person she loved most in this whole world. Whatever love Sophie had she owed to him, not to her, her mother said with so much feeling and tears in her eyes Sophie had to believe her. It was another tone she used with her father, simpering, affected, lapsing into baby talk— a tone her father detested. Her father disapproved of her mother, and Sophie was made to be her father's ally. She was glad her mother had admirers and a nice friend like Zoltan. No matter what her mother said, and no matter what people were saying against her mother—that she was a bad wife and mother—Sophie felt her mother was a woman wronged, robbed of her child. She was relieved her mother had a lover. To think of her alone, banished from the house, was intolerable.

Zoltan Vithezy wanted to marry her mother. He was different from mother's other boyfriends because he wasn't so pronouncedly athletic, and handsome, and always tanned. He was tall, fair and kind; not dashing or mannered in the expected way. His smile was always surprising. Maybe he wasn't really handsome. What struck Sophie most was that he was big. People said her father was tall but Vithezy stood at such a height that to enter through a normal doorway he had to draw in his head like a turtle for which reason he was nicknamed Teenie. Otherwise, he had no distinguishing features, unless his baldness which, however, due to his extraordinary height, went unnoticed. Sophie, who rode piggy-back on him, was in a position to note both his bald pate and the long blond hairs which still adorned it. Papi treated Zoltan in a friendly but somewhat patronizing way and he didn't make fun of him. They had long discussions and seemed to respect each other.

Zoltan behaved toward Sophie differently from the others. Even if her mother was divinely oblivious to Sophie, sometimes Zoltan liked to pretend that they were a family. He went about it in a funny way, perhaps because Sophie was a funny little girl or because he was so tall and in a funny position. Also he was a quiet, thoughtful man, brooding, not talkative. It was her mother who would start him, joking about his being taciturn. But even though he was preoccupied with himself and then with her mother, suddenly he would want them to be three people and he went about it in a big way, lifting Sophie up and dancing—holding her by the waist while her feet dangled in the air, he waltzed or put her on his back, riding piggyback, even when she was too big for that. They were putting on a show for her mother. Or he put on a show with her mother for Sophie. Sophie and her mother didn't have to put on a show for him, that would have been impossible. Ordinarily, she would have been embarrassed especially to watch him putting on a show with her mother, but she was too impressed by his strength and suddenness. He lifted her mother like a feather. "Shall I throw her out the window?" he asked. She saw even her mother was stunned and confused, protesting, giggling hysterically.

She knew that she mustn't like her mother's lover too much even if she wasn't clear about why. Even with Zoltan who was like a second daddy it was safer to be on joking and playing terms. Long before the divorce, her mother asked her how she'd like him for a daddy. While she was ready to oppose, displease, deny her father for a cause, she couldn't hurt him. And to prefer another man to your father was a hurt. No one asked Sophie if she preferred Zoltan Vithezy to her father, but even to ask her if she liked him was like asking her how she felt about something she was not ready to feel, like asking you do you like oysters—someone who hasn't tasted oysters and isn't ready to.

THE DAY everything changed it seemed like it happened to someone else, another child, an undefined stranger, was trying to grasp the deception, the endless loss; the loss of both the world and the person to whom it naturally belonged who was beginning to feel at home in the world which was strange enough, with its meadows, trees, and sky and the only world there was. Then suddenly it was brought home it didn't belong to Jews: it was other people's world—Hungarians, Germans, French, Russians—and they might let Jews live on their earth and even own a house or a shop for a while but then they'd want them to move on and nobody really wanted them. It had to be so, the Jews weren't meant to feel at home anywhere; the fields, orchards, horses, cattle, rivers and sky were not for Jews and not what Jews wanted or should want because they were singled out by God to be different, singled out for a different destiny.

The double loss of a world and of the person who belonged to that world was experienced by an anonymous schoolgirl in a sailor-blouse uniform and high brown laced shoes. Sophie Landsmann, the name on the trolley pass, who was she?

In the gymnasium a child's eyes were studying the legs extending from the black shorts of the class lined up against the wall: their form and proportion, the different skins—pale and ruddy, hairy, smooth—asking what were the distinguishing signs, because one pair of legs didn't belong in the room, in this building in Budapest or anywhere on earth.

From the fall of 1938 till the spring of 1939 no one knew whether Rudolf Landsmann and his daughter would really be going to America. School occupied most of her days, and the long trolley ride from Pest to her school in Buda and back. Everything hinged on a piece of paper.

One Sunday morning in the spring of 1938 her mother invited Sophie to her bed.

"Would you be very unhappy," her mother asked, "if I left the house and married Zoltan?" They had been discussing the question of the divorce, her mother continued; her father and she had decided it would be for the best, but they wouldn't do anything against Sophie's will. Her father was worried that Sophie would be unhappy if they separated. "But I know you wouldn't be unhappy—" her mother was smiling, she spoke with great verve. "We were always good friends," she told Sophie and she hoped they would be even better friends in the future, however she was quite sure Sophie wouldn't miss her. She would want to stay with her father, naturally; she had always preferred her father. Her mother understood how Sophie felt. The conversation they were having was just a formality; it was to reassure her father. In a sense she was asking for Sophie's permission but really telling Sophie that it was to her advantage.

"You will have your father all to yourself like you always wanted," her mother said gaily; "you will have two fathers."

The divorce wouldn't change anything, her mother went on; Papi and she would always be the best friends, and whenever Sophie needed her mother or felt like seeing her...

She was staring at her mother's rings which had always fascinated her. She heard the sound of the gardener raking the gravel under the window. Looking up she noticed her mother's breakfast tray with the broken eggshells on the chair. She had eaten and her face was painted; she was wearing a peach-colored satin bed jacket, the same color as the pillow case. Her mother's eyes were very bright, her mouth quavered.

"Aren't you a little sad I'm leaving?" she asked.

Her father asked her afterward if her mother had spoken to her and told her.

"Well, that's how it is," he said. "A divorce is not a good thing…
But under the circumstances…" He spoke in the tone he used for
unpleasant matters, as if he were talking about other people's troubles.
"I couldn't live with your mother any more," he said, "we are too
different. I want my peace."

She sensed uneasily her father's new position and that he was not
the sweet, good man her mother and his family made him out to be.
He was getting rid of her mother because she annoyed him; fortunately
there was someone who wanted to marry her. But he didn't like the
whole thing. From the way he pronounced the word "divorce," Sophie
sensed it was something ugly, sad and terrible; but she didn't know
how to apply it to him or her mother or herself who were never really
a family.

It was both sad and exciting to think of her mother marrying
Zoltan. Sophie was impatient to see her mother's new house; she
looked forward to living in two houses. She wondered if when her
mother left she would have her room or whether her father would
sleep there. But her mother didn't leave right away; even after she was
married all the furniture and some of her things remained in her
room. She didn't visit her mother and Zoltan—their place wasn't
ready or they were away on a trip. Her father told her that he might
go to America. Uncle Isidor and his family were definitely planning
to leave Budapest. He hadn't decided yet. Perhaps he and his brother
would join them in America a year later. They would decide about
all this in the fall.

She spent the summer with her father and his sister in Dubrovnik.
When they returned to Budapest she learned that the villa was going
to be sold. They stayed there briefly. There was a lot of packing to be
done. Sophie went to live with her grandmother. Her father came to
see her there. After the house was sold he stayed in a hotel and she
saw him only at Grandmother's with the family. Uncle Isidor, Aunt
Olga, and their two sons whom she didn't know very well before came
to visit at the same time. They talked about Hitler, money matters
and whether her father would get his visa. Sometimes Uncle Isidor
addressed her in his loud, unnatural voice that made the most ordi-

nary remark sound preposterous. "You will go to America on a big boat, can you believe that," he boomed, his round, childish face frozen in a military mask. "You, Landsmann Sophie, will go to America. And do you know what you'll be called in America? A 'kid'! A 'kid'!" he bellowed woefully, then burst into laughter. Sophie would deny this, insisting that a kid was a small goat. Then Uncle Isidor and her father would give imitations of a typical American, slouching, hat pushed back, thumbs behind suspenders, chewing gum and picking their teeth; soon cousin Gabor joined in. The men enjoyed this game. But Aunt Olga got mad when Gabor put his feet on the table. He was only showing how men sat in America, but his mother was really offended. "In my house you will not put your feet on the table," she said.

She was leaving; it was almost certain, probably in March, maybe as soon as February. They would go by ship. For a whole week they would live on a ship as big as the Duna Hotel, with shops, movies, a swimming pool. Her father brought her pictures of trans-Atlantic steamers. When they talked about going to America she didn't think about leaving Budapest or what it would be like in America, but only about living on a ship and actually crossing the Atlantic Ocean. By the middle of March it was certain that they were going, there were the tickets for the *S.S. Aquitania* leaving Le Havre on April fifth and the train ticket booked from Budapest through Paris.

Sophie's meetings with her mother during these months were infrequent and irregular. Her mother's involvement in her new life apart from her father and herself, lent her a new allure and even created a new closeness between them. On the few afternoons they spent together Sophie observed that her mother dressed more simply, living in fact under more modest circumstances than in her father's house. She seemed more affectionate than before, and at the same time gentle and subdued. Now her mother was like a friendly stranger with whom she in turn could be friendly, and for the first time she felt they were intimate, discussing things she did not talk about with her father and his family because she did not feel this respect between them and herself. The possibility of Sophie's going to America may also have created a new sense of closeness. But when her mother suddenly exclaimed, "You will go to America and leave me!" she didn't know what to say. She endured in silence her mother's tears at their separation, her ambiguous reproaches against fate and herself—against her daughter who was tearless; she couldn't entirely believe her mother's sincerity, that she was inflicting such a blow by going to America. She had not chosen to go to America with her father, but her mother demanded that she assume the role of a child she invented. Her mother had her own story of the wonderful, adorable, handsome Rudi going off to America with his lucky little girl; and even if she couldn't entirely believe in her father as a demigod, she wanted Sophie to believe it. But her mother understood that her tears only hardened Sophie's heart and surprised her by taking her side: her mother loved and respected the person she was who had no patience for a mother's tears, who had her own will and destiny, who would let no one, neither father nor mother, stand in her way and in whom her mother took pride. At exalted moments Sophie would be torn between two temptations: to incarnate her mother's vision of her strong-willed ambitious daughter, whose lack of attachment to family was not only forgiven, but encouraged, and to entrust herself to her mother who truly understood and would help her attain whatever ambitions she had envisaged for her. But if secretly she considered that she might be happier staying with her mother, she also understood that this was not a real possibility. On occasions her mother would daydream with her about their life together—but only supposing her father was not granted the visa. Her mother's wistful make-believe, Sophie understood, was not only conditional, but predicated on its denial: on the child who could not be swayed, who would not be groomed or guided by her mother. However touched and tempted by these seductions, she understood that her mother wasn't serious—she made it clear enough by breaking off each time she reached the climax of her invitation— the issue had been sealed by her daughter. Sophie listened to her mother, now charmed, now angry, but all the time looking behind her mother's words for the real reason why she couldn't make a genuine offer: whether she was lying to her or helpless or both. And finally, looking into her own heart, where she couldn't find any truth either, left her baffled and resigned. Everything had become so strange. From the time of her mother's marriage to Zoltan she had seen nothing of him; he vanished like the house. Whenever her mother burst into tears, Sophie lapsed into angry silence, thinking: In America I won't see you cry. I won't miss you. I'll never feel sad. She was going to America where everything was white and very modern; in America she would speak and write and think in English and forget Hungarian.

But sometimes after seeing her mother it was she who cried, waiting at the trolley stop in the early evening, suddenly every portal, tree, shop window, chance passer-by seemed unspeakably beautiful and happy. And to think that all this was made meaningless for her because she was Jewish; her walks through the city, the long trolley ride twice a day, crossing the Chain Bridge, the school day, her pride in her homework made questionable when they began talking about leaving, then made totally meaningless when it was certain that she was going. She was waiting, counting off the days till she would get on the train. And at the same time she did her schoolwork with the same care, precisely because it was meaningless. At Grandmother's she spent her time playing endless games of Monopoly with cousin Tibor, Aunt Lea's thirteen-year-old son. After a while she moved into cousin Tibor's room in Aunt Lea's apartment. Aunt Lea brought them their meals in the room because they wouldn't leave the game. Her husband was cross at how Sophie's presence upset the household, but they let it go since it was only for a short time before Sophie was going to America.

The morning of departure you feel nothing. This is how it should be, must be: the curious absence of feeling on the morning for which there had been so much preparation; drinking your hot chocolate, only half aware of the voices and faces of aunts and cousins you are leaving behind. Should a spoon feel different in one's hand this morning? Everything is unnatural. Immune to the excitement that possesses relatives accompanying you to the station. It's their day. You are departing and invulnerable. Unresponsive to their asking eyes. Cousins' babble, aunts' sentimentalities and repeated commentary that today was the day, crying out, "You are leaving us!" Voices repeating the old instructions and what to tell her father in Paris and what things to remember—none of this annoyed. It was the same pleasant numbness like before you were operated on. This is how it must happen, at such moments you should be absent. It's like when your tonsils are taken out.

On the train platform just before mounting the wagon, the numbness was shattered by the hissing steam and sudden excitement, the real hands, bodies of the last embraces clutching, admonishing, till once again safe inside the train compartment. These last awful moments that had to be endured, standing still like a statute before the window, family cluster on the platform waving hankies, making faces, mouths shaping words. The thought occurs that the train will not move, this moment will be prolonged into eternity, of the family cluster waving handkerchiefs and Sophie standing expressionless by the window like a statue forever. Slowly the train begins to move, a jolt and a few chugs; you stand solemnly for a long time, as the train picks up speed, wheels sing, buildings fly past, now her journey was beginning.

It was a strange venture for Sophie Blind to write about what it was like to be a child in Budapest. The person who would be writing it wasn't there, not as she was now. She was writing in English in a New York City apartment. The child was in another country, in another language. She who was writing had not been there, couldn't be there, then. But she could go back. Sophie Blind now in New York could go back. The child cannot, never having left. There is always that part which remains, continues, captive in its moment, and another that escapes. Someone else has somehow entered into the coming moment, a shadowy figure hurrying along a train platform with a suitcase, clutching her handbag and coach tickets. A woman in a traveling cape or a child holding on to her, they blur in the steam rising from the wheels, hastening along the train platform to their coach, one among the crowd of figures, passing, unregistered, as a gentleman sitting by the window of one of the first-class coaches looks up from the page of a book to rest his eyes for a blank instant and returns to his reading.

FOUR

A BRIGHT flurry in the hall. —Mummy, look! Presents! They can't wait, running from their suitcases, unwrap the packages themselves. Toby, all legs, laughter and flying hair, waving a woven mat before my face; Jonathan, like an apple-cheeked, curly cherub out of a painting, brings a bowl.

—I made it myself, do you like it Mummy?

—Lovely... I'm astonished at their splendid, solid limbs.

—Did you weave that, Toby?

—Sure, we have a loom, it's easy. —Look Mom! Joshua spreading a pile of large glossy prints on the living room floor, beautiful faun-faced dancer. And the way his eyes light up suddenly, the bold ironic look like Ezra's old magic in the room.

—Joshua, is that you?

—And here I play a drunken peasant. I helped direct it too. Can we mount them and hang them up?

—Mummy where are you going to put my bowl?

—Oh Mummy you must buy me some yarn...

—Children, take off your coats, you've just arrived...

—I'm going to see my room.

—Me too.

—And then let's talk...

—Did you know Cherie had a colt and we named it "Especially-me"?... and did I write you about the bears? Yes! They really come right up to the fence.

—Say, the apartment looks nice!

—So let's talk, Mom. Any good movies in town?

My ears hum. Enlarged to a mere outline, I'm barely in the room reading Jonathan his father's postcard.

Here for a visit from their Adirondacks country childhood; they've found the TV and their doodads, discovered the goodies in the fridge and poke around my desk. The word "home" still rings strange. They unpack their toilet kits and I give them each a towel...

Cornflakes under the sofa, footprints on the wall, the doorknobs sticky with jam...Why is Jonathan's shoe on my desk? Toby rushes down the corridor to look at herself in the hall mirror, got up in my fur hat and textured tights.

—Gross! she shrieks. Oh gross!

—On you it looks good. Now will you please sweep up—

—I will. I will, she sings, rushing off. —Anyway it wasn't me.

—Jonathan, put away... He can't; Joshua tied him up in his sleeping bag, he is happy regressing. —Oh Joshua, you beast! Joshua come here! Doesn't hear; glued to the idiot tube in his room, shades drawn, crouches hypnotized at the foot of the unmade bed surrounded by comics, candy wrappers, half-eaten cupcakes and empty Coke bottles. Looks up absently.

—So what are the plans? Can we go to Palisades Park?

—Children I want you to settle down.

—But Mummy, we're on vacation!

A small delegation from another world, they sit on my bed while I drink my coffee. They count the cigarets I smoke; tell me my hair is too red; want to know how much money I have in the bank; they ask why I don't get married again. —Don't you think Bill is handsome? Do you see him when we're not here? I haven't the heart to tell him his hero is queer.

—Mummy is there anyone you like?

—Don't you get lonesome living all by yourself? Jonathan asks.

Toby says, When I marry I'm going to live in a big house in the country with animals and have lots of children and I won't send them to boarding school.

—So what are plans for the summer?... But Mom, aren't we going to Europe with you?... But why?

—Because it's Daddy's turn this summer...

—Have you planned things for us to do for the month we're in New York? Toby asks.

—Mom, I wish I could go to Europe with you, Joshua sighs. We've had such nice times together... Remember Greece? And the boatride from Dubrovnik to Venice?... The first time I was on a boat and you tied me to some post on a dog-leash—oh, I remember that so well! Was I only two? Wasn't Yugoslavia cool, and remember the house of the Turk on that long bus trip we took... Yes, Mostar—remember when he showed us his grandmother's underpants, big enough for an elephant, to show us what women used to be like in the good old days? Oh it was gross and we had to pay for the rosewater; and you wouldn't let me dive off the bridge when the local boys were doing it for money... And remember in Ibiza in that farmhouse the night the bottle of butane gas burst into flames; Toby and Jonathan were asleep upstairs and I was so scared I started screaming; you said we had to get it outside the house because it could explode and you told me to go outside and wait and I saw you come out carrying that thing all in flames I was so scared it was going to explode before you threw it down the cliffs and afterward when I asked you whether you weren't scared and if it could have killed you, you just said, "It didn't explode so why talk about it? Now go to bed"...Yes you did, in exactly that tone. God!...and then in the Barcelona flood, oh I'll never forget that—the water streaming and crashing down and you were pulling me in the dark, remember it happened while we were in the movie the water was up to our waist—

—Don't exaggerate.

—Listen I was only seven, it was up to my waist and then I stepped into some kind of hole and the water came up to my chin and I said, "Look, Mummy, look!" and you looked at me perfectly calm like everything was normal and said, "Joshua, stop screaming, this is a flood." God! I couldn't believe it. My own mother...Well you know you were not an easy mother...you have to remember that I was just a little boy and you were this big tall silent woman in black with angry eyes and hair like a witch—Mom, you were scary!

—Anyway, Joshua, you were always a good traveler. Remember the time we missed our train connection on our way to Rome from Brindisi?

—Oh yes, the great chess game! We got off at this place in the middle of nowhere at midnight and played chess till three in the morning and I won!

—Who is that? Is that you? Voices call from the living room. The box of old photographs spilled on the floor.

—Mummy come here you have to tell us; we don't know most of these people. Tell them about Omama and Grandfather Moses...

—My ancestor. Cool. Joshua fascinated by the picture of Reb Smuel of Nyitra. —He has a face just like Lenin.

—No other resemblance I'm afraid.

—And he was a very great rabbi?

Tell them what a creep; petty provincial reactionary...

—Look Mom you have to think of the times he lived in, you can't judge him by our standards... So he was for the *ancien régime*...

My tolerant American children.

—I mean when you study history you realize... Take Stalin for example...

—C'mon Mummy show us all the pictures. What happened to the ten children? Tell them the sins of the fathers; the sons whose teeth turned on edge. —I guess our grandpa is the only one who made it...

—Uncle Joske isn't a failure. Look, he did his thing. A professional soccer player, that's not a bum. Now he's over eighty and still working as a doorman for a swank hotel. I bet he is happier than Grandpa because he isn't so lonely...

—What's a concentration camp? Were they your cousins? Did they really do that to people? But why? Why did they want to... The look of incomprehension and horror on Jonathan's face like my father's.

—What about the three daughters? Did he ruin their lives too?... You mean they couldn't marry anyone they liked... Oh gross! I'm glad I don't have to live in those times... Oh here you are!... Mummy and Daddy gazing at each other tenderly.

—Yes, just after we were married.

—Was that the style?

—Did you and Daddy ever take a vacation together? Tell them about the summer in Maine—the one time Ezra came with me, only because a French Hegelian was there, hitching to the post office twice a day hoping for a letter from a colleague when he wasn't talking *en-soi* and *pour-soi* with that Paris pothead ... the one time he came to walk with me on the beach at night, doing me a big favor, it was full moon, I begged him, dragged him, and he stood behind the tide-line, wouldn't take off his shoes and after a moment's profound meditation said, Nature is silent. And turned back ...

—Not even before you started fighting? Toby asks. But how come?

—You know Daddy; he liked to be in cities with libraries and bookstores and cafés, to sit around and talk.

—God! Joshua exclaims, why did you marry him then—I mean you're just so completely different. How can you marry someone with whom you have nothing in common! ... Why can't you explain to me then what you had in common ...

Those were strange times, my bunnies, when your father preached dialectical theology and we both lived it. —Someday I'll tell you ...

—I hate parents who say that ... and what about all those mysterious trips you took with Daddy, Joshua pounds on, you know what I mean, before I was born ... Is this a trial, what's eating him? Listening, his eyes narrowed as I tell him, no mystery, son, your father taught at different universities and so ...

—Why did you like traveling so much? Did you really like being in Jerusalem? It sounds gross. Just when you should be making something of yourself, when you were about to become an actress—how could you go to a gross place like Jerusalem?

—Oh peace, Joshua ... You won't till I explain how I could be so stupid ... But everything was so different when I was growing up—no, I don't mean like old-fashioned. It was the war. We were just stunned. The things that had happened and that after they happened everything could just go on as before ... it made one's personal future somehow irrelevant. I don't know how to explain.

—I guess I'm different, he says. My personal ambitions are more important to me than anything that happens in the world . . . If the whole human race is destroyed, then of course . . . he concedes. But did you want to get married and have children? Oh I'm just curious. I can't wait till I'm old enough . . . Can I have a girl when I'm seventeen? Sixteen? Did I tell you, I kissed a girl already. Please don't go yet. I never have a chance to talk to you, you're always busy with Toby and Jonathan. Tell me, when you went out with Daddy before you were married . . . Did you go dancing and to the movies? . . . You didn't! . . . What did you talk about? . . . Tell him. Nihilism. The sanctification of life. The death of God . . .

—You liked the way he talked, he says understandingly. That's one thing about Daddy, he is intelligent. No one can beat him in philosophy.

The gaiety of table setting with Jonathan's puppets helping, Toby's prettily folded napkins. —Thanks for remembering the ketchup, Mom. And the gooky juice we like. As Joshua brings it in with some fancy juggling. Nice children. Why suddenly this awful feeling when everyone is seated. Of just this. Just us. Always at family meals. With Ezra too, only then the burden of the awfulness wasn't all on me.

—How is the roast?

—Very tasty.

—Mom, let's talk about something. Let's have a conversation.

—Well?

—I'm thinking.

Jonathan says, Daddy writes he has a room for you. So why can't you come and stay with us?

—Because she doesn't want to and little children should mind their own business, Joshua tells him, disgustingly condescending; then crisply, changing his tone for the debating society: Tell me, Mom, what are your opinions on the war in Vietnam; are you for escalation or . . .

—Let's not talk about depressing subjects like war, Toby protests.

—Why not? It's a major national issue.

—Because you're going to quarrel and I don't want to get killed in an atomic explosion and words I don't understand give me a headache.

—Don't get upset, baby; we'll talk about . . .

—That's right, humor her! Let's all humor her.

—Leave me alone, she screams.

—Joshua, I said enough! Too late, the ketchup is flying.

—It's all right, Mom, I have her under control.

—Joshua, you beast!

—That's right, she spills ketchup all over the place, he says mopping it righteously, she scratches me on the face and I'm a beast. Look!

—I'm glad you're bleeding, Toby bawls.

—Toby, leave the room.

—Why don't you tell him to leave the room . . .

—And Jonathan is the good boy, the good boy, Joshua lays it on, viciously patting him on the head.

—Can't you make him shut up! Toby cries.

—Yes! Why can't you? Joshua taunts. C'mon Mom let's have a showdown. Springing gaily on the table, does his karate chops. An authority crisis! he announces. And look at her: imperturbable; inscrutable.

—Get off the table and you, Jonathan, don't giggle when your brother behaves like a—

—A clown! Now watch me do . . . He's off on another tangent, imitating Chaplin.

—Enough! Next year you go into summer theater and that's all. That's all!

—All this screaming has really given me a headache, Toby complains. Just tell me where the aspirin is. Jonathan, his face in the bowl, still in stitches. His turn to go mad.

—You should really meet Elizabeth, Toby chatters on, drying the dishes. You'd like her, Mummy.

—Elizabeth?

—You know, Elizabeth, Daddy's new wife; I don't know if she is really his wife but she lives with him and it's like they're married, anyway you'd like her because she is very sensible; she is a teacher and drives a Porsche—you should see it. Oh it's really beautiful, white outside with red leather seats, and she plays tennis and goes horseback riding with us and she tells Daddy what to do. She really makes him behave. Like suppose we're doing something and Daddy rushes in with a catastrophe, she just raises her index finger like this and says, "*Moment!*" and that stops him ... You know it really stops him. He doesn't shout and curse when she is there. It's only when she isn't there that he starts carrying on, calling us bad names ...

—No Toby, he wasn't like that when I married him ...

—Can people change that much? Mummy, when you marry some-body can't you know what they're going to be like? Because when I get married I want to be absolutely sure. Did you think when you married Daddy that you might ever get divorced? ... So ... she ponders, even when you think you're absolutely sure ... But you changed too! ... except if you hadn't married Daddy I wouldn't have been born and I wouldn't like that, so I'm glad you did ...

Jonathan in the bathtub. —I hate the way the boys at school tease me ... the things they tell me ... It's so disgusting I have to whisper it in your ear ...

—I thought you knew, Jonathan. Why disgusting? Our bodies are made for it.

—You mean it's true! Did you do that with Daddy?

—Of course; how do you think you were born?

—How disgusting. I'll never do it. (Wrapped in a towel, a desert saint at nine.) Do you still do that with men?

—Of course.

—How often? he asks.

—That's none of your business.

—There is something else. The boys said there is something even worse than fucking. But I can't tell you. Do you know what?

—No. Worse than fucking? ... then whisper it ...

—It's when boys do it to each other. Is that true?...I think it's disgusting. I won't get married when I grow up. I'll be a priest...

—But Mummy, you're not leaving us all alone!

—I told you I was going out for dinner with a friend.

—Why can't we go too?

—Why can't you tell us who? What's the big secret?

—She has a date and it's none of your business, Joshua tells them. My advocate. —You're going like that? he asks. How come you're not dressed up?

—Really! You behave like the worst parents...Tell them I'm just meeting an old friend at a deli...Now they're really indignant.

—That's all! Leaving us alone just to...Big schmear!...next time I'll put on my mother's fur coat and tell them...

—Just go, Mom, and leave everything to me, Joshua with an evil gleam in his eyes.

—Mummy, you can't! He'll torment us! Toby cries, but she is already screaming with delight as she leaps aside, casting hopeful looks at her tormentor.

—Well, why don't you go! Giggling, they push me out the door.

Variety at least, one would think—or the married woman would suppose, like the settled person supposes the traveler has variety at least—but it's the sense of repetition that saddens, even when it's very pleasant she has the old feeling, here I go again; it seemed all right for many years, it seemed the very essence of herself to feel here I go again getting laid, the limbs twining, the fingers running up and down tracing ear, shoulder, haunch, the womb beginning to rise; pulled along with it, the spirit remains an observer on a dizzying ride. To feel here I go again being laid like every woman since Eve and enjoying it was how it should feel in marriage, all right if it's not going anywhere, it's a reaffirmation, a repeat, the old lay. And now it's again like this; except it's not carried into sleep and through the next day, giving the daily chores and cares, all the varied offices of this strange coexistence of two, its impertinent validity. The ease with which she leaves the scene because she isn't chained to this room by marriage or love feels so odd. Riding up Broadway in a taxi, a free woman, if this moment she is less lonely than she had been with Ezra, does she miss the heavy old misery? Even when it has a kind of perfection like with X—it was in his country, she made the voyage, successfully transplanted and transformed into a creature of his planet, the phantom image of her alienated self persisting through the act and for days after... And that won't do either.

—Why aren't you in bed, Joshua? It's three in the morning.

—Mom, I'm so sad. Stay with me a little. Do you think life has any meaning?

—You behave like a clown all day and at three A.M. you ask me if life has any meaning.

—What do you expect? Fourteen, he says. *C'est l'âge bête.* I know I'm horrible and give you a hard time but I can't help it.

—You're not even trying.

—I know. Don't you think I know. I don't even try to improve myself. Oh I feel sick. I keep thinking that I'm going to die. One day I simply won't exist. Nobody will remember me. So why bother?

—We all have to die, I say, savagely cheerful. Disgusting how he wallows like his father.

—God! you're a real comfort.

—If you thought about death seriously for one minute...

—Why don't you believe I'm serious? You think I'm shallow, don't you? Maybe you don't care. But I hate to have to die. If we have to die—life is stupid.

—And so?

—What do you mean, "and so?"

A closed figure, hands clasping knees, his mother, I sit on the floor the incarnation of life's stupidity. The silence growing vertiginous, my body's surface like a black cloth absorbs his angry baffled look. I am the abyss. Can't tell him I mean Yes, life is stupid, fifteen years ago in a furnished room in London pleading with Ezra I wanted to run out of this world and he said, Yes, I'm going to give you a child this time to root you in life; I didn't believe it was possible; life couldn't begin in such darkness and he said, Yes, in just such darkness. And in uttermost exhaustion of all hope and love and understanding, his father explained with dialectical theology. And now here you are, my boy.

—Don't you really care? he asks, dismayed.

—Don't you know that I do and that I love you and that I know that you're a good boy; even when I seem annoyed and don't come up with answers, you must always know that.

—I know, Mom. I just like to talk.

—Joshua, lovey, it's very late.

—I'm sorry, Mom.

—Let's have some hot chocolate and go to sleep.

—I'll make it, he says. Mom, aren't you really afraid of death?

—Of dying, yes, when I cross the street. But the thought that I'm going to be dead one day, that doesn't bother me at all, I feel it's right and just as it should be. Sometimes I think women find death less of a problem than men. The real problem is not death—

—Well naturally, he cuts in. Because a woman has less to gain from life than a man.

—You don't say...

—A woman's life, after all...The fact is it's a man's world. Solemn, wide-eyed, telling his mother the obvious painful fact. When you think what a man can achieve, I mean...

—But Joshua, can you imagine living forever? Can you really?... That's wonderful.

—Kids stop that racket I'm on the phone. It's Kate.

—Oh can we go to Kate!

—She promised to hypnotize us.

—Oh please!

—I told you we're going Sunday. We're just discussing it.

"Think it over," Kate says, "he is well-preserved for fifty-two and—"

"No Kate, not a shrink and hung-up on Jung—please!"

"O.K. O.K. No shrinks; no Hindu gurus, no Jewish intellectuals or media men, over thirty-five and available...Lady, forget it!... What a pity," she sighs. "You really do like men don't you...But when you think of all the ways of creative self fulfillment, the many many worlds without and within—is twoness all that important?"

"The presence is important."

"You can get one in Japan."

"What do you mean?"

"Didn't you know they made them in Japan absolutely life-like, body temperature at 96.8 with secretions and everything—weight, skin and hair texture—a beautiful quiet presence; and doesn't talk..."

"But I want him sometimes to talk."

"He could easily be programmed to say something every ten minutes."

"I don't believe it. You know people who actually own one?"

"Sure, rich people in Hollywood. They cost from a thousand dollars up. A Marilyn Monroe dummy might cost..."

"How ghastly..."

"But it works. Men swear they can't tell the difference. Now I don't know any woman who has one but there's no question they'll have the perfect computerized dummy in another twenty-five years—maybe ten."

"Too bad. Right now I could really use a rent-a-vacation mate..."

"It's no joke. They're working on it. He'd be programmed to speak in several languages, of course, drive a car, take you boating, play tennis..."

"I think I still want the mystery of the other..."

"Oh, they'll program the mystery of the other too...And of course they'll have to build in some kind of anti-suicide device; you can see how in a situation like this a person would get suicidal...Isn't it depressing?"

"The most depressing thing I've heard since Hiroshima."

"But it's inevitable. Isn't it awful! I really think romantic love is

the great cul-de-sac of creative evolution. God's big booboo. O.K.
You better get back to your children. See you Sunday for dinner."

—Grandpa's on the phone—

"You're not going to Europe again this summer!" his voice crack-
les on the New York–Garfield line . . .

"But Father, one has to get out of America at least once every two
years to keep one's sanity." How some lines get repeated . . .

"I don't." Delivered ponderously from the somber living room at
the other end . . . "But you've always had this obsession. And suppose
war breaks out? Remember wherever you go you must immediately
register at the nearest American embassy and if you don't, well—you'll
just have to suffer the consequences because you're on your own, I'll
be eighty next fall; I just had a complete check-up, they looked into
every hole and took a hundred fifty dollars' worth of X-rays and do
you know what they found? Ear wax . . . Well, now you'll be scattered
to the four winds . . . But it's how you wanted it and I give you my
blessings . . ."

In the sensory deprivation chamber. Visions, hell. Enjoy the peace
and quiet. Supposed to be pitch dark but actually looks milky. They
say pitch dark when you can't see your own hand in front of your
face. Raise hand: true. Can't see but phantom hand promptly appears—one, two, six phosphorescent skeleton hands. Halloween
game. Stare in the void. Milky and webbed. A bog. Rain drops in
puddle. Mud. Straw. Inside some kind of stable. A long dark slit just
above my face, the lips widening: a sow giving birth. Scary when you
see same image, eyes open or shut. Perceive tiny eyes and whiskers,
some chicken feathers in the hay, again the rat and rain down the
mud walls, on the mud floor; the slit widening huge now and tumes-
cent, something trying to press through. Shift image from above my
head to the front; labor continues . . .

Back in the living room, watch the children sit, eyes shut, writing
in the air: Joshua trance. Toby trance. Jonathan trance. —Down—
down—down, Kate's voice drones on—floating down a river, your

arm is getting so light it rises without effort—up—up—rising, rising...They sit with sleeping faces, one arm raised high.

...Up, up, you're soaring high above the earth, higher—now you're
sitting on a cloud so high you can see the whole world stretching
below you...Now look down and tell me what you see, Jonathan.

—My shadow, he says.

...you are before a heavy oak door. Behind this door lies your
personal paradise. You press down on the brass handle gently, the
door opens. You have to step over a high threshold. Have you stepped
over, Joshua? He nods. You're inside? And what do you see?

—A maze.

—A maze! I ask you to imagine your personal paradise and you
see a maze...

—Yes. A maze, he murmurs solemnly. It goes on and on; there is
always more to see...different styles and epochs...

—Amazing! Kate says. Your children are amazing. Toby tell your
mother...

—Mom, how was it in the sensory deprivation chamber?

—Interesting.

—Sophie did you have a rebirth experience? Kate asks.

—I suppose you could call it that. I'll write it up for your files and
let the computer decide.

—Mummy, you should have let Kate put you in a trance...

—We had a cool time. Kate, don't you really want to have children?

—Me have children! Oh no. One of me is enough...So kiddies,
you're off to your papa tomorrow...And what about you, Sophie,
have you decided where you're going this summer?

A small train station in Europe. People hurrying past.

Waiting outside on the platform, colorless, sad, impersonal, of
some foreign town; the station house, some trees, sky; struck by their
quiet fixity; the calm, spacious world of people not waiting at train

station. Startled when I see that the conductor stands before me. He is asking me where I want to go—but suddenly I can't remember. Stare at the rolls of tickets in his bag, all different colors. "Where do you want to go?" he repeats impatiently. Everybody is in such a hurry, I can't remember at all—the place—the name of the place—anything; but I have already disappeared.

Wake up in my room as the platform sinks—the backdrop removed some time ago, never distinct—a building, trees, sky ... Leaving New York this morning. The Pan Am flight ticket to Paris, return open, on the table. Awake, packing toothbrush, comb, pills; check passport; call to find out when the bus ... disconcerting how the urgencies of dream and waking life correspond. At home in neither. The one who got up no more myself than the one dreaming.

Because I'm not awake yet? ... Not truly awake. Of course, she thinks, going out on the street to hail a cab. And what presumption to expect in this life to be perfectly awake. In the taxi she recalls with a tinge of regret the tantalizing colors of the roll of tickets in the conductor's bag, the anguish of abandoned dream places lingers on, the scene left mysteriously, will-lessly ... The irrelevance.

Seat belt fastened, watch the handsome high-tailed jets skate slowly and stately to cocktail-hour music.

TITLES IN SERIES

For a complete list of titles, visit www.nyrb.com or write to:
Catalog Requests, NYRB, 435 Hudson Street, New York, NY 10014